## Other Titles by *Langaa* RPCIG

**Francis B Nyamnjoh**
*Stories from Abakwa*
*Mind Searching*
*The Disillusioned African*
*The Convert*
*Souls Forgotten*

**Dibussi Tande**
*No Turning Back. Poems of Freedom 1990*

**Kangsen Feka Wakai**
*Fragmented Melodies*

**Ntemfac Ofege**
*Namondo. Child of the Water Spirit*

**Emmanuel Fru Doh**
*Not Yet Damascus*

**Thomas Jing**
*Tale of an African Woman*

**Peter Wuteh Vakunta**
*Grassfields Stories from Cameroon*

**Ba'bila Mutia**
*Coils of Mortal Flesh*

**Kehbuma Langmia**
*Titabet and The Takumbeng*

**Ngessimo Mathe Mutaka**
*Building Capacity: Using TEFL and African languages as development-oriented literacy tools*

**Milton Krieger**
*Cameroon's Social Democratic Front: Its History and Prospects as an Opposition Political party, 1990-2010*

**Sammy Oke Akombi**
*The Raped Amulet*

**Sammy Oke Akombi**
*The Woman Who Ate Python*

**Susan Nkwentie Nde**
*Precipice*

**Francis B Nyamnjoh & Richard Fonteh Akum**
*The GCE Crisis: A Test of Anglophone Solidarity*

# THE FIRE WITHIN

Emmanuel Fru Doh

*Langaa* **Research & Publishing CIG**
Mankon, Bamenda

**Publisher:**
*Langaa* RPCIG
(*Langaa* Research & Publishing Common Initiative Group)
P.O. Box 902 Mankon
Bamenda
North West Province
Cameroon
Langaagrp@gmail.com
www.langaapublisher.com

ISBN: 9956-558-18-4


First Published 2008

## Dedication

*To the memory of my grandparents:*
Marcus and Kamah Awah Njoya.

*Praise and Glory to God Almighty*

# Content

# Prologue

From a distance Pa Anye, Ndomnjie, Yefon, and her uncle Dr Wirghan could see the smoke rising slowly to about five to six feet before spreading out like a rejected offering. Then what appeared to be a pile of clothes by the side of a makeshift hearth moved slightly. As the group of four approached, the scene became clearer.

"He is the one!" exclaimed Ndomnjie. "Yes, he was in the bus as we came up." He gently nodded his head several times. "It is almost two years now, but I can recall that he was with us."

"Are you serious?" questioned Pa Anye.

"He is the one," Yefon confirmed.

The pile of clothes was, in fact, a tall young man in his mid twenties. As Ndomnjie stared on, he noticed the young man's very black and somewhat overgrown hair, which looked shaggy at the top. It had, at one time, been neatly trimmed low around the upper tips of his ears and below to the back of his neck. Eyes with very clear whites, though partially covered by heavy eyelids like those of a person struggling to stay awake, lighted his long face. His long nose ended in a tip comfortably lodged on a sprouting moustache crowning his upper lips. His broad shoulders and V-shaped chest narrowed to a thin waistline, and the muscular thighs convinced Ndomnjie that his subject of interest had once been much involved in sports.

Pa Anye was still wondering about his pair of trousers which, unlike most mentally disturbed men's, was not threadbare, but had been rubbed all over with something black. "What is he rubbing on his leg like that?"

"It's charcoal," answered Ndomnjie.

Occasionally the young man would look around him with a very confident, if not defiant, smile and then he would sigh, moving his head from side to side. He was lying down on his side, with his left elbow propping the upper half of his body from the hard and cold tar on top of the brickwork, which formed the heart of the Sunshine Chemist roundabout. In a way, the roundabout itself is in the heart of the town of Batemba, the capital of the Savannah Province. As he lay there, the different roads leading out of the roundabout were like the network of a spider's web. He himself, in the centre of the roundabout, looked like prey, the surrounding houses and people, spiders of different sizes and shapes, creeping threateningly towards him.

The vehicles that zoomed past the roundabout with screeching tyres meant nothing to him. Occasionally a passer-by would briefly catch his attention and he would tail the person with his eyes until distracted by something else. Up in the distance, above the houses on his right, lay the Station Hill from which the roofs of houses in the government residential area glittered. On the cliff where the almost flat top of the Station Hill comes to an abrupt end, dropping down about 60 feet, were many shades of green. The fresh leaves of tall trees that seemed to vie with each other for a greater dose of the sun's rays were visible from a distance, and so were a few waterfalls running down the slope like tiny silver threads. On his left was another hill, although not as pronounced as the Station Hill. On it stood a mesh of haphazardly constructed houses with footpaths snaking in and out of the different compounds. Occasionally a storey building disrupted the regular nature of the height of the houses. People were all over the place and milling around the streets, without paying any particular attention to the solitary figure that seemed at home in the street.

His fireside was much alive as bright red flames leapt up almost engulfing the dirty pot on the hearth. Pa Anye, Ndomnjie, Yefon, and Dr Wirghan approached cautiously, wondering what Pa-pa (as people called him) could be muttering to himself. They were just two paces behind Pa-pa when he burst out laughing and then the clapping of his hands followed the movement of his head from side to side. Then the muttering, but this time his words were audible. "Beauty! Beauty! When they talk of beauty, she had it: ebony black and glittering like a polished carving. A-a-a-a-h! Then when she smiled, ah! But I told you, I denied, yes, I said we should keep it, I even promised telling my people, but you would not listen. You said you would not hurt Mommy's memory. You didn't want to see me in trouble, but which is more painful, which is worse—losing you two or having both of you and to hell with what people say? Why have you left me alone?" Pa-pa paused for a while before continuing sadly, "I can take off my pair of trousers eh! I can do it, or rather I feel like running along this straight street. No, I won't. People would think I'm ma-a-a-ad ha-a-a-a!" He laughed aloud.

All of a sudden, Pa-pa jumped up as if struck by a thought. With grim determination in his looks, he started marching purposefully along Central Avenue. This main street leads from his residence—the roundabout—into the commercial nerve-centre of Batemba. Pa-pa marched with his chest jutting out and his head held high like a disciplined soldier on parade. The supercilious look in his eyes and his commanding bearing gave the impression he was above everyone else around him. Then he began talking threateningly as he marched on, "Just let me get there, fools. I'll make them know their right from their left. I'll make them know how to guide and not dictate their foolish superstitious whims to others. Mad people!" Pa-pa never really got anywhere for, each time after marching for a while, he returned to his hearth where he started all over again, warming and painting himself black with charcoal.

"This is just a case of acute depression. If only we had psychiatric units in this country, this is a young man who should be functioning well with the right treatment," Dr Wirghan lamented. "You say he's been like this for over a year now?"

"Yes," answered Yefon.

"What a waste," Dr Wirghan lamented.

"True!" Yefon agreed. Yefon had not given up on Adey, and so had brought her uncle who studied in Sweden and had been practicing there as a medical doctor for over 20 years to get his opinion.

"So you say there is only one mental health hospital in the whole country?"

"There is only one in the capital city of Nayonde—Centre Bonaparte," Ndomnjie put in.

"And they've not been able to help this young man?" Dr Wirghan questioned in disbelief.

"His parents and I have been there with him four different times. First of all, nobody speaks English there and so we could barely communicate. They kept him there for about a month without any changes. A doctor saw him once in all that time. We had no choice but to bring him back. All his parents can do now is pray for him while I hoped you would someday see him during one of your visits back home."

"What a shame! I wish I were here permanently. Not being resident at home, I can hardly do anything."

"That's alright uncle, I just wanted you to see him ... just in case ... one never knows."

"So that's how he spends his time?" asked Ndomnjie.

"Pretty much. His parents have done everything to keep him at home but failed. Sometimes he goes back home where he is given good food and urged to bathe and have a change of clothes, but then there are times when it is a lot more serious, like now, and he just walks away from home and does not return, sometimes for weeks. His mother sometimes brought him food and money, but since it is not at all times that she met him at the roundabout, she now walks past from time to time and when she sees him, she gives him money."

"What a shame!" Dr Wirghan echoed again as the small group walked helplessly away from the roundabout.

# Chapter One

It is difficult leaving the warmth of thick bedding during the intensely cold dry season in Batemba. As if the cold was not enough, thoughts that had been with her all night also kept Mabel in bed. It struck her that her stepsister's vomiting seemed to follow a certain pattern. She vomited in the mornings and in the evenings. Thinking it might be worms, Mabel had procured worm-expellers, but the vomiting only intensified.

All through the night, Mabel had wondered what could be wrong with her younger stepsister, Mungeu'. There was a nine-year gap between Mabel and Mungeu', but in spite of this, they were so close that they lived more like friends than stepsisters.

Mungeu' was the only one who cared genuinely about her, the only relative who understood when she could not distribute money to members of the family every end of the month. It is true that her salary was substantial, but she had been trying to save before beginning to help the family so as not to sacrifice her peace of mind.

The rest of the family had damned her, calling her selfish while others completely boycotted her home. This, however, did not bother Mabel at all since it left her to herself to plan her life in her own way. She wondered at this ridiculous attitude of her family members. Against all odds, a child is born and brought up by her parents, during which period she gets assistance from nobody besides them. Then as soon as the child grows and is successful in life, long before she can think of helping her own parents who had to forgo a lot to bring her up, other family members curse her for not giving them her money to squander. Moreover, she had hardly seen or heard from these relatives before.

Mabel was already dressed for the day. She wore a white transparent blouse through which one could see the brilliant white straps and lace-reinforced edges of her brassiere. Her well-ironed grey skirt, with the pleats standing out, was distinctly professional. Her white high-heeled shoes matched her blouse and gave her leg a delicate appearance. Mabel was at the dining table taking her favourite breakfast of fried plantains and eggs, which she always washed down with a cup of tea. Just then

Mungeu' came back from the toilet, bent over and staggering into the sitting room with her left hand gripping her mid-section.

"Munny! What's happening?"

Mungeu' could only stare at Mabel weakly. Her uncombed hair completed the picture of misery she painted.

"This vomiting, let it not be that you are pregnant? I am sorry I have to be that blunt, after all you are no longer a child. Think about it and we will talk when I'm back, okay! Did you hear me?"

"I heard you. Bye-bye," said Mungeu' as Mabel stepped out of the house on her way to work.

"Bye!" answered Mabel.

Mungeu' was midway through her now tasteless breakfast when the events of her life came surging into her mind. She had never known her mother who died shortly after she, her only child, was born. After the delivery, the placenta of the child would not be born, and the nurses claimed only the doctor, who was away, could do something about it. Nobody knew the house of the doctor on call, not even the driver of the only rundown ambulance the hospital had, and so Mungeu's mother bled slowly to death with the nurses only being able to change the bedpan into which she bled.

Mungeu' remembered growing up and feeling alone with her father's eldest and first wife who reduced her to a slave virtually. This caused her to escape from home and, on her own, register as a student in a home-craft centre at the age of fourteen. Years before, her father had refused sending her to college like Mabel because Mabel's mother, Angwi, who brought her up, had poisoned his mind against her. Angwi had described Mungeu' as lazy, dirty, and, worst of all, fond of men. To her father, therefore, sending such a child to school, especially as she was female, was a complete waste of money. "After all you are growing up really fast. Are those not breasts I see already lifting up their heads on your chest? Instead of wasting my money, there are many husbands waiting." Mungeu' could still hear her father's sentencing voice as she stood some distance away in tears.

Her fate was sealed – to be some old man's breeder. "For how many young men would leave all the young women who too were beginning to go to college these days to marry her just because she went around brandishing a pair of breasts," Mungeu' wondered. With this in mind, she decided to talk to the Reverend Sister running the Holy Rosary Home Craft Centre (HRHCC) in Bari, a neighbouring town to the northeast of Batemba. The centre accepted her, on condition she pays her way through by, because she could not come up with the cash for tuition, working for them during the holidays.

Two years later, at the age of sixteen, Mungeu' graduated from the HRHCC skilled in all she had been taught. She could cook, farm, knit, and, above all, sew clothes. As Mungeu' prepared for her graduation, Reverend Sister Anne-Frances advised her to sew baby clothes—because babies will always be born—and to open a small store for her goods as soon as she was in Batemba town.

Mungeu' would never forget her graduation day—June 30th 1975. When at last it came and all the formalities were done with—speeches, awards, and the handing of diplomas and prizes won—the loneliness of her life struck her once more, like a blow in the face. While the parents of the other students rushed to congratulate their daughters and walk them home, Mungeu' found herself searching the faces of the visitors in vain for her father. He was nowhere to be found. Not one of her stepmothers had come to congratulate her on her day of success.

When all those graduating and their friends and relatives had left the ceremonial ground, Mungeu', with her certificate in her hand, picked up the basket containing the prizes she had won for her brilliant performance. As she wondered where she was to go now that she was sure she meant so little, if not nothing, to her family, she saw the solitary figure of a woman about one hundred metres away. She was still staring in doubt when the figure beckoned her to approach. About thirty metres from the woman, Mungeu' dropped her basket and ran forward shouting.

"Mabel! Mabel! Where are you from? What are you doing here? How did you know?" Mungeu' rained questions at her.

"It is a long story and we cannot stand here talking about it. Let's go home first," urged Mabel smiling happily as she took Mungeu's hand into hers.

Mungeu' sighed before she spoke: "I have no home yet. Even then, I'm still to collect my belongings from the dormitory."

"Leave them there. We'll come back for them later on. Come!"

Mabel had not changed one bit since Mungeu' last saw her several months ago. Her build was still that of the athlete she used to be, and she was full of feminine beauty. She looked well fed, with a plump appearance that could not pass for being fat. Her eyes, which appeared small because of her thick eyelashes, gave her a sleepy appearance. The hair on her head, though low-cropped, crept down delicately by her ears almost to the level of her jaws, confirming her hairy nature. That confident look on her face was still there and Mabel looked as calm as ever, with a tendency to smile all the time. Her legs, though powerful, had an effeminate appearance, almost ethereal. From her ankles upwards, her dark brown complexion assumed a fairer tone. Her hips narrowed into a surprisingly slim waistline, which gently broadened upwards to accommodate her ample bust. She was tall enough not to be called short, although Mungeu' was some inches taller, slimmer and more fragile looking in spite of the hard work at the HRHCC. Mungeu's thinly set lips betrayed a certain firmness in character which almost came out in the way she walked with short firm strides that swung her slightly broad hips from side to side. Like Mabel, Mungeu's beauty as a woman lay not just in her appearance but also in her character—a very friendly, generous and hardworking girl who would shoulder another person's burden as though it was her own.

It was a long walk from the bus stop, where they had dropped off from Bari, to Mabel's newly acquired apartment situated just before the hubbub in the heart of the town. As they walked home, Mungeu' furnished Mabel, in detail, with some of her experiences during the three years at the HRHCC, during which time they had met on a few occasions only. Completely disappointed at the nature of things at home, Mungeu' had spent her three years at the HRHCC with visits to her family stretched far apart. Mabel, on her part, visited her at least once each year when she herself was on holidays. During the holidays, Mungeu' stayed at the HRHCC doing different odd jobs to earn some private pocket money which she used for her personal needs and her fees. Occasionally her father sent her some money and so did Mabel, whose pocket money was always more than she could use since after her father had given, her mother who traded in petty household items would also give.

They had been walking and talking for about thirty minutes when Mungeu' found herself at the threshold of the town. There were a few houses here and there, newly constructed, with glittering tin roofs. Further, towards the heart of the town, Mabel turned off the road from Bari and together they followed a footpath that emerged onto a new building.

"If it was a vehicle it would have come in the other way." Mabel spoke while forming a curve with her hand to show the direction a vehicle would follow. She dipped her hand into her purse and brought out a shining new key before stepping out of her muddy pair of shoes onto the veranda. Mungeu' followed her cue.

"This is a very beautiful building Mabel. You don't mean this is your house?" asked Mungeu' wide-eyed.

"Yes, I just moved in here," answered Mabel unlocking the door.

Mungeu' could not believe what she saw. Mabel's parlour was well furnished. A very new set of couches had been carefully arranged in the parlour, as well as a dining table with chairs for the diners, a reading table to one end on which stood a reading lamp and a cupboard with glass windows through which one could see different sets of plates, dishes, teacups and spoons. All this furniture was resting on a reddish rug, which covered almost every inch of the tiled sitting room. Mungeu' stood in the centre of the parlour awe-stricken and unable to move. She had never seen the inside of any house like this before.

"What's wrong Munny? Why are you looking so surprised?"

"Nothing is wrong; I'm just surprised you could have acquired all this property in so short a time," answered Mungeu'.

"Well, you will remember it has taken a lot more time than just money. I was planning to acquire all these things, which is why I could not give our father a single franc after I brought my first salary to him. Of course, you will remember what happened to all that money: it was distributed to different members of the family. As Pa put it, it was to 'buy' my head from a bunch of wolves who want to reap where they never sowed. To them, unfortunately, the money was like the first course of a meal as now they are asking if that was the first and only salary I ever received."

"Don't mind those idiots. They can go to hell. After all, I don't see why a family should spend all it has bringing up a child and then just when they should begin reaping what they sowed, some clowns emerge in the name of relatives and take total control of the atmosphere."

"Munny, who cares? I have done my part, for which reason I could care less about all their recent talking. Well, now you see for yourself what I have been trying to do. I am through with the parlour and the bedrooms, only the kitchen and the bathrooms are left. I saw all these in a magazine. Of course, it's not exactly as it was in the book, but it is close enough to what I saw."

Mungeu' followed Mabel into the first bedroom. There was a big bed beautifully made with sheets and a very thick blanket. At the lower end of the bed was what looked to Mungeu' like a huge cupboard set in the wall, but when Mabel opened it, Mungeu' saw to her astonishment dresses hanging from an iron bar that went across from one end to the other. On the floor were about ten pairs of ladies' shoes, some low and others high. Her eyes caught a small delicate table leaning against the wall across from the bed, on which stood a mirror big enough to reflect a life-size image. In front of this mirror stood about a dozen little bottles containing perfume and different kinds of make-up. Mungeu's breath hissed through clamped incisors as she relaxed after having taken in enough.

"Do you like it Munny?" asked Mabel.

"What kind of question is that? Where is the woman who can see such things and not like them?"

"In that case, follow me."

Mungeu' followed Mabel into the neighbouring bedroom. It was a replica of Mabel's room, but when Mabel opened the wardrobe, after she was sure Mungeu' had seen enough of the room, the dresses that were in it were Mungeu's. Not yet sure of what she was seeing, thinking it was a coincidence, Mungeu' went closer to the wardrobe. No, it was not a coincidence. The dresses in the wardrobe were hers. At least those were class shoes and, hanging at one end of the wardrobe, her uniforms. Mungeu' could hardly talk. She stood staring and when it occurred to her that she was not seeing the contents of the wardrobe as clearly as before; she blinked and tears trickled down her cheeks.

"Why, Munny? Don't you like it?" asked Mabel worried when she noticed her stepsister in tears.

"No, not that," answered Mungeu'.

"Then what?" urged Mabel as she gently turned Mungeu' to face her, holding her by the shoulders.

All efforts to speak failed Mungeu' as she struggled with whatever was blocking her throat. She swallowed and burst into sobs. Mabel's arms crept round Mungeu's body as she locked her in an embrace.

"Why have you done this Mabel?" asked Mungeu' after her sobbing had subsided.

"What do you mean? Don't you like it?" Mabel asked with a look of surprise.

"No, that's not the point. You have younger sisters and brothers from your mother's womb, why then did you prefer me?"

"Munny, you will be pretending if you say you do not understand my situation. Even as a student didn't you see me spending my money on my brothers and sisters? How many of them were grateful? They thought it was their right that I, being an elder sister, had to spend my money on them, right? You may also think that way, but I don't. We are all children and have been given equal chances, at least those from my mother's womb. If I should endeavour to help a brother or sister, then they have to show they appreciate what I do for them.

"Are you telling me you appreciate all that I did for you when I was in school because your mother is not there, or is it because you are from a different womb? No Munny, gratitude is gratitude and should be made manifest irrespective of the relationship between the parties concerned. Above all, the person you are has made you more than a sister to me—you are my best friend. How many people were willing to understand when I said I was trying to settle down before helping my relatives anymore? Is it not these same relatives who went around saying because I had now left college I didn't care about them? But you, you who needed all the help, told me not to bother and even advised me to look for a house for myself since, as you suggested, it would take me away from all the talking relatives? Is that not what I have done Munny? Answer me! Is that not what I have done?"

"Yes, Mabel."

"Then why all the tears when I give you a place in that house? Or do you want to go back to our parents' place and continue swallowing all that rubbish our father's numerous wives have been giving you?"

"No, that's not the point Mabel. It is just the way I'm touched by all you've done."

In a bid to change the topic and the prevailing atmosphere, Mabel reminded Mungeu' that she was yet to see the visitor's room, the toilets, and the kitchen.

They moved from the one to the other. Mungeu' was impressed with the gas cooker in the kitchen which could carry different pots at the same time. She felt the same about her shower and the water system toilets.

"But there's one more thing Mabel. How did you get my things and how did you know I was to graduate today?"

Mabel's calm look, as she stared at Mungeu' with a gentle smile on her lips, was penetrating. "Munny, I am not surprised you do not seem to know who you are to me. Yes, possibly you think because they say I'm very much like my mother in looks I have also inherited her ways, not so! My mother, her harsh ways notwithstanding, is my mother, but our characters are not in any way similar. As a younger sister of mine, I saw you grow. I witnessed your attitude towards all the difficulties that came your way, your realization that you were motherless, the torture my mother made you undergo, and the neglect you suffered from our father's hands because of what my mother said to him about you. Munny, do you know that in spite of all this hardship you've never said anything ill against these persons? How many people do you know who are like that? Instead, you struggled all these years alone, and without any bitterness. You fought for your admission into the HRHCC and spent your holidays doing odd jobs for three years to pay your way through, with occasional assistance from Sister Anne-Frances and our father. Is this the sister of mine that you think I should neglect with all that I have today? No Munny, it is my wish to do that which is correct where our parents went wrong as concerns you, for your mother was kind hearted, gentle, and loving. To her, children were all one, not A's or B's children. And in you I see your mother: that determination, that patience, the will to survive in spite of the tough times she faced as our father's fourth and youngest wife. Yes, this is how I feel and this is how I felt when Sister Anne-Frances contacted me."

"She did?" asked Mungeu' surprised.

"Yes she did."

"How did she get your address?"

"I have friends in this town, don't forget."

"What did she say?"

"Well," Mabel observed, "she had carried out investigations and had found out that I was your sister and, as she put it, the only one who cared about you. So she asked me to help. She pointed out how wonderfully well your performance had been at school and also said she was aware of the fact that you didn't like the idea of going back to our parents."

"Yes but—"

"Yes she told me you were planning to set up a small business for yourself, but she felt you needed someone to live with until you could afford to open the business. She was very glad to hear me say it had been my intention to help you out in one way or the other. She then told me when you were to graduate."

"She did?"

"Yes she did, about a week ago."

"Now tell me how you got money to furnish this house."

"Munny! I hope you don't think I stole or have a fat ugly old man in the background."

"That's not it, but you'll agree that in so short a time you've acquired so much."

"I agree, but it's all a matter of how one plans one's life. As you know, while I was undergoing this training to come out and be a banker I was earning some money, all of which was given me after I passed out of the training school for workers of the African Progressive Bank. I have also been working for the last four months. The money that accumulated while I was in our training school, my salary for the last four months during which I have worked, and the financial assistance from our bank due every new worker in the field is what I have used in equipping this house which is meant to be ours – you and me."

With every passing day Mabel and Mungeu' settled happily into their new home and the routine of their daily lives. Mungeu' was still in bed one morning when the sound of a vehicle stopping in front of the building brought her back to the present with a start. She was waiting for a knock but got a ringing sound coming from the short corridor which formed a passage leading from the parlour into the exterior behind with the kitchen door on the left. She rushed out of bed and peered through the window after shifting the blind unnoticeably to one side before opening the door. Two young men were standing on the veranda with a cupboard between them.

"Good morning, Sister," greeted the younger man who must have been somewhere around fifteen.

"Good morning. What can I do for you?"

"Are you Miss Anye's sister?" asked the young man.

"Yes I am," answered Mungeu'.

"Well, this is her cupboard meant for the kitchen. Can we take it in?"

"Yes sure!" Mungeu' moved to one side to make way for the young men.

Both boys, gasping and grunting, struggled with the cupboard into the kitchen and positioned it where they thought it should be.

"Thank you," said Mungeu'.

"Thank you," answered the boys as they walked back to their pick-up delivery truck and drove off.

Mabel returned home about midday. The house was sparkling clean and food was ready. Mungeu' had used some of the fabric she had designed and items she had knitted while at the HRHCC to decorate the heavily cushioned chairs in the sitting-room and to cover the centre and dining tables. Mabel dropped her handbag on the table and crashed into the nearest chair. After eating she crossed the parlour into her room to relax for a while before going back to work.

"Those carpenters have brought that cupboard." Mungeu' pointed out.

"They have?" asked Mabel excitedly as she shuffled into the kitchen. "Oh, it looks good, don't you think?"

"Yes, it's beautiful," answered Mungeu'.

"Wait a minute, how come food was ready even before I got here Munny? It means either you didn't go to your business place today or you returned much earlier than usual."

"I didn't even go. I haven't been feeling well, I must confess."

"*Ts-s-e-u*!" Mabel sighed. "What is really happening to you Munny? Please tell me," begged Mabel with a worried look on her face.

"Mabel, don't look like that, please. I wish I knew. I just feel strange – vomiting all the time and ... I don't know."

"Munny let it not be that you are pregnant. What about your period? Is it normal?" asked Mabel.

"I don't think so."

"When last did you have it?"

Mungeu' tilted her head to the left as if listening to a voice from above. "Let me see, I haven't really bothered checking." She finally answered, but it was as if she was talking to herself.

Mabel looked questioningly at Mungeu'. She was staring at the wall above Mabel's head with a far-away look in her eyes. "Yes?" Mabel urged.

"I think I last saw it o-o-o-on the 25th," she concluded energetically.

"25th of last month?"

"25th of April!"

"What month is this?" questioned Mabel unable to believe.

"Today is the 29th of June."

"*Ts-e-u*!" Mabel sighed, shaking her head from side to side. "I think you are pregnant. Munny, please tell me, have you been seeing any man?" Mabel questioned.

Mungeu' hesitated.

"Tell me," urged Mabel "at your age, you are no longer a child. Have you?"

"Mungeu' was now staring at the ground like someone in a trance.

"You think and tell me when I'm back from work this evening," suggested Mabel. "I am already very late." Mabel spoke as she walked out of the house after snatching her bag that was hanging on the dining table chair.

Two hours of her break time had gone by without her usual nap and she hoped to spend at least twenty of the remaining thirty minutes walking back to the bank since her colleague Mambo had said it would not be possible for him to stop by and give her a lift as usual.

Mabel's afternoon at the office was a most boring one. She lamented this useless idea of going to work in the morning, returning to spend about two hours at home during which time one could hardly rest before it was time to go back to the office for the afternoon shift which was spent by most workers sleeping on their tables, that is if they were present at all. It was a strange kind of working schedule being introduced. She thought of a colleague of hers who explained that she could hardly find time to spend with her family, especially the children. She saw them early in the morning as she prepared them for school and briefly during her break as she prepared their lunch. By 6:30 pm when she finally got home from work, she was too tired to spend time with the kids. She thought of the days just before the arbitrary establishment of the United Republic of Caramenju when people worked from 8:00 to 3:30 pm straight, with only a thirty-minute break and wondered who changed those hours that gave one enough time for one's family.

As Mabel walked back home from work, her head was pounding. She had not slept that afternoon and when she went back to work, she had been busy with figures and preoccupied with Mungeu's state. She feared her sister was pregnant. The usually clear evening was dark, as if some barely transparent material had suddenly shrouded daylight. The sun, which should have set by this hour, was blazing red just above the western horizon. It looked like the eye of an earth that had spent the whole day weeping.

"Munny! Munny!" called Mabel as she thumbed the doorbell. She could hear Mungeu' shuffling along. She pulled back the bolts and the door glided open with a prolonged creaking sound.

"Mabel!" Mungeu' greeted.

"Hmm! How are you?"

Mungeu' jerked both shoulders up at the same time while leaning her head towards her left shoulder in response. "How was work this afternoon?" she asked.

"Tedious! I had to fight with figures while attending to customers one after the other. Our demanding periods are the morning hours, speaking generally, and when customers are expecting their salaries or when a big feast is approaching, but some days, for no obvious reason, our afternoons can also be very busy."

Mabel had changed into her nightgown and was sipping at a cup of *Ovaltine* beverage when she introduced the topic she so much dreaded discussing.

"Munny! I'm sorry I'm giving you so much trouble, but you know if anything happens to you now that you are living with me, even if nobody asks me any questions, I will hold myself responsible."

"I understand Mabel and I'm sorry to make you go through all this."

"So you see why I must know what is happening to you. To tell you the truth, it seems to me Munny that my fears are true. I think you are pregnant."

"I don't know. You know, I really know nothing or rather very little about these things. But I must confess that I have slept with a man, although just once, about two months ago."

"Were you safe before that?" questioned Mabel with raised eyebrows.

"Safe? What do you mean?" Mungeu' looked confused.

"O my God! You mean you are that naive? You mean all your time at the Holy Rosary Home Craft Centre was spent on all the other things of the world and nothing about your own body? Nothing about men? Nothing about men and women? How long since you saw your menses before you met this man?"

"About two weeks, I think," answered Mungeu'.

"And of course since you met him you've not seen your menses." It was more of a statement than a question.

"No."

"Munny, we are in trouble. I am very sure you are pregnant."

Mungeu' remained calm, like one who did not grasp the intensity of the situation. "Are you sure?" she questioned at last.

"I am very sure, else why all this vomiting and spitting around the place? Oh, how unsuspecting I have been. These are all symptoms of pregnancy."

Mungeu' remained silent.

"Well, we are where I think we are and I trust you agree with me that we have to tell Pa about it," Mabel suggested.

"He will kill me."

"So what do we do?" questioned Mabel.

"I don't know," Mungeu' answered.

"Whatever the case, he will find out sooner or later so why don't we tell him now? Who is this man anyway and how did you meet him?"

"It is a very long story Mabel, but I will tell you all that I can remember. You see, it was my third year at the HRHCC when a young teacher who was taking us for Fine Arts and Economics, Fon, approached me. He told me how he loved me so much and would like me to be his girlfriend and, if all went well, marry him later on. He looked very serious to me Mabel, for he went on to tell me about his plans of going abroad to study economics for a degree. It was his hope to return and work with any of the banks that he believed would soon be dotted all around the place. His idea was that we would get married before his departure and then I would, in due course, join him overseas."

"Did you tell Sister Anne-Frances?"

"How could I tell her such a thing? It would have meant Fon's job and he was a very good teacher."

"Okay, okay," Mabel answered impatiently, "go on with the story."

Mungeu' went on to tell about how she was tormented by Fon's persistent approaches: he coaxed, taunted, threatened, but all in vain. Mungeu' spoke of how he had ceased troubling her for a while, only to reappear one day at her business place, shortly after her graduation, talking fervently about his love for her and the need for him to get married.

"Mabel, after all these months, I believed he was serious and gave in to an invitation to his house which is not far from the business site. Mabel, are you listening?" she questioned while staring hard at Mabel who had her forehead in her left hand.

Mabel didn't answer but placed her left hand on her mouth and was staring at Mungeu's chest with unseeing eyes. Completely beaten by her sister's inexperience, she was thinking of how terrible men could be. She thought of all the lies they would tell, and the extremes they would go to just to get their way with women, after which the women should count themselves very lucky to see them again. She did not care very much if they told all these lies to girls who had some experience, but when the victim is a naive girl like Mungeu', Mabel just could not understand. She wondered when women would learn to neutralize the power of that word "marriage" over them, which like a passe-partout opened all doors. Mabel's mind went to this very beautiful girl, Mafor, with whom she attended the training school for African Progressive Bank personnel. Mafor gave in to a mate of theirs in whom she saw nothing good, simply because the man promised marriage as soon as they were out of school, only for her to discover on the day they were graduating that Kadiri was already married. As if this was not enough, he went ahead to whisper behind his wife that he could take Mafor for a second wife or if she wanted it, send away the first wife whom he described as a dull illiterate. Mabel was still thinking of whether to blame the men, the women, or a tradition which had raised marriage to a very potent religion and spouses, especially the men, to the level of gods to be worshipped, when Mungeu' questioned if she was listening to her.

"I'm listening Munny, but why didn't you ever tell me this?"

"I was confused ... I mean ... I don't know what to say."

The brief silence that followed was palpable. While Mungeu' silently regretted all she had done, Mabel was blaming herself: she should have found time to talk to her sister about men and sex instead of hoping she would come by it somehow; she had, and the consequences were seeming catastrophic.

"Whatever the case Munny, I think we have to tell Pa. Meanwhile, we must make ourselves ready for whatever comes our way after we've told them, alright?"

"I understand."

"Don't feel too terrible in any case for this is life. I must go to bed, Munny, since I'm really tired and I've got to go to the market at Bansei tomorrow."

"I know. Good night Mabel!"

"Goodnight," returned Mabel as she pushed back the chair with her buttocks in the process of standing up, before walking into her room.

Mungeu', very heavily, got up from her seat, made sure all the doors leading out of the house were secured, switched off all interior lights and walked into her own room. She was thinking about Mabel's market trip to Bansei, a village about some twenty-five minutes drive from Batemba, with a market not only rich in foodstuffs, but one considered cheap compared to the rest of the markets in the neighbourhood of Batemba.

## Chapter Two

Places were still dark. The wind raged outside and heavy raindrops played a lullaby on the tin roof. Mabel struggled out of bed. As she swung open the room door, the bright lights from the passage into the kitchen forced her to shade her eyes with her left hand. She was sure Mungeu' had forgotten to turn the lights off, but then she caught the smell of meat frying. Mungeu' had not heard Mabel leave her room and went on with her cooking without knowing that Mabel was standing at the door of the kitchen. Mabel coughed and Mungeu' spun round squawking.

"Hey, you've frightened me."

"Just by coughing?" asked Mabel laughing, knowing full well that had been her intention.

"Of course, I thought I was the only one awake and I was even backing the door, just to hear someone cough right behind me. If you were in my place, you would have screamed, you who is frightened even by a mouse."

"When did you get up, and why so early?"

"Well, since you said you had to go to market I thought you would need an early breakfast and some food to take along since with these bad roads during the rains, one can hardly tell what can happen. You were very tired when you went to bed so I didn't think you would be able to leave your bed early enough to do these things."

"Thanks for everything Munny."

"There's hot water in that pot there; you can cool it to your preferred temperature. By the time you are through bathing, breakfast will be ready. You said they are picking you up at 5:30 am, right?"

"Yes," answered Mabel as she poured the hot water into a bucket to take it into the bathroom.

In less than twenty minutes, Mabel had bathed, dressed, and was at the table taking her breakfast. Although it was still too early to eat, they grew up learning from their father that they should never leave their homes for any journey or business without at least a little food in their stomachs. Meanwhile, Mungeu' was in the kitchen parcelling Mabel's lunch, should anything go wrong and cause her to need food while on the way.

Batemba to Bansei is supposed to be done in twenty-five to thirty minutes, but because of the state of the roads it could take about two hours and anything could happen to the tired, haggard, and overloaded transport vehicles that ply the road. Just then, they heard the sound of a vehicle stopping in front of their apartment. "Br-r-r-r-ing" went the doorbell. Mungeu' hurried to the door, pulled back the bolts and held the door open.

"Good morning," said a young woman on the veranda, who looked slightly older than Mabel.

"Good morning," answered Mungeu'. "Come in."

"Is your sister up yet?" asked the woman just as Mabel was shouting "Hey come in," from the table.

"Yes she is," answered Mungeu' moving aside for the woman to step in.

"Morning Munna," greeted Mabel as she struggled to stand up pushing back her chair with a grating sound.

"Morning! Are we ready?" asked Munna.

"Yes we can go," Mabel suggested as she went back for her basket that had spent the night under the dining table. "This is my sister, Munny," said Mabel.

"I knew as soon as I saw her. Who can fail to see the resemblance after all the time you spend talking about her."

"Munny, I have also talked to you about Munna. She is my colleague, and her husband also works with us."

"You are welcome Sister," said Mungeu'.

"Thank you," answered Munna. "We are not going with her?"
She questioned, addressing Mabel.

"No we're not. We can't just leave the house like that," answered Mabel.

"That's true," confirmed Munna as she stepped out of the house.

"Okay Munny, it's time for us to go. As soon as I am back then we will go to Pa hm? Don't worry too much okay! They will scold you, but that is as far as they can go, what else? Moreover, we are together."

"Is there any problem?" asked Munna.

"No, just some point to straighten out with our parents" answered Mabel as she and Munna walked out of the house into a white station wagon 404 Peugeot in which the driver was snoring.

"Tita!" Munna called out.

"Madam! Madam!" answered the driver as he woke up with a start, immediately adjusting himself in his seat.

"Let's go. I hope you are not feeling sleepy because I don't want to end up in a ditch," warned Munna.

"No Ma! It's just because I was idle."

"Okay let's go."

"Munny, see you later on," Mabel called out as the vehicle rolled out of the compound.

Mungeu' stood watching until it went out of sight. As necessary as it was, she did not like this trip to the market in all this rain. Even more troubling was the howling of a strange dog that disturbed her sleep almost all through the night; people believe this to be a harbinger of doom within the vicinity thus disturbed. When she could no longer see the vehicle's rear lights in the distance, Mungeu' entered the house and bolted the door behind her. She went into her room and curled herself up under the blanket to wait for daylight.

It was only when Mungeu' woke up that she discovered she had slept. The powerful rays of the mid-morning sun, like blazing arrows, had slanted into her room and settled on her face. She squinted as she jumped out of bed dazed by the bright rays. Mungeu' was expecting Mabel back latest by midday, and the morning was already halfway gone. She hurriedly refreshed the house by opening the windows, sweeping, dusting the furniture, and mopping the rooms before settling down to prepare lunch. She was sure Mabel would be very exhausted when she returned, so to make her eat well and enjoy her meal, Mungeu' decided to prepare Mabel's most favourite dish: boiled plantains and stewed fish.

Mungeu's anxiety started mounting when by 3:30 pm Mabel was not yet back. At 5:00 pm, she could no longer hold her calm and so after several years, Mungeu' decided to visit her father's compound. Her idea was to inform her father that Mabel was yet to return after leaving for the market at Bansei very early in the morning. She did not want to meet Mabel's mother, Angwi, who hated the idea of her putting up with her daughter. But when Mungeu', after walking for some forty minutes, got to her father's compound, he was out visiting and so she was forced to tell her fears to her stepmother who only listened because her daughter's name had been mentioned. Even after Mungeu' had finished talking, Angwi only looked at her angrily and said nothing.

As Mungeu' walked back home, she tried to figure out what really she had done to Angwi but could hardly put her finger on anything concrete; or was it her late mother? She wondered. Were her mother the second wife then such profound hatred could have been justified. The impact of the arrival of a second wife is usually more powerfully felt by the first who finds herself face to face with an archrival against whom her anger is usually impotent as she now controls at least half of the husband's attention, which all used to be fixed on the first wife. However, her mother was fourth and did not even have the fortune of having a baby in her marriage as soon as she would have loved to. When the baby came, at last, it claimed her life and as if that was not tragic enough, it was a baby girl. Her only regret, however, was that her mother died while giving birth to her. She sometimes wondered if Angwi hated her for being a girl and for taking after her mother so much. For people who knew her often talked of her and claimed if one saw Mungeu' then there was no need trying to look for her mother. "Again, Mabel, her daughter, is better placed than I am ...." As Mungeu' walked back home, all her efforts to seek the cause of Angwi's profound hatred for her were futile and so she resolved never to let it bother her again.

Her mind floated to and from Bansei as she wondered why Mabel and her friend had taken so long to return. Although the idea of an accident kept on bugging her, Mungeu' did not want to think it possible. "Everyone knows how bad that road is and so the chances of a driver speeding along are zero. Furthermore, the car used by Mabel and her friend was so new a technical fault was just not likely." Whatever thought crossed her mind, Mungeu' was sure that by the time she got home Mabel would be there.

It was very dark when Mungeu' got home and all the hopes of a brightly lit house to announce Mabel's return were frustrated as she saw the house's silhouette against the last traces of daylight in the horizon. It looked like the finished job of an unskilled artist—a splash of ink against a greasy background. Mungeu' stamped her feet hard on the ground in an effort to clear her sole of mud, all the time hoping Mabel had arrived but was trying to worsen her fears by leaving the house in darkness. After all, it would be all joy if after the delay it turned out that she had returned. But no, when she opened the door and switched on the lights, it was obvious Mabel had not returned. Her room was empty, there was no mud on the floor, nor were there the usual food items from such "bush-markets" in the kitchen. Mungeu's worries turned into her worst fears, for anything short of a serious accident should have been rectified, even if it meant coming back to Batemba for a mechanic to take to Bansei. Her mind raced like a whirlwind through the landscape of her memory flinging events that had marked her life and their consequences all about like dust particles and bits of paper in a tornado. She crumbled into a cushioned chair begging God not to let anything happen to Mabel. Now she was pregnant and only with someone like Mabel beside her would she be able to take all the rubbish society would heap on her as soon as the pregnancy was found out. How she wished people could only be realistic and accept certain occurrences in life. People go around sleeping with one another, but nobody wants to hear that a girl is pregnant. What hypocrisy! "Why don't people even mind their own affairs?" wondered Mungeu'. She was convinced of the wicked and poisonous nature of humankind as people pried into the affairs of others not to give a helping hand but to gossip and paint a more unfortunate picture of the culprit. "To hell with society and what it thinks and expects of me!" Mungeu' sounded determined. The idea of something having gone wrong with Mabel frightened her to the core. As these thoughts stormed her mind, Mungeu' failed to hear the vehicle that pulled to a stop in front of their door.

"Br-r-r-r-i-n-g!" the doorbell sounded.

Mungeu' jumped up from the chair. Throwing away her characteristic caution, she flung the door wide open but was deprived of all excitement. It was not Mabel, but a man she had never seen before standing at the door. Her disappointment was so profound that had the stranger not greeted her she would have unconsciously shut the door in his face.

"Good evening," greeted Mungeu' in return.

"I'm the husband of Mabel's friend with whom she went to market. May I come in?"

The looks in Mungeu's eyes were hollow, like a deep abyss. There was fear, confusion, and hope, all in one look.

"May I come in?" Mambo repeated.

"Where's Mabel?" Mungeu' asked confused. "I'm sorry, please do come in," she urged after recollecting herself.

Mambo walked into the house and took a seat before urging Mungeu', who was still standing at the door with a look of surprise and expectation, to come in and sit down. "I don't know how to –"

"Please, if there's anything that has gone wrong just tell me." Mungeu' was already trembling as she spoke.

Mambo looked closely at her for a while, walked over and took her arm before speaking. "There's been an accident."

"Where's Mabel?" asked Mungeu' in a very weak voice. She herself looked very calm like one resolved to accept whatever is reserved anew for her by fate.

"She is in the hospital."

"Your wife?"

"Also at the hospital."

"Please, can you take me there?" asked Mungeu'.

"Yes, of course, that's in fact the reason why I'm here."

Quietly Mungeu' stepped into the shoes she had on when she went to her father's compound. When Mambo was on the veranda, she locked the door and followed him into the car. The drive to the hospital was in silence'. Mambo did not know how to begin telling Mungeu' about Mabel's state, while Mungeu' feared asking and preferred waiting to see for herself. Mungeu' used up part of the time she spent walking to the hospital ward praying that Mabel's condition not be serious. Then she started bringing up reasons why she should believe Mabel's state was not very serious: "else Mambo should not have been looking so calm; he should not have come to me so soon for he would have been busy at the hospital." It did not occur to Mungeu', however, that the accident could have taken place much earlier on in the day and that Mambo could just have found time this late to come over to her place. At the Casualty Department, as they walked past, Mungeu' heard two female nurses discussing a very serious accident that had occurred along Sapda hill. The

Sapda hill is the death trap between Batemba and Bansei and the districts beyond. Besides being very steep, this long and winding hill is exceedingly slippery during the rains and full of dusty gullies for potholes during the dry season. Vehicles have been known to burst into flames as they toil up the hill, or to skid into the frightening valleys bordering this very narrow road. According to the nurses who had just walked out of the direction of the wards, the women were still unconscious.

The crowd on the veranda of the female accident ward was, from its size, enough to tell the tale. Mungeu' was already sniffing as tears rolled down her cheek. Mambo followed her closely as she fought her way through the crowd until she got to the door.

"Get back!" snapped a nurse standing at the door.

Mungeu' who could not even say a word just started crying. It was common knowledge around, especially with nurses who enjoy mystifying their job, that when relatives are denied access to their patients then the patient is virtually dying.

"Excuse me please," said Mambo addressing the nurse-sentry, "We are relatives of the patients: one of the ladies is in fact my wife and the other her sister," he said pointing at Mungeu'.

"So what?" barked the nurse. "I've said you can't go in."

"My goodness!" exclaimed Mambo breathing in deeply.

"The doctors are inside." The nurse quickly added, Mambo's reaction having frightened her for they are used to fawning relatives and not those who sound like they know what they are doing.

"Is that the simple information you could not give me politely?" shouted Mambo, his anger mounting.

The nurse decided it would be better if she kept quiet and so she turned into a wall. The creaking sound of wheels being forced to turn and the sudden withdrawal of the crowd from the other door shattered Mambo's contemplation on how to tackle this wall. He turned to see nurses hurrying out with a gurney—the nurse in front dragging, and the other pushing. There was a third nurse holding a bottle from which a very clear liquid flowed through a transparent tube into the hand of the patient on the gurney. It was Mabel. There was a thick bandage on the left side of her neck, the dressing of what must be a serious cut for the bandage was soaked in blood, and so was Mabel's long black hair which now looked unkempt. Mungeu' followed, crying, until she was stopped by a young male nurse at the entrance to the operating theatre. Mambo took her by the shoulder and they walked back to the female-private-accident-ward where Munna, with both legs hanging in the air, tied to some pulley mechanism, was moaning in pain and babbling incoherently.

Just then, Tita, a tall strongly built man, walked into the female-private-accident-ward. Besides the thick layer of plaster which crowned his right temple, his left hand, which he carried in a sling, was also in a plaster of Paris from the wrist to the shoulder joint.

"Good evening Sir," he greeted.

"Evening Tita! How are you feeling?"

"Much better now, Sir. I just wanted to say I am very sorry about madam and her friend, Sir."

"Tita, I think you should be resting instead of talking after everything you people have gone through today," said Mambo very calmly.

"I think I am alright, Sir. I am lucky to have escaped with only a wound in the head and a broken arm."

"Yes you obviously are. I think you must also understand that I am not blaming you at all. An accident is an accident, and twenty years as a driver coupled with the fact that you have a big family yourself eliminates the possibility of you having been careless."

"That's true, Sir," confirmed Tita.

"What you don't know is that a friend of mine happened to be driving directly behind the truck that hit and pushed you people into the valley. He told me everything about how you made way for the driver of this truck, who had been threatening you from behind, to pass on, but since he had come too close, not knowing your intention, he tried in vain to slow down his heavily loaded vehicle. He skidded in the mud and crashed into the side of your car, sending your vehicle tumbling down into the rocky valley. Because their trucks are very big, they think that in case of any collision with smaller vehicles, they cannot get hurt and so they go around driving recklessly, jeopardizing the lives of other road users. That driver, on this occasion, met with the wrong person. I'm going to see to it that he is taught the lesson of his life. If ever he drives again, there wouldn't be a more careful truck driver. He is already in police custody."

"Thank you, Sir."

"Okay, you go home and get some rest. I'll see you tomorrow."

"What about the car, Sir?"

"I'll get people to pull it out from the valley tomorrow. That friend of mine who witnessed the accident also succeeded in gathering much of what you had bought from market, so don't worry. Good night, Tita."

"'Night Sir."

It was late in the night when Mabel was brought back from the operating theatre, but instead of returning her to the accident ward, she was carried off to the newly constructed wing of the hospital that had well kept private rooms. A nurse stood sentry and nobody was to see her. Mungeu' who had been around the accident ward and the theatre—shuttling to and fro—was now known to the nurses on duty and so they listened to her when she said she had to stay around in case they needed some help. Mungeu' pleaded with the nurse at the door to kindly let her see her sister's face. Moved by the fact that Mungeu' had been crying for the last three or four hours, the nurse easily succeeded in making her promise to be quiet and calm as a prerequisite to seeing Mabel.

"Come in but do not make a sound."

Mungeu' pulled off her shoes and walked quietly to the side of Mabel's bed. With her hair cleaned and fresh dressing around her neck, Mabel looked so calm one would have thought she was just sleeping. She was yet to regain consciousness about ten hours after the accident. Satisfied, Mungeu' turned and left the room. Nobody was to stand within ten metres of the room although there was a lot of movement back and forth as nurses and doctors brandishing X-ray films came and left. Mungeu' spent the night shuttling between Munna's bedside and Mabel's room. But for the pain, Munna was now talking sense, although some nurses were saying certain things about her left hip and her right femur.

The following morning was calm, but people were beginning to throng the corridors of the hospital, hurrying in different directions: some were hospital staff and others relatives, taking care of patients, with their baskets, food flasks and so on. When Mungeu' saw Mambo approaching, there was nothing else she could do other than show recognition. She was so tired she could barely stand and her eyes were red and swollen from lack of sleep and weeping.

"How's she?" asked Mambo.

"She's still the same," answered Mungeu' with tears in her voice.

"I have not come here to make you cry, Mungeu', and besides, crying does not help now so hold yourself together. Who are those rushing like that? Do you know them?" asked Mambo suddenly staring above Mungeu's head.

Mungeu' turned to see Angwi rushing towards them. Her hair looked uncombed and she had her loincloth firmly secured in place by a head-tie tied around her waist. She was muttering something as she approached, half-running half-walking, looking like one in a trance. She did not even see Mungeu' as she went past, but Mungeu' heard her repeating the words: "That what has happened to my child?" in a hushed tone.

"Madam, what is it?" asked the nurse who was in front of the room.

"My child! I want my child!" Angwi sounded frightened with her strangled voice.

"Madam you can't see her, the doctor has said she should not be disturbed."

Just then, Pa Anye who had been outpaced joined his wife at the door. "Good morning my son," he greeted the nurse at the door.

"'Morning, Pa!"

"I hear my daughter had an accident yesterday and she is in here. Can I see her?" Pa Anye asked very much under control.

"You see Pa I know how you feel, but because of the serious nature of your daughter's condition, the doctors have said nobody should be allowed to go near her. I'll let you see her in any case, but only on condition that there will be no noise and you'll stay by her for just a minute."

"I agree," answered Pa Anye.

Just then, another man who was tall and looking well fed joined them. He was sweating profusely and seemed to be in a mad haste.

"Good morning," he greeted. "I presume this is 15 B?"

"Yes sir," answered the nurse. "Can I help you?"

"I am Ebot Tanyi Ebot, the manager of the African Progressive Bank here in Batemba. One of our senior personnel was involved in a motor accident yesterday. I must see her in connection with documents for her immediate evacuation abroad."

"But Sir – "

"I know. I have this document from Dr Mbangne, the Delegate. He asked me to show it to whoever was on duty when I got here."

"Come in Sir," said the nurse after glancing through the sheet of paper handed him. "Pa you can come in too, but make sure your wife does not produce any sound," he said to Pa Anye with emphasis.

After looking at Mabel's calm face on the pillow for a few minutes, Ebot turned and, walking briskly, left the room. "Thank you nurse," he said at the threshold.

"Pa! You people should come out now," the nurse urged Pa Anye.

Pa Anye took Angwi by the elbow and they walked out of the room. Pa Anye was as calm as ever, but Angwi was already sobbing, whistling quietly and tracing light dance steps as she made her way out of the room. Outside the room, her eyes fell on Mungeu' who was sitting on the veranda with her heels drawn up against her buttocks and her knees almost under her chin. Her arms hung loosely by her sides. She too was sobbing.

"I knew nothing good could come out of this union between you and my daughter," Angwi shouted at Mungeu' who sat as if she was not hearing either because of exhaustion or because she was used to such stupid effusions from Angwi. "I knew there was nothing but the shadow of ill luck over you and now you've transferred it to my daughter. What were you doing that she was the one to go to market? You stay with my child, feeding on her money and growing fat, and at the same time letting her do all the work? Now you sit here pretending. Leave this place!" shouted Angwi. "Leave this place I said." Angwi's loud and angry voice, as she hurled abuses at Mungeu' and her late mother, calling them all sorts of names, had drawn both patients and visitors to the scene. But not until Angwi called Mungeu's mother a prostitute, did she budge. Mungeu' looked up at Angwi with flame-red eyes and flaring nostrils, ready to pounce on her. On second thought, she maintained her calm lest she be blamed someday for raising her hands against Mabel's mother. The fact that she was old enough to be her mother and therefore an elder against whom Mungeu' could not raise her hand also entered her mind, but Mungeu' brushed it aside as rubbish. "If an elder wants to be treated like an infant, then it should be given him or her. Anyone who could not behave herself should be stripped of all respect and treated accordingly," Mungeu' argued with herself. She had had more than enough from this woman who should in fact have handled her like a daughter but almost ruined her life instead.

As the nurse pushed Angwi away from Room 15 B, Mambo took Mungeu's hand and pulled her off the floor. "Come, go home, bathe, eat and have some rest. Your sister is not dead yet," he said.

Mungeu' walked to and opened the door of room 15 B without permission from the nurse. The nurse, still surprised and full of awe for this girl who could take so much insult without as much as a word in reply, did not say anything. Mungeu' approached Mabel's bed, stared steadily into her face for a while and then touched her arm. "Mabel," she whispered, "had I known it would come to this you would not have taken a step out of doors yesterday, but divine will is supreme. With you in this state, I cannot say for sure what will happen to you or me, but now I know my troubles must begin again. I have loved and will always love and be grateful to you Mabel. Let me go back home for now dear sister." As Mungeu' walked past the nurse at the door, she thanked him for everything. She then stopped by to tell Munna that she was going home for a bath.

"How's Mabel?" questioned Munna who did not seem to be herself yet, even though her words made sense.

"She's still there. I'll see you in the evening," said Mungeu' as she walked away from Munna in the company of her husband.

At the gate leading out of the Casualty Unit of the General Hospital, since this exit was more in the direction towards Mabel's house, Mambo said good-bye to Mungeu'. "Try to rest. You need it, for nobody knows how busy you might have to be very soon so take my advice."

"Thank you sir," answered Mungeu' "and see you later on in the day."

# Chapter Three

When Mungeu' walked back to the hospital, the sun was already setting. She had bathed, eaten the food she had prepared the previous day and rested for some hours. She came ready for any eventuality, even if it meant spending the night again at the hospital. Approaching the private room where Mabel was, it occurred to Mungeu' that room 15 B looked deserted. Her left hand came up gently to her chest. For a moment, she appeared confused, and then she started running. Just then, however, she saw a nurse leave room 15 B with slightly hurried steps towards her direction.

"Evening Sister!" Mungeu' greeted.

"Good evening," answered the nurse as she strode off.

Rushing after the nurse, Mungeu' questioned, "What about the patient in that room?" Mungeu' questioned.

"What about the patient? Who are you anyway?" questioned the nurse at the threshold of the nursing station.

"I am her younger sister."

"Well, she has been evacuated."

"What do you mean?" asked Mungeu' trembling.

"She is a very important person where she works and so they have decided she should be treated abroad. They've carried her to Bari where a plane will take her to the Bongola International Airport and then overseas."

Mungeu' stood with glazed eyes like someone under a spell. "Oh God!" she whispered, "they wouldn't even let me see her should it turn out to be the last time?"

"Are you alright?" asked the nurse who had been looking at her.

"Ye-e-yes, I think I am," Mungeu' spluttered as she turned round to walk to Munna's room in the female accident word. She was sound asleep, but Mambo was there and said but for the pain and the inconveniences involved in responding to nature while in bed, there was a lot of improvement. She had repeatedly asked about Mabel and Tita and she was glad to hear they were not very badly off. Mambo feared the consequences if she were acquainted with the gravity of Mabel's state.

It was already dark when Mungeu' took leave of Munna who, after getting up from sleep, had found time to explain what happened from start to finish. As Mungeu' walked all the way home she wondered why things of little consequence never happened to her. She had hardly had any happy moments in her life, but the months she spent with Mabel, now death had come to take away the only one to whom she meant something. Mungeu' only became conscious of herself when she climbed onto the veranda of their building. She opened the door and went straight to bed.

★★★

A whole week had gone by after Mabel's evacuation, but no news had reached them yet. Mungeu' had spent time shuttling between home, her business place, which was now being run by Yefon, the most devoted and reliable of her four apprentices, and Munna's room in the accident ward. Although Munna was still in hospital, she could now walk around a little with the aid of crutches. Tita's head was much better, and in a few more weeks, they would remove the plaster of Paris from his arm. News of Mungeu's pregnancy had already spread around town like brush fire. Even Sister Anne-Frances had heard and had personally written a letter to find out from Mungeu' herself if it was true. The talking had been too much with people pointing her out furtively when she went past, while others visited her to find out for themselves whether it was true or not. Their pretext was that they had come to find out if she had heard anything about Mabel. It pained Mungeu' to think of how mean people could be, even those girls who slept with men as often as they ate in a day were now talking of how terrible she was, just because she slept with a man once and, because she did not know what to do, got pregnant. Nevertheless, Mungeu' made up her mind that nothing people said was going to bother her. It was true she was pregnant, but she knew she was several times better behaved than most of the girls who now went around laughing at her and pretending to be better behaved. Mungeu' wondered if indeed these girls were mocking the fact that she was pregnant or that she did not know what to do to continue appearing like one who had not slept with a man before.

One thing, however, pained Mungeu' above all else: the fact that she had not seen or heard from Fon again since the day he took her to bed. With Mabel away, she knew she was alone, and alone she meant to face the tide of events coming her way. She was beginning to hate Batemba because of all the talking going on about her. She was convinced it was the budding town's scanty population that caused people to be interested in the affairs of others. "If things go on like this," she thought, "I'm sure to leave this town soon." Mungeu' could not help wondering why a people like these, friendly and hospitable, would suddenly become so vicious in the way they gossiped about others. She smiled alone as the real problem became obvious to her. It was like the light of an electric bulb rescuing someone who had been groping about in a dark room loaded with many pieces of furniture. The real problem, it dawned on Mungeu', was not with the town as a whole but with a particular sex—the female. "Yes," thought Mungeu', "being a woman in this town is the problem. Women hate one another, for no reason in particular, so much so that they would go to any length to shatter the integrity of a woman they've only seen and admired even though they've not met before."

On Saturday, about a week later, after Mungeu' had gone to her business place, she suddenly felt tired and nauseated. She decided just before midday to go back home and rest. Just as she approached the veranda of their home, she saw a woman sitting there whom she recalled walked past their home every morning, carrying vegetables in a basin, to sell at the market.

"'Morning madam, can I help you?"

"Good morning! Yes. On my way to the market this morning, your mother asked me to tell you that your father wants to see you today, any time before dark."

"She didn't say why?" asked Mungeu'.

"No!"

"Okay, thank you. I'm sorry, I'm just returning from work and do not have anything to offer you."

"A cup of cold water, if you have some, would do," answered the woman who looked tired after trekking to and from the market. One could still see traces of sweat that dried up as it trickled down her face while droplets still bubbled on her nose and upper lip and reflected the sun's rays.

"Come into the house," invited Mungeu'. "You are quick in returning today."

"No please, thank you, just let me stay here. My feet are dirty. You are right, you know today is Saturday and the market is always crowded with buyers who rush to stock for the week.

Mungeu' went into the kitchen and returned with a glass and a bottle of cold water from the refrigerator.

"Thank you very much," said the woman after almost emptying the bottle. "I'll go now," she said as she picked up her empty basket, which she balanced neatly on her head.

Mungeu' wondered why her father wanted to see her. It is not that she could not guess. She was just unsure whether it had to do with her pregnancy or with Mabel's accident. Mungeu' decided the former was more likely to be the reason, for what else could she say about Mabel's accident which would not be the same old story they had heard from Tita over and over again? Whatever the case, she was resolved that nobody was going to make her cry, and she would give it to anyone who pushed her. After all, her father had barely been in her life whereas all Angwi had done was tell lies about her and torture her emotionally. Now she was a woman, and she would not take any nonsense from anybody. Mungeu' wept as she lamented Mabel's absence. Had she been around all would have been different, at least under control. Now, here she was alone to wage war against a family that never cared about her, and a tradition that seemed to go all the way out to victimize rather than redress. "All that they are interested in is identifying the father of my child who would then be condemned to try and win over my so-called parents by giving them repeated gifts of money and drinks." Mungeu' was determined to remain quiet about her baby's father's identity.

It was 2:30 pm when Mungeu' woke up from sleep, feeling as exhausted as she was before going to nap. Nevertheless, the will to go to her parents' and settle, once and for all, whatever was at stake there pulled her along. In less than thirty minutes she had bathed, dressed and was ready to start the long trek to her father's compound after the heart of the town on the way to Bachiri.

When Mungeu' entered the courtyard of her father's compound, the sun had disappeared and although there was still daylight, darkness was pushing the last of it into the horizon. Her father's building, the main building in the compound, formed one wall and on either side of the father's house stood two buildings belonging to all his wives. Even the hut belonging to Mungeu's mother was still in place, although looking abandoned. The toilet, had it not been a little too far away, would have completed the square, leaving a kind of opening surrounded by buildings. It was into this courtyard that Mungeu' walked only to find three elderly men, her father included, and three old women seated and sipping raffia palm wine from horns and glasses respectively.

"I'm greeting you all," said Mungeu'.

"We have heard," answered the assembly.

Mungeu' walked past straight to her mother's house which had only a single room serving as kitchen and bedroom, and pushed open the door. Rats scurried around her feet. Mungeu' stood still in the centre of the room depressed for a while, during which she thought of her mother, calling her to help her solve the problems that were going to come her way. Since Mungeu' heard of this summons, she, without being able to explain why, kept on feeling that something was going to go wrong. Mungeu' personally confessed to her mother's spirit all that had happened to her since her death and said she was sorry she had let her down by becoming pregnant without a husband. She confessed it was a new kind of music playing around these days and she, for the first time she tried dancing to the tune, fractured her leg. "Mother, had you been around it would all have been different," Mungeu' wept. She was still communicating with her deceased mother's spirit when she heard her name. It was her father calling.

"I have heard," Mungeu' answered.

"I think I am the one who asked you to come here today and not your mother's house."

"I know that," answered Mungeu' calmly although not without sensing the trouble brewing while also hinting at her unwillingness to tolerate any insults.

Two of the three women who had been drinking with the men in the courtyard exchanged glances and then looked at Mungeu' in disbelief as she walked out of her mother's house towards the group. Mungeu' could read the questions in their looks: "Since when does a woman answer back when a man talks, let alone a daughter to her father?"

"Sit down there," ordered Pa Anye pointing to a chair which had just been brought out while Mungeu' was in her mother's house.

Mungeu' sat down quietly, but awkwardly, since she had to part her legs to accommodate her bulging stomach which looked bigger for its age, and she dared not part her legs directly in front of the men, especially elders like these. In just one quick move Mungeu' parted her legs and at the same time turned her body to one side so that those sitting in front of her were facing the right side of her body. As if responding to some invisible signal, her father's three wives emerged from their different houses with their stools in their hands and joined the rest in the centre of the courtyard. Mungeu' could hear her younger stepbrothers' voices coming from the different houses belonging to their mothers. It occurred to her how strange it was that she would not be able to recognize some of them if given the chance, yet they were her siblings. Some of the children were quarrelling, others just shouting as they played, and then a child was heard crying. All the noise drowned Pa Anye's first words as he spoke while making to stand.

"Sit down, sit down," the others protested.

"Will you all shut up there," Pa Anye shouted at the children but to no one in particular. "Let me just get anybody's voice again and the person will tell me who brought the other into this compound, fools!"

There was total silence.

"A-a-h! What is becoming of the world and children of today? With all the elders out here, you idiots have no sense of respect to go on disturbing." It was obvious to some of those present that Pa Anye had overreacted to the situation at hand. He was, indeed, just getting himself ready to tell Mungeu' his mind since he was still smarting from Mungeu's rather bold and almost rude answer when he asked her to come out of her mother's house.

"My parents," started Pa Anye, with his attention directed at the older members of the group. "You all know that when an ordinary snake is killed, it is an issue concerning only a household, but the death of a python is reported at the palace. I have killed many snakes in this compound before and none of you heard of it, but because it is a python that has now been killed, you must all be informed. Have I spoken correctly?"

"We are listening," the visitors answered.

Pa Anye now narrowed down to the matter at hand. He pointed out how serious an offence it is, according to tradition, for a daughter to get pregnant while still under her father's roof. He spoke about the disgrace Mungeu' had brought on his family. He went on and on before asking the elders what they thought should be done. Angwi was already crying and talking about the terrible things Mungeu' had done to her by flinging away all her efforts to make her grow up into a good wife. Such hypocrisy was too much for Mungeu' who had been listening to the family's pretended concern with a suppressed sneer. Her mood suddenly changed into that of an offended mamba ready to strike. From one elder to the next, all gave their views about the gravity of Mungeu's offence, emphasizing the fact that she had brought quite a lasting disgrace to the family. Only one woman kept quiet all through, one of the three elderly female visitors. A slim and tall woman who to Mungeu' was very kind, for she fed her in her childhood whenever Angwi beat her and kept her out of doors for hours without food. It was this woman who always spoke to Mungeu' of her mother's physical and spiritual beauty and her having taken after her. Mungeu' could see the tears in her eyes as she listened to the abuses poured on her. Then suddenly Nemo-aku', as she was called because of the kind of cocoyam she sold at the market, made to speak and everyone listened.

"My daughter!" she called out to Mungeu'. "You have heard all that has been said against you, what do you have to say?" Without her initiative, Mungeu' would have ended up at the receiving end without the opportunity to tell her own story.

Mungeu' cleared her throat before speaking. "Thank you mother for thinking I might have something to say, yet I wonder if there's anything to be said. I am simply surprised at how much blame people can be willing to heap on someone else without questioning the role they themselves played towards bringing the person to where she is today. I have fought hard to be where, and who, I am today. It was no small battle because I did all that I did with my own private initiative, as the child that I was. Were my mother alive I would certainly have been a different person. Even my father sitting here never bothered to find out what was happening to me. He listened more to his wife who herself didn't care one bit about what happened to me after she had, as she claimed, fed me. But because of all the concern and love shown me by your daughter, my sister," Mungeu' directed her words at Angwi with her chin, "I will never disrespect you. However, today I am sitting here in front of you all having been condemned because I am pregnant. How many times did you my father, or you who claim to have been a mother to me, alert me as a daughter, of the possibilities of such a thing happening to me? What—"

"That's enough!" shouted Pa Anye jumping up. "Who do you think you are to say all that rubbish in front of elders? Yes, that's the stubbornness Angwi complained about all through the days you spent with her, and now you have the guts to sit there and blame your irresponsible behaviour on us. That is not relevant here today, have you heard? I'm sure you are all with me?" Pa Anye asked turning his head from side to side to look at the other elders present.

Nobody uttered a word. Mungeu's words made sense to the elders. Some of the men held their hands in their hands—the right wrist, with the palm facing the ground, in the left palm—which they hung on their slightly protruding stomachs as they stared at the ground. Others held their foreheads between their thumbs and the rest of their fingers.

"Yes," continued Pa Anye, "how you have grown or tumbled up is not important here today. What is important is the name of your bastard's father. We must have his name." Pa Anye emphasized.

Mungeu' kept calm as she stared into the group in front of her without looking at anyone in particular.

"You don't have anything to say? Are you suggesting you don't even know the man who is responsible for your pregnancy?" asked Angwi.

Mungeu' smiled at the implication of Angwi's words. Her mind wondered at the apparent unfairness of nature: for her to have gone to bed with a man just once and to find herself being thus abused. Pa Anye's shout interrupted her thoughts.

"You will not say anything to us?" Pa Anye jumped from his chair with his right hand in the air, but the old man sitting between Pa Anye and Mungeu', Pa Ntseh, with unexpected agility, sprang up and placed himself in Pa Anye's path. "You will do no such thing. How dare you strike a pregnant woman?"

"Then let her get out of my compound now. Get out!" shouted Pa Anye, "And find out for yourself the difference between sleeping with a man and delivering a child. Idiot! I said get out. Leave, now!"

Quietly Mungeu' stood up from her seat. She had tears in her eyes and felt like crying, but she was determined not to give her father or any of his wives the pleasure of knowing they had hurt her. She walked over to her late mother's neglected house, shut the door and walked out of her father's compound without a word to anyone. As Mungeu' walked back home with tears blurring her vision, she thought of the crossroads at which she now found herself and kept wondering at how unfair things could be in life. For once, she understood why some people take their lives. She wept as she thought of all she had gone through and cried even more when she remembered Mabel, the only person to whom she meant something, now gambling with death. She had heard nothing from anyone about Mabel and so did not know what to think. In the darkness Mungeu' pulled herself along.

Mungeu' was completely exhausted when she got home. The key of the door was in her small red purse. She took it out, opened the door and switched on the veranda light which they usually left on all through the night. Whose footprints are these? She wondered. Somebody had called in her absence and the mud from the caller's shoe was on the veranda. Unable to guess who might have called, Mungeu' pushed open the door, but her attention was again caught by a screeching sound on the ground as she locked the door. Whoever had called had sent a note under the door. Not knowing what to think of it, Mungeu' picked up the note. It was addressed to her from Mambo. He lamented the fact that he had not been able to see her mindful of her state. He blamed it on the maximum attention he had to give his wife as soon as he was not at work. He hoped Mungeu' was well. He mentioned the possibility of his wife leaving the hospital within another week. He was going to go on and write something, but he changed his mind and pointed out that he would call again later on in the day. Mungeu' was still wondering what he wanted to write about when she heard the sound of a car in front of the building. Mambo banged shut the door of his car.

"Oh you are back, that's good. Where were you?" he questioned with a concerned look.

"My family sent for me," answered Mungeu'.

"I hope nothing is wrong?"

"There's always something wrong with my people. Please sit down for a minute. I want to heat some food. I have hardly eaten all day."

"And that's not good for a pregnant woman," said Mambo.

"Thanks for the advice. I'll be out in a few minutes," Mungeu' spoke as she shut her room door after her.

When Mungeu' re-emerged from her room, about twenty minutes had gone by, but she had bathed and changed into fresh wear. She smelt and felt fresh. "I'm glad to hear of the progress your wife has made," said Mungeu' as she walked into the kitchen. "You don't mind eating some rice this late I hope?"

"No, no, thanks. I just ate. It's just that I thought I had to give you some information. That's why I came back."

Mungeu' walked into the parlour with a plate of rice on which she had sprinkled some stew and sat right across from Mambo. "You have something to say to me?"

"Yes, it would have meant a lot of writing so I preferred to call again. It is about Mabel."

"What!" asked Mungeu' with a start, at the same time setting down her plate.

"No, nothing bad. Just to say we got word from her doctors abroad. Her branch manager was at my place this afternoon and told me her operation had long been carried out. In fact, upon her arrival, an ambulance took her straight to the hospital and into the operating theatre at once, but all efforts to get us by phone failed. The operation was successful, but she was yet to regain consciousness three weeks after. This morning however, a call came through from one Dr Raineer who spoke about Mabel for a long time. The good news is that Mabel, unlike we were told, regained consciousness one week after the operation although a complaint arose: she could not seem to remember everything all at once. Dr Raineer is, however, positive that she will recover fully. It is a matter of time even if it takes a while. We got this news today, and I didn't think I should go to bed without letting you know since we've all been very worried about her condition."

Mungeu' leaned her head against the upturned palm of her left hand with her elbow firmly planted on the armrest of the chair.

"Mungeu', I think you should eat. I didn't consider this bad news at all, that's why I didn't hesitate telling you. After all, did we think Mabel was ever going to regain consciousness? If now she is conscious, can sit and talk, then that is remarkable progress, her failing memory notwithstanding. Dr Raineer thinks they will keep her until she improves since she has to be closely observed."

"Thanks for everything, Sir. It is just that a lot has gone wrong with me especially ever since Mabel's accident and I know had she been around all would have been under control. So at the mention of her name, all the problems I have encountered and am still likely to encounter, just flooded my whole being."

"What kind of problems have you been having? I hope they are not financial?" questioned Mambo with so much concern."

"No, Sir, not financial, it has to do with my family. You see ..."

Heavy banging on the door caused Mungeu' to swallow her words.

"Who's it?" she questioned alarmed.

"Open this door," Angwi shouted.

Mungeu' and Mambo exchanged glances.

"I say open this door or I'll break it down," screamed Angwi.

"Who could that be?" Mambo was totally at a loss.

"Mabel's mother," answered Mungeu' with a pale smile as she walked across the room to the door. "Just some of the problems I was trying to talk to you about," she added.

The door was brutally pushed in as soon as Mungeu' pulled back the bolts and this sent her crashing on to the ground. As Mambo jumped to assist Mungeu' who was struggling to get up from the ground, Angwi dashed into the house. Her headscarf tied around her waist and with arms akimbo, she stood staring at Mungeu' who was now on her feet, as if she intended setting her ablaze with her gaze.

"Ma Bih, what's the matter?" questioned Mungeu' completely shaken, meanwhile using Mabel's surname to address Angwi as a sign of respect.

"What is which matter?" questioned Angwi panting. "So this is what you use my daughter's house for, not so? Somebody decides to help you and now you want to own her house not so? Even with her accident and your pregnancy, you still bring your men into her house."

"Now wait a minute Madame," said Mambo.

"Wait which minute, wait which minute?" Angwi retorted.

"Just leave her alone, Sir. I suggest you go now. Please say hello to your wife. I'll see you people tomorrow."

"You better go with him, because you are not spending another night in my daughter's house," said Angwi.

Mungeu' looked at her in disbelief. She had feared it would come to this someday, especially should Mabel die, but it had never occurred to her it could be this soon. "What did you say Ma Bih?"

"If you no longer hear well, ask your man to tell you what I said. I said I want you out of my daughter's house now," she had her words emphasized by pointing to the ground as she spoke.

"Okay, I have heard. Can I pack my things?"

"Pack which things? What is in this house that is yours? Is it not my daughter's clothes and her shoes that you put on? "Pack my things," she sneered at Mungeu', repeating her words with a disgusting twang.

"Could you do me a favour, Sir?"

"Sure! What's it?" asked Mambo with disbelief in his looks.

"I would be grateful if you would kindly drop me off at my place of work."

"That's no problem at all."

"Thank you, Sir," said Mungeu' as she walked back into the room which had been hers until a few minutes ago.

When Mungeu' re-emerged, she was dragging two big

boxes with her. Mambo got up from his seat and took the much bigger box, which was obviously heavier, from her. Before Mungeu' stepped out of the house, she asked Mambo to be her witness and take note of not only what had happened, but the fact that she had taken only her boxes and nothing else. Still shocked as to what was happening in front of him, Mambo was a willing witness.

"I've seen and heard all," Mambo assured Mungeu', with an attitude towards Angwi as if she did not even exist.

After Mambo had loaded the boxes into his vehicle, he sank into the driver's seat and was waiting for Mungeu' with his fingers drumming a strange tune on the steering wheel.

"Ma Bih," called Mungeu' as calmly as ever, "whether you've been sent, or this decision is yours, it does not matter. All I want to say is thank you for everything, but take care of Mabel's property for she is not dead yet. In fact, she is recovering. That's the message brought to me by this man whom you do not know but are so anxious to call my boyfriend. I will leave word, whenever Mabel returns, for her to come to you for her property."

"Yes," retorted Angwi "send her to me. She is my child and she knows her father."

Mambo zoomed off as soon as Mungeu' banged her door shut. "Did you say this is Mabel's mother?"

"Yes she is," answered Mungeu', "but they are two very different people," she quickly added.

"So what are you going to do now?" Mambo questioned.

Mungeu' made to laugh, but it was a short gesture as if she was sniffing at something, then her face hardened. "I don't know yet, but at least I have the whole night to think about it."

"I think you should come to our home. We would be very glad to have you with us," Mambo assured her.

"I don't doubt that Sir, but I would rather spend this first night alone. It will give me time to come to terms with what has just happened, and possibly a plan of action."

"Could you let me in on whatever decision you arrive at?" Mambo's voice sounded as if it were a statement instead of a question.

"Thanks for the concern, Sir. I will."

As Mungeu' lay on the small five-spring bed in the back

of her workshop where she and her apprentices took quick naps when tired, her mind was racing, but it did not take her long to decide on what to do. She had to leave Batemba and stay somewhere else where she would be free from the chains of culture, tradition, and the strain of living in an area where everyone knows or is anxious to know, and modify according to his or her machinations almost everything about the other.

Early in the morning, on his way from hospital, Mambo dropped in with breakfast that had been prepared in his house.

"Good morning Sir!"

"I hope you slept well."

"I am at least refreshed."

"Good. Here is some food for you." In an effort to brush aside Mungeu's thanks, Mambo continued talking. "I have spoken to my wife about what happened yesterday and she is insisting that you have to move into our house, at least until Mabel's return when everything can be sorted out."

Mungeu' bowed her head for some seconds and when she raised it again she spoke with tears in her voice. "I thank her very much for that, Sir, but I would need a little bit more time to think about it."

"You are free to, but remember that it's a good idea if you can put up with us, because especially now, you need someone around you," Mambo suggested.

"Thanks again for everything, Sir."

Mungeu' transferred the food into other dishes which she always kept in her workshop and made to clean those in which Mambo brought the food.

"Don't worry about cleaning them." Mambo took the dishes from her. "Good-bye Mungeu' and see you in the afternoon. I'm almost late for work."

"Good-bye, Sir."

Mungeu' spent the rest of the early hours of the morning thinking about the kindness of Mambo and his wife, but she dreaded the way society was more likely to interpret the whole situation. She was not only going to be branded a second wife Mambo was grooming, he was likely to be held responsible for her pregnancy. As kind and understanding as Munna was, such gossiping, Mungeu' was convinced, was bound to turn Munna against her before long and possibly poison their successful relationship. It would be an opportunity to destroy Mambo and Munna's much-envied marriage. "I wonder why some people just can't bear seeing others happy without making it their duty to deform their happiness. Some would even go to maddening heights to realize this demonic goal." Mungeu was talking to herself.

Mungeu's mind settled on a very pathetic case that bore peculiar similarities at the initial stages, to that of Mambo and Munna. Musa, a presentable young man with a promising future as a pilot fought against all odds to marry Ngwe, a young and exceptionally beautiful high-school student. Her beauty was not only too much for Musa's sisters but for his mother as well. After their marriage, Musa thought he had conquered those relatives of his who preferred anyone else to Ngwe and so became less apprehensive of the vicious insinuations of his relatives who felt Ngwe was emptying their son and brother's wealth. For those who knew how much Musa loved Ngwe, they were more than shocked when Musa not only complained about his wife's increasing beauty, and her tendency to spend money carelessly but went on to beat her up. When Ngwe, unable to account for this change in her husband, moved out, Musa was later found hanging from the roof in his bedroom. Mungeu' shuddered at the thought of such a thing happening to the Mambo's with all fingers pointing at her as the root cause. She did not dismiss the possibility, bearing in mind how well marital conspirators can frame a story about a given situation. As a result, Mungeu' made up her mind to turn down this kind offer. She could be blamed for anything else, but she could not stand the idea of being accused of any unfavourable developments in Mambo and Munna's marriage. Consequently, Mungeu decided to leave before Mambo could pass by again to insist that she joins them.

When Yefon, Mungeu's apprentice, came in later on that morning, Mungeu' narrated all that had happened to her from the summons by her father, the day before, until how she found herself spending the night in the workshop. She told Yefon of her plans to leave the town and Yefon, a girl with a history similar to Mungeu's, an orphan without a guardian, decided on the spot to go along. Accordingly, Yefon rushed back to her single room apartment, a few blocks away from the workshop, to pack her belongings comprising of a box, a bed, a dining table, two cane chairs, a kerosene-stove and some dishes before returning to join Mungeu' at the workshop.

Mungeu' was just emerging from behind where she had spent some time talking to her landlady, Mbanya, a motherly widow in her early fifties, with penetrating looks that tell of wisdom and an understanding nature, only to find Yefon at the threshold of the workshop looking confused since Mungeu' was nowhere to be found. After telling her landlady she had to leave, Mungeu' paid the rent she owed for the first two weeks of the present month, and then thanked her for giving her the opportunity to use her house for business. With tears in her eyes, Mungeu's landlady returned the money she had just received as rents from her.

"I wish I had more to give you my daughter," Mbanya spoke as Mungeu' held the money in her hand in disbelief. "I had heard some women on their way to market talking about what Angwi had done to you, but what can I say? Not every mother has the heart of a mother."

"Thank you Ma!" Mungeu' replied.

"Go well my daughter, and do not let anything change your ways. Forever, remain firm, friendly, and as hard-working as you have been, and I am sure all will be well with you."

Mbanya swallowed Mungeu' up in an embrace before disappearing into her room as if she did not want to witness Mungeu' leaving. "Mambo will get the note," she assured Mungeu' as she walked away. Just then, Kebila, the landlady's last son, a boy of about seventeen, came running towards Mungeu' and Yefon who were both sitting on the edge of the veranda with their legs dangling below in front of their now empty workshop. Mungeu' had quickly written off her other apprentices. She was lucky she was yet to accept any money from them. Had she, it would have been more difficult sending them away without paying back a certain percentage.

"I've seen a vehicle. The driver says you should get ready, that he'd be here soon."

"You didn't tell him we have packed our things already Kebila?"

"I told him sister."

"*Ts-s-e-up*!" sighed Mungeu' anxious to leave before many people could find out.

"Yefon, you really don't have to go with me. I can have you settled in with another mistress as is the case with your friends."

"That's out of the question, I'm going with you."

The sun was right overhead when the taxi arrived. That was about an hour after Kebila returned, but Mungeu' was glad for all the other passengers were already in the bus and so as soon as their things were tied onto the carriage, they would be on their way.

"*We-eh*! Sister, I'm sure you will kill me now," said the driver as he jumped out of the bus playfully and at the same time looking apologetic. "You know how difficult it is to get passengers. In any case, I have already started compensating you by reserving for you the seat behind me, which everybody likes." The driver joked along. Indeed most passengers prefer the seat behind the driver because there is enough room for one's legs. This seat used to be second in passengers' scale of preference only to those beside the driver, but these are now most unpopular since the passenger's comfort is jeopardized each time a uniform brandishing individual, rank notwithstanding, arrived. Such uniform men, thinking only of themselves would demote one passenger from the front seat to the back, if they were going to pay the complete transport fare, or else squeeze themselves in with the other two passengers if they had no money to pay their way. The idea is that they protect unworthy vehicles from the money-snatching claws of most police officers, at checkpoints, who would let a car without a driver continue on its way provided the car could give them a bribe. No wonder citizens have now come to see uniform men on the roads as illegal toll collectors whose idea of the work involved in their job is to harass drivers and passengers. One would wish the money they collected went into public coffers to help pay their undeserved salaries. This, unfortunately, is not the case because the location of their makeshift roadblocks is strategic: in front of Off-License liquor stores.

When their cargo was secured in the carriage, the driver, like a diplomatic orderly, jokingly ushered Mungeu' and Yefon to their seats and slammed the door shut. All through the journey, Mungeu' was troubled each time she thought of the unknown she was travelling into. She was waiting for the slightest opportunity to question the driver about Nju'nki and the accommodation situation there. Nju'nki is a coastal town reputed for its position as a melting pot for cargo ships along the West African Coast and the richly supplied giant shops which benefit from the to and fro movements of these ships. She got her chance when the driver stopped at Mbikam for the passengers to relax themselves for a while. Mbikam is a small roadside village, which is about halfway the distance between Batemba and Nju'nki. Almost every vehicle plying this road stops in this village for the passengers to rest and refresh themselves with food and drinks.

"Sister," he called out," let me finish paying you for the delay now and that child you are carrying will be named after me for all this punishment I'm working," said the driver laughing.

All Mungeu' could do was a weak smile.

"Come! Come! Let's get something for you to eat or else you can wait in the bus and I'll buy all the food you need."

"No, I'll come with you."

Mungeu' could not help wondering at how different people's temperaments could be; that one could be so choleric like Angwi and the other an embodiment of humour and understanding like this driver. Yes, it occurred to her that that was life and only those determined to survive, make it.

"I'm Ndomnjie," said the driver.

"I'm Mungeu'"

"So what are you going to do in Nju'nki?" asked Ndomnjie.

"It's a long story. What is more urgent and important to me now is finding a house to rent. How difficult do you think it would be for me to get a two-room apartment?" asked Mungeu' seizing the opportunity.

"Why?" Ndomnjie looked surprised. "Do you mean you don't have people in Nju'nki?"

"No, I have never been to Nju'nki before. Anyway, like I said, it's a long story and I don't need to go into that now. So how can you help me get a two-room apartment when we get to Nju'nki?"

The look in Ndomnjie's eyes was explicit. He was convinced Mungeu' was a wife running away from a husband with whom she has quarrelled. "I'll see what we can do," said Ndomnjie still wondering at what could be behind this.

"Ndomnjie, I think I know what's on your mind, but I'm not anybody's wife. I'm someone just looking for peace of mind so you need not be afraid of helping. If you can help me, I'll appreciate it."

"Just let me take care of that then," Ndomnjie assured her.

"Thank you," said Mungeu' feeling greatly relieved and more relaxed than before.

With roast meat, plums, and plantains in their hands, Mungeu' and Ndomnjie walked back to the bus towards the other passengers who were already trickling back, munching away at different food items and sipping at their drinks.

## Chapter Four

Months had gently rolled by since Mungeu' and Yefon found themselves at Nju'nki. As it had turned out, Ndomnjie was himself a landlord with houses sprinkled around Nju'nki. His newest house, which still had rooms to be leased out, was around Sokwa, the heart of social and economic activities in the town of Nju'nki. It was to this house that Ndomnjie drove Mungeu' and Yefon late in the evening when they first arrived. Ndomnjie's family lived just a few buildings away and it was with the assistance of this family that Mungeu' found herself quickly settled in her new apartment. Of the two rooms she was to occupy, Mungeu' quickly transformed the outer room facing the road into her workshop. Her four machines, which Ndomnjie had transported two at a time during subsequent trips from Batemba, were lined two on each of two opposing walls. Along the third wall, was a broad shelf on which cloth materials of different colours and textures were displayed. There was enough room between the shelf and the door leading into the second room for people to try on their new clothes before carrying them home.

Settling down had not been easy, but Mungeu' was now much relaxed, being away from the mind-racking looks and whispering voices of gossips in Batemba. Through Ndomnjie's family, Mungeu' easily made new acquaintances and this ensured, in a short space of time, a large supply of customers for her: women coming to have their babies' clothes tailored and those bringing their own materials to have their dresses made. However, this was the ninth month of Mungeu's pregnancy and if her doctor in Batemba was correct, then her baby was due any day now.

Yefon, on her part, was occupying a single room in another of Ndomnjie's houses situated closer to the sea in a business cum residential area called West Beach. In all, Mungeu' and Yefon felt themselves very much at home among these coastal people.

It was a Saturday and as dusk approached, a very refreshing wind from the sea tore its way across the town forcing trees and flowers in its path to bow in humility. The atmosphere, which had been so hot and humid during the day, became cooler and more accommodating with the wind. Mungeu' and Yefon had just finished a review of the week's activity, since Sunday was their resting day, and had closed down the workshop for the day. Together they ate supper in Mungeu's room before Yefon left to walk back to her home. It was at least a kilometre away, but since her route was through the buzzing town, there was a lot to distract her and make the trek interesting.

All alone, with Yefon gone, Mungeu' accepted to herself that all the awkwardness during the day amounted to symptoms, she had learned during her clinic sessions, of impending labour. Quietly she put into a small briefcase all the items she had been told must be present with her whenever she was sure it was time. The cramps were beginning to be frequent and so Mungeu' thought it was time to walk to Ndomnjie's wife, Ndolo, and tell her how she was feeling. Ndomnjie, who had lived in the coast for at least fifteen years, had met Ndolo during his struggling days as a young man. After ten years in marriage, Ndolo had not changed much from what she looked like when Ndomnjie first saw her: a tall woman with a slim build yet with broad hips that bulged to the sides. Behind smooth eyelids tipped by clusters of long black eyelashes were islands of black surrounded by very clear soothing white pools, which gave her a gentle appearance. Her delicate yet slightly pronounced cheekbones narrowed down to a small chin. Her full lips always parted in gentle welcoming smiles, revealing dazzling white teeth that lit up her facial features. The gap in the upper row of teeth was simply tantalizing. In spite of her screaming beauty, Ndolo was gentle, understanding and very friendly. After three children—two girls and a boy—with a gap of two years between each and the younger, Ndolo looked like a girl of twenty-three.

When Mungeu' knocked on Ndomnjie's door round about 9:00 pm, Ndolo, a primary school teacher, was busy correcting children's scripts; she was holding some in her hand when she opened the door.

"I knew! Looking at you in the morning I was sure you would not last until tomorrow," said Ndolo smiling. "How is it? Bad?"

"Not really," Mungeu' answered with a weak smile.

"I pray it waits until these children's father returns. He went up (meaning to Batemba) yesterday but said he would be back today."

"Well, I just thought I should let you know how I am feeling. I'll call as soon as I think we should get going."

"That's alright. *Ashia ya!*" said Ndolo comfortingly.

It was about an hour later on when Mungeu', briefcase in hand, met Ndolo heading for her house. Ndolo was coming to find out how Mungeu' was feeling but was equally ready to accompany Mungeu' to the hospital straight away should the need suddenly arise—a distance of about a kilometre along a gently climbing slope. Mungeu' could barely stay erect. But as luck would have it, after just a few steps, which brought them to Half-Mile, the converging point of all major roads in Nju'nki, they met Ndomnjie dropping off his passengers. Without a question, after his wife explained things to him, Ndomnjie, even after his long and tiring trip from Batemba, immediately turned right around and carried both Mungeu' and Ndolo to the hospital.

When Ndolo and Ndomnjie finally went to bed it was 4:00 am, an hour after the uneventful arrival of Mungeu's baby girl.

After the delivery of her child, Mungeu' was more determined than ever to succeed in her business and with the assistance of Yefon, the business flourished. She found herself with both money and time, much of which she spent on her daughter—Ndolo-Mabel. As a way of showing her gratitude to Ndomnjie's family and her stepsister, Mungeu' had named her child after both Ndolo, Ndomnjie's wife, and her stepsister, Mabel. Mungeu' wished for one thing—that Ndolo-Mabel would get the parental love and education she did not have. Therefore, as the years went by, Ndolo-Mabel grew up with her mother supervising her every step.

★★★

Ever since Mungeu's departure from Batemba, nothing had been heard of, or from her. In her family nobody, apparently, cared about her, but Pa Anye's mind occasionally went to this child of his whom he knew, deep down in him, he had neglected. Each time his eyes fell on Mungeu's mother's house, he thought, with guilt, of both mother and child, both of whom now seemed dead to him.

Munna had long left the hospital and, although feeling much better, walked with a slight and barely noticeable tilt to the left with each step. Mabel too had returned, and she was almost as sound as ever, even though it took her slightly longer to recall events that had taken place, or persons she had known. A little probe from her listener did the trick and she never forgot again. In any case, with the passing of time she soon recovered fully. Her return was indeed victorious.

It was a quiet, calm Saturday afternoon with a very bright sky when a pick-up belonging to African Progressive Bank glided into town heavily loaded. Beside the driver, a young man of about twenty, sat a young woman who took in the town and inhaled the warm afternoon air with so much joy and relish. To the occupants of the town who saw the truck, it was just one of those vehicles always coming in with cargo from the coast. However, to the young woman who sat beside the driver, it was coming home after months during which she met, wrestled with, and struck a truce with death. It was a very happy day for Mabel because only a very few and extremely lucky persons are given audience to by death, and left to return to the world of the living. If anything else, one thing kept her happiness bubbling in her chest all through her journey home: the thought of meeting Mungeu' again. The thought of Mungeu's pregnancy which was, at first, vague to her was now clear and she was sure the baby would have been born. How she longed to meet both mother and child and to find out how she braved the storm that was already brewing before her departure.

After stopping at her manager's house where even the manager wept for joy, they stopped at Munna's place where they shed more tears. Munna wept and smiled as her temperament changed. She vividly replayed, mentally, everything they had gone through. She had hoped Mabel would not be deformed in any way. Her eyes searched every exposed spot of her friend's body. At last, she could heave a sigh of relief. But for a thin scar on her scalp, slightly above the right ear (Mabel had to part her hair to expose it), the scar on her throat, and the fact that Mabel's speed of recalling was yet to return fully, she looked very well. Mabel would not eat without seeing Mungeu' and so she said she had to hurry home. The Mambos feared giving her the news about Mungeu's departure and so preferred letting her find out in her own way. They promised, in any case, to call on her later on in the day. To buffer the effect of not finding Mungeu' at home, Munna hinted at the fact that a lot had gone wrong in her absence and promised to explain what they knew later on.

Mabel's heart missed a beat as she stepped onto her veranda twenty minutes later. Although her blinds were still there, the thick layer of dust on the veranda was ominous. It was easy to see that for a very long time nobody had stepped there. When this thought struck home Mabel rushed back into the van sniffing.

"Let's go," she ordered.

"I hope nothing is wrong madam," put in the driver.

"My sister, John," answered Mabel.

The driver drove off to Pa Anye's place following Mabel's directions. Before they got there, she had managed to put herself together. When the van pulled to a stop in Pa Anye's courtyard, his wives, Mabel's mother included, with a number of dusty, half naked children with tears and catarrh trickling down from their eyes and nostrils, emerged from the different buildings. Never before had a vehicle come that far into the compound. Whatever the reasons-maybe her return was too sudden, or she had been considered dead—the welcome she got was calm and quiet. The women and children walked up and embraced her, and then her mother came up last.

"My child," she called.

"Mother!" answered Mabel with a weak smile.

"You have returned." It was a statement.

"Yes I have. Where is my father?"

Just then, Pa Anye was stepping out of his house. He had been lying down in his bed resting when he heard the sound of a vehicle driven into his compound. After waiting in vain for someone to bring him news about the vehicle, he decided to come out and see for himself.

All had gone well so far. The driver who brought Mabel had eaten and was drinking a bottle of Special, while Mabel sipped at very fresh raffia-palm from a glass. The calabash of raffia-palm was standing between Angwi and Mabel herself. They were all in Pa Anye's parlour, a room slightly bigger than the other two rooms in the house with their doors on the left and right walls. Inside the parlour were five wooden chairs, with one double the size of each of the other four, which were meant to take a person each. A very solid cupboard, just before the entrance into the room on the left, betrayed glasses and plates of different sizes through a glass window. The walls of the parlour were covered with black-and-white pictures, the ages of which became obvious at a glance. There were pictures of Pa Anye and his first wife and others in which members of the entire family were present. The most pronounced picture was one of Pa Anye in the police uniform of his days as a policeman serving Her Majesty the queen in the colonies, with four medals of honour hanging from his left breast.

After waiting for a while to hear mention made of Mungeu' in vain, Mabel decided to question.

"Where is Mungeu'?" The question was directed at nobody in particular, but both her parents were present.

"Child won't you bathe, eat and rest for a while first?" suggested Angwi.

"How can I bathe, eat and rest without seeing Mungeu', mother?" questioned Mabel. "Where is Mungeu'?"

"It's a very long story and I think we should talk about it tomorrow," suggested Angwi.

"Let me know what I can now," Mabel was determined.

When Mabel, after taking her keys from her mother, left her parents' compound for hers that evening, she had heard her mother's version of what had happened to Mungeu' in her absence, but she was sure there had been a lot of distortions, for Mungeu' would never insult Angwi, never! Mabel was sure. Moreover, to authenticate her conviction, her father had said nothing all through but had sat pensively, staring within himself. Mabel knew her mother had hated the idea of her living with Mungeu' but had never thought she could go as far as sending her away. What grieved her more was the fact that they did not even know where Mungeu' had moved to and had not cared to find out, in spite of the fact that she was pregnant when she left. "What grief is this?" Mabel wondered. "How can a girl go on suffering all through her life and yet one cannot find what she has done wrong? Things just keep going wrong for her all the time?" Mabel stared at the dismal sky as if questioning nature why Mungeu' had to suffer so much.

Besides the staleness, Mabel's house was intact when she got into it. While John, the driver, offloaded the cargo straight into the room formerly occupied by Mungeu', Mabel took her bath. When finally she emerged from her room, John was sitting on the edge of a chair beside the dining table.

"John, you will wait for me to prepare something for us to eat before you can go and rest, okay."

"I have already eaten at—"

"No! No! You can't come and go like that, just wait."

Mabel was still talking when the Mambos arrived. There was a girl of about fifteen holding a basket containing food dishes.

"Sorry we are not letting you rest," Munna apologized.

"What rest Munna? I have been resting for months."

"Anyway, I brought food for you. Lum, bring those food flasks from the car," said Munna, addressing the girl who came with them. "There's some jollof rice and your favourite fried fish in here and in the other dish, fried plantains and eggs. Sit down and eat at once before they get cold."

Mabel went into her kitchen and came back with plates for everyone, but the Mambo's said they had had their share before coming. Mambo, however, ate very briefly from Mabel's plate wishing her a good appetite.

"You must rest now Mabel. We will see you tomorrow," said Munna. "We will see you tomorrow," she added as if to emphasize her promise.

"Thanks Munna. I will wait for you. Morning?"

"Yes as soon as Mambo is off to work I'll come. You are welcome," she said, grabbing Mabel's head and pressing it against her bosom. Mabel who was still sitting on the dining chair grabbed Munna round the waist and they stayed like that for a while. "Before I forget, Lum will stay and help you until you settle down. Say a week or two would be alright I guess?"

Mabel could not speak. Overtaken by her emotions, she only nodded. After the Mambos, John also left with Mabel urging him to visit as often as he wished.

## Chapter Five

Time passed, and as the days went by, Mabel's life, gradually and without any fresh setbacks, returned to normal, and but for the gap created by Mungeu's absence, she was her old self once more. Mabel, however, was bent on finding Mungeu' without publicising it, but so much time had elapsed and she herself feared she might hardly meet anyone with any vital information about Mungeu'.

With his wealth increasing, Ndomnjie had moved to a more secluded compound he had built for his family at One-Mile on the way out of Nju'nki. Mungeu', meanwhile, had transformed her business into one more lucrative. She now had twenty girls learning to sew from her. She had also added another section to the business—the knitting unit. In this unit the ladies called thrice a week—Monday, Wednesday and Friday—and for hours each day were taught knitting. Accordingly, Mungeu' had occupied two more rooms. She got all her materials from Nigeria, travelling with other traders by sea in powered canoes. Ndolo-Mabel had started nursery education at Girls Nursery School in West Beach. Like her mother, she was a quiet child with gentle looks that belied her strong personality, which was already beginning to worry Mungeu' who did not think it was good for a child to be so firm in her ways. However, Ndolo-Mabel's gentle smile, whenever Mungeu' looked troubled about her, calmed her fears. It was one such encounter which Mungeu' was trying to deflate when she decided to go out for a brief walk with the intention of meeting some of her business partners so they could finalize plans for their trip to Nigeria early the next morning. Nigeria was a neighbouring country to the Northeast of Caramenju.

When Mungeu' returned, it was already very dark. She put two dresses, two loincloths and two blouses into her small traveller's bag alongside her bathing items before going to bed. As usual, she had been telling Ndolo-Mabel a whole week before that she had to travel again. She did this to prepare her daughter's mind for the hour of departure so she would not cling to her in tears. The first time this happened, Mungeu's spirit remained at low all through the trip. The trick worked. After repeating very often that she had to travel, Ndolo-Mabel got used to the idea and sometimes even turned around to ask Mungeu' if she was not travelling again. Thus prepared for her mother's departure, when she woke the following morning and did not see her, it was easy to convince herself that her mother had travelled according to her plans.

This night, when Mungeu' returned from seeing the other traders, she went into Ndolo-Mabel's room, peered at her as she slept, and sighed to herself before gently placing her lips on Ndolo-Mabel's right cheek. Yefon, who always stayed behind with Ndolo-Mabel whenever Mungeu' went on such trips, was already asleep too, but she turned to welcome Mungeu' before going back to sleep.

★★★

Whenever Mungeu' travelled, she took about a week and usually there was no anxiety on the part of those back at home. But this time, the Ndomnjies and Yefon were worried for word had come that many canoes returning from Nigeria capsized because of the very bad weather, while others were attacked by armed robbers to whom human life meant nothing. Mungeu' was now two days late, given that she was always away only for a week. Secretly Yefon had her fears for two days ago word came that robbers had attacked a canoe, killed all the traders and carried away their cargo. Her fears heightened when it occurred to her that for the last two nights Ndolo-Mabel had been disturbed in her sleep by dreams during which she always cried, calling out to her mother. Ndomnjie, to whom she had complained, had calmed her fears by assuring her that sometimes because of unforeseen circumstances a business trip could be prolonged. But Ndomnjie himself could no longer hide his fears when five days after her due date Mungeu' had still not shown up nor had they heard from her. Ndolo and Ndomnjie, whenever he was in town, had been spending their evenings at Mungeu's place, with Yefon and Ndolo-Mabel, waiting for Mungeu's return.

It was slightly above a week after Mungeu's due date when they, Ndomnjie included, had been sitting like this, playing the game of *Ludo* one cold and rainy evening when a knock came on the door.

"Ye-e-s!" answered Ndomnjie glancing at his wife questioningly. "Who is it?" he asked.

"It's me Sir. Ejike is my name."

Ndomnjie pulled back the bolts and saw a young man of about twenty drenched from head to toe with his teeth clattering. "Yes, what can I do for you?" asked Ndomnjie tensed.

"I would like to see the owner of this house, Sir," said Ejike.

"She is not around, but if there is anything, you can tell me," Ndomnjie assured Ejike as he stepped out to join him on the veranda, shutting the door behind him.

"It's very cold outside and you are wet, why don't you come in?"

"No Sir, it's alright since I won't be long. I'm already very wet. Thank you."

"Okay, if you choose."

"I am just returning from Nigeria and things went wrong. I was with Sister Mungeu' when we were attacked by armed robbers. For days now, I have been in police custody, detained because I brought news of the attack. Only two of us managed to escape and it took us about three days to finally get to Nju'nki and I went straight to the police with the story."

"Where you were detained?"

"Yes Sir."

"But why were you detained?"

"You know the police. They thought I was part of the whole plot instead of another trader who managed to escape from the attack."

"So where is Mungeu' now?" questioned Ndomnjie completely shaken. It was not as if he did not understand what Ejike was saying. He was confused and felt the need to hear Ejike tell him in plain terms that Mungeu' was one of the casualties of the armed bandits' attack.

"She was sitting right in front of me when the thieves started shooting from a distance. I heard her scream before her body hit the floor of the canoe. Then the man on my right fell right on me. I remember hitting my head, and that was all. When I woke up, there were so many bodies—men and women—all around me. We had been dumped in the creeks, which we were trying to avoid when we were attacked. As I sat there trying to recollect myself, a man of about forty started moaning beside me. He had a bullet wound around the left rib cage and the inner side of his left arm was also badly affected. With this man, two days after we had been running in the bushes, I signalled a custom patrol boat that brought us to Nju'nki. The rest were taken to hospital, while the police who all this while have been questioning me, kept me in custody. They've only released me today so I thought I should find out if Sister Mungeu's family was already aware of what happened since we normally travelled together even when in Nigeria."

"Thank you," said Ndomnjie as he leaned against the wall for support. "So Mungeu' is dead," he thought aloud in disbelief.

When Ndomnjie became conscious of his surroundings again, he found his wife holding his hand and asking him what happened. Since it was late and obvious that nothing could be done that evening about Mungeu's corpse, Ndolo only went back to her house to check on her children before returning to Mungeu's house where she and her husband spent the night with Yefon and Ndolo-Mabel.

# Chapter Six

Early the following morning, hardly having slept, Ndomnjie opened the door of Mungeu's house to let out his wife who thought it was necessary for her to go to their own house before the children woke up. Ndolo had virtually spent the whole night crying, and so the first thing she did as she stepped out into the street was to blow her nose before taking up the loose end of her loincloth to dry her eyes, finishing up with her nostrils. As Ndolo walked away in the direction of her house, it occurred to Ndomnjie that she had disappeared too soon from sight. He slowly swung his head from right to left, his eyes taking in the atmosphere from shoulder to shoulder, and it struck him that it was still unusually dark although it was already some minutes off 7:00 am. Then his eyes caught the very thick layer of rain clouds that frustrated every effort by the rays of dawn to reach the earth. Very slowly, confidently, and with an air as if everything else was beneath them, the clusters of rain clouds spread across the atmosphere sealing off the sky. Ndomnjie shuddered as the chill morning wind hissed past him.

Many questions flooded Ndomnjie's mind as he stood in front of Mungeu's door gazing at nothing in particular. He wondered about the people to contact to get some assistance in handling Mungeu's corpse, since she was already a woman and a mother although not married. He wondered how things sometimes happened. Mungeu' who hardly talked about her family had strangely brought up a conversation about them just before this trip. It was on this occasion that she spoke about her father, her own mother, her death, and how she had to struggle to survive without her. In detail, she had also mapped out her plans for the future, to the astonishment of Ndomnjie.

Ndolo, on returning, was not exactly surprised to see her husband standing where he was when she walked off.

"What are we to do?" she questioned.

"Well, an idea just occurred to me. First of all, I will, at 8:00 am, hurry to the hospital to identify the body. As soon as that is done, I will inform the members of our traditional meeting– *Nda- got* –about the death and together, I think we will be able to solve the problems that may arise according to our tradition. Today is Saturday?"

"*H-m-m!*" Ndolo mumbled.

"Then I better hurry up, else we might have to wait until Monday. Meanwhile, ask Yefon to help you pack her belongings into those trunks she brought back from Nigeria the other time. Her clothes, shoes and other personal items must be neatly packed. Clear the parlour so that her body can lie in state there while we empty the workshop. When you've done that, hurry and put a few things together for ourselves, since we have to go up with the body, okay?"

"Okay. In that case, I will have to send word to the village, or go myself, for Mbamba to come and take care of the children and the house while we are away." She was referring to her mother.

"Okay you do that, and quickly too, since we must leave this afternoon."

When Ndomnjie got to the hospital, the nurses were just beginning to settle down for the day's work. He figured it must be about 8:00 am already. He found his way into the casualty unit where a few elderly nurses were consulting patients with minor ailments.

"Good morning!" greeted Ndomnjie aloud.

Only the elderly nurse closest to him responded. Ndomnjie did not care. He had more serious business at hand than to care about the whims of nurses.

"Please, who am I to see about the bodies for identification in the mortuary?"

The nurse looked at Ndomnjie before speaking. "Just follow the corridor until you get to the end of that building you see there, then turn left and walk straight to the building you'll find at the end of the corridor. That's the mortuary and the attendant's office is next to it. In fact as you approach the building, he is likely to call your attention through the window."

"Thank you."

Ndomnjie followed the nurse's directions and when he was a few paces from the mortuary building, a man sent his head out through one of the three windows facing Ndomnjie's direction.

"Good morning!" he greeted. "May I help you?"

Two ideas ran across Ndomnjie's mind as he approached the window through which the man had addressed him. He was convinced this man's training emphasized politeness or else he was specially chosen to operate the mortuary because of his manner. Ndomnjie could hardly remember any time in his life when he approached any other wing of the hospital needing help and the staff on duty greeted him first. He smiled to himself at a recent experience he had with the nurses at the labour room, when Ndolo was to put to bed their last child. "The nurses behave as if their womanhood is threatened by the idea of a different woman other than themselves having a baby. They insult and say many horrible things to women undergoing the pangs of labour, instead of being of help to them" he thought. One nurse had asked Ndolo, as she paced naked around the labour room, if she did not know the results of what she was doing with a man, hanging both legs up in the air. Ndomnjie was positive that this polite mortuary attendant was put here because of the delicate and sensitive nature of this unit. "People coming to the mortuary usually have battered emotions and no patience to deal with these nurses," he thought.

"Good morning, I need help," answered Ndomnjie.

"Come in. What can I do for you?" The attendant went on with a politeness that Ndomnjie was convinced would be better employed in the wards. In the wards, visitors walk a tightrope, not knowing whether their patients will make it or not and could do with a polite staff person there instead of in the mortuary where visitors already know the fate of their patients. Ndomnjie stepped in through a double door into a room almost empty, but for a writing table and two small chairs one of which the nurse was sitting on. On the writing table were books that looked like registers and the day's issue of *The Caramenju Tribune,* which the nurse must have been reading before Ndomnjie interrupted him. Behind the nurse, as he sat at his table motioning Ndomnjie to the other chair, Ndomnjie noticed two doors—one to the left, the other to the right. From behind the door on his left, he could hear a faint humming sound like that of a refrigerator.

"I have just heard of the presence of some corpses from the armed robbery attack in the sea between Caramenju and Nigeria. I'm here to check if my neighbour is among them. She travelled about a month ago to Nigeria and until now we are yet to hear from her." Ndomnjie spoke after sitting down.

"Can you describe her? Anyway, we have only two women here and both their national identity cards were found in the pockets of their gowns. Come and see for yourself if one of them is the one you are looking for." The nurse spoke as he walked to the door on the right bound to be leading to the documentation room of the mortuary unit. He pulled out a drawer from a file cabinet, sighed as if he had done the wrong thing, pushed back the drawer and pulled out the one immediately below. He took out two identity cards neatly coated in black plastic jackets. Both had, on one edge, tapes of different colours glued together on the jackets amounting to the national colours—green, red, yellow. "Have a look," said the nurse as he handed both identity cards to Ndomnjie.

Ndomnjie's hands were shaking as he sent both hands forward, undecided whether to use his left or right hand in taking the identity cards from the nurse. The first card he looked at was that of a much older woman who in no way resembled Mungeu'. With a thumping heart because of a strange kind of happiness he felt at the first lady not being Mungeu', Ndomnjie hurriedly switched the positions of the identity cards, moving the one whose owner he could not recognize to the bottom and the other to the top. The eye is usually too fast. Ndomnjie was yet to concentrate on the second identity card when his eyes fell on the long pale face on the card which, unlike Mungeu' as he had known her, was strangely without a smile. The photographer must have reminded her not to smile else the photograph would be rejected. Yes, although she looked much younger, Ndomnjie knew it was Mungeu' as soon as he saw the picture. With his hands trembling more violently, Ndomnjie walked back into the neighbouring room where they were originally and leaned on the lone table from which position the attendant commanded a good view of the only entrance into the mortuary. He tried talking, but his voice failed him. Then he took out his handkerchief and wiped away the sweat on his face. Outside, the thunderclap increased in intensity with lightening cracking and flashing from horizon to horizon. Suddenly a heavy shower of raindrops was heard on the mortuary roof, but it lasted only a few seconds. Looking through the window Ndomnjie could see the shower rushing from the mortuary block away into the distance. In his mind, he saw the buildings as part of a big field with a sprinkler positioned in the middle slowly spinning round and occasionally giving each area within a given circumference an opportunity to cool its thirst.

"I'm sorry," said the mortuary attendant to Ndomnjie.

"Thank you. Can I see her?" asked Ndomnjie.

"Yes sure! If you wish."

"Yes I would like to."

The attendant led Ndomnjie through the door to the left, across from the documentation room. The humming sound doubled. They walked down a corridor with a series of doors on either side of the corridor, and then the attendant stopped in front of the last door on their right. The double door opened in both directions, but the attendant pushed it in. Ndomnjie found himself inside a large room with the humming sound vibrating his person as if it were coming from within him. The first things that caught his attention were the gurneys and then a cement slab with a depression the length of its middle and a tap on the top left edge. Then it occurred to Ndomnjie that what he took for a wall, from the other end of the room, was indeed compartmentalized.

"Come this way," said the attendant as he went ahead to the middle of the compartmentalized wall. He picked up a small square card hanging on a string from the handle of one of the small compartments, read it, dropped it, picked up the next one to the left, read it, then turned and looked at Ndomnjie. Ndomnjie who had kept a safe distance behind the attendant came up close and read the tag for himself: "Mungeu' Anye." The attendant pulled out a kind of stretcher on which lay a human form covered with a thin, green plastic sheet.

"You want to see it?" asked the attendant, the idea being that Ndomnjie should brace himself.

Ndomnjie could only nod.

The attendant, with some care, held the edge of the sheet away from the body and folded it once down to the level of the chest. Ndomnjie stared in disbelief, the body, but for a cut on the left shoulder, looked very much as if she was just asleep. Ndomnjie stared hard at her chest and indeed, it was not dancing to the rhythm of life. Her face looked white, almost as if a thin layer of powder had been dabbed on it. There were very tiny drops of water on her face and body, giving the impression that she was sweating. Ndomnjie's head was resting on the left side of his body in his left palm and the elbow of his left arm on his right wrist that gave it support somewhere at the level of his lowest left rib bone.

Suddenly, Ndomnjie jerked as if he had received a prick.

"Wait! Wait! Wait! Let me see." He pulled out the stretcher almost completely and then positioned himself with his back against the cooling plant, to get a better look at the corpse. "Something is wrong. This is not Mungeu'. She is not the one!"

"Calm down Sir. Don't get yourself worked up. Just stay calm and all will be fine. Are you sure about what you are saying?"

"I am convinced. I know Mungeu' very well. It is true there is some resemblance, but Mungeu' has more hair on her body than this. At first I thought it was the cold, but now I'm convinced she is not the one. Mungeu' is even taller. Let's check all the female corpses here."

"No, we can't do that. I'm positive about our documentation system. At best we could look at the other corpses from the same attack, but I can assure you this is the owner of the I.D. you saw because I personally took it out of the pocket of the *caba* she had on. Come, have a look." The mortuary attendant had dragged out the stretcher in the compartment to the right of that which to him contained Mungeu's corpse as they spoke.

"She is not the one either." Ndomnjie was certain. "This one is fatter. So what do we do now?"

"It's hard to say because the rest of the corpses are male and are from the accident which occurred around West Beach yesterday. All I'll advise is that you make a report with the police."

"What will they do? Those people who hate leaving their offices to investigate petty theft cases around town, you think they will bother with such a complicated issue?

"Just make your report so that somebody should not ask you someday why you didn't inform the police. That is the least you can do. Whether you believe in our police force or not, you would have done your part."

"Thanks for everything."

"Thank you and good-bye. Please do let me know should anything come up.

"I will," Ndomnjie answered as he hurried out of the mortuary. His mind raced as he tried to decide on what to do and tried to understand the confusion in the mortuary. In this state of mind, he walked right to his car without being conscious of his surroundings. He sighed as he tried fitting the wrong key into the door. Then he heard the call.

"*Monya*!"

"What is this?" Ndomnjie questioned in a whisper as he turned slowly in the direction of the call that came from behind a bus. His heart must have stopped beating for only Mungeu' and his mother-in-law addressed him "in-law." That was not his mother-in-law's voice. He saw his wife first and then Mungeu' emerged from behind her. Ndomnjie's face went through a dozen unrelated expressions following the rhythm of his feelings: from sadness through confusion to happiness and, as he saw Mungeu's heavily bandaged left arm, alarm.

"O my God!' Munny, what is this? What happened?"

Mungeu' only had time to gesture by twisting her head slightly to the right and showing her right palm to the sky as a way of saying "just as you see it," before she was swallowed up by Ndomnjie in an embrace. They were locked up like this for quite a while with Ndolo staring unseeingly from behind her tears.

"Thank God, thank God," Ndomnjie kept whispering as he loosened his grip. "You don't know what we have gone through," he said turning to look at Ndolo who was drying her eyes.

"I can imagine," answered Mungeu' calmly.

"I delayed a bit after you left, trying to get the children something to eat and just when I was about leaving to ask Mbamba to come and stay with the kids, Yefon rushed into the house to tell me she had arrived. I immediately told her what we had heard and she decided to join me since I thought I had to stop you from raising a false alarm."

"Just give me a few seconds. I'll be back."

When Ndomnjie returned, he was almost running as if by the time he came out the scene would have faded away. The mortuary attendant was behind him.

"Munny!" Ndomnjie called out, as if to ensure it was indeed Mungeu' he was seeing.

"*Monya*!" she answered.

"Welcome madam," the mortuary attendant greeted. "You are indeed very welcome. I'm glad to see you. Ndomnjie will tell you what we've gone through. You must rest. I'll see you later on. I know the house. This is your identity card."

"Oh yes, thank you Sir. The police officer who looked at our documents before we left the shore here made the mistake. Because both identities are the same, he mixed them up and we, on our part, didn't check. Hers is with me also. Here you are," said Mungeu' after foraging her bag for a while.

"You must rest madam, we will talk later on."

"Thank you."

After every two or three steps, the retreating mortuary attendant turned, looked at Mungeu' and clapped his hands in disbelief.

Before Mungeu' went to bed that afternoon for a nap with Ndolo-Mabel who would not let her out of her sight, she had asked Yefon and Ndolo to help prepare a large variety of dishes for at least fifteen to twenty people and to get drinks for that number.

When Mungeu' left her bedroom with Ndolo-Mabel still tailing her, it was getting dark and some of the guests were already arriving. Ndolo had brought in her sisters to help. Mungeu's sitting room had been rearranged, with many more chairs brought in from neighbours to accommodate visitors. The cooking was almost done with too. She drove the sleep from her face with cold water before changing into another *caba*.

"We are waiting for *Monya*," she told Ndolo who was beginning to question about the delay with her eyes.

"That has to be him," Ndolo observed after they heard some car doors banging shut.

"We will begin as soon as he is here."

Shortly after Ndomnjie brought in the last group of friends and was himself comfortably seated by his wife and kids, Mungeu' stood up and cleared her voice in response to a wink from Ndolo. She stretched her neck to look at the dining table behind the chairs of the guests on her right, before beginning. "My dear parents, brothers, and sisters who are sitting here today, because I know how much you have all contributed to my success, because I know you all care and have always wanted to know what is happening to me, a new phase is beginning in my life and I owe you all an explanation. That is why you are here today. My story is a painful one that I can't go on repeating each time I meet a new friend. It is for this reason that my benefactor here, Ndomnjie, and I agreed that this is just the right forum for you to get my story. I will not even let a day go by before I tell you myself. Many of you are wearing strange faces already because you have noticed only a stump where once I had a left hand. It is for this purpose that I have asked you all to come, hear my story, and join me in thanking God that I can, at least, be here with you today when those who were with me on this trip, but for a few, are now history. In fact, the news my God-given family here received was that I was dead."

"Wa-nda-ful!" exclaimed a guest

"The kind informant, one Ejike with whom I always travel, was correct, for only a miracle saved me. Ejike is in here, and before I proceed, I want to thank him for the effort he made to inform my family of the trouble that had befallen me.

"Ejike saw me shot and heard my cry before I fell to the floor of the canoe. Of course, you know of my repeated trips to our neighbours for our needs. I must have fainted because I only discovered myself amidst other bodies on the shore. Even before I could gather enough energy to moan, I heard our attackers debating on what to do with us. They settled on burning our bodies. They had taken us all for dead. One of the robbers had been instructed to carry out their decision. He had, in fact, returned with a jerry can of fuel from their launch and had started sprinkling it on our bodies when the sound of the others struggling and quarrelling over the loot got to him. He dropped the container and rushed over to our canoes. What made me not cry out when I felt petrol on my body and knew what was coming next, I can't say. I can't equally tell you from where I got the energy. However, with all my might, I dragged myself into the nearest bush, tied my battered left arm with my gown and started running away naked. I had no sense of direction. I had, however, been running for quite a while when I was hit by this strange sensation, and then, all of a sudden I was falling as everything turned black.

"When I woke up, I was in a small but well furnished room. I tried to move but couldn't, then again I felt the pain in my left arm. When I looked at it, it was heavily bandaged and appeared shorter, as if almost everything under the elbow was gone. Then I remembered what had happened to me and I knew for certain that my arm had been amputated. My scream brought a young man rushing into the room. 'Oh, you are awake at last. Thank God,' he said as he gathered me comfortably into his arms. He introduced himself as Dr Abonkem and told me I was in an offshore hospital belonging to Sklumbager, one of the oil prospecting companies along our coastal waters. He made me understand their dog had found me lying about fifty metres from their picnic site and it barked until they arrived at the scene. From there, as he told me, I was rushed to their hospital in a speedboat. The bullet had heavily battered my left arm. The bone in the middle, between my wrist and elbow, was in splinters. The offshore medical team had no choice, they agreed, but to immediately cut off my arm." Mungeu' paused for a while to let silence return as some women were already weeping and blowing their nostrils. "The doctors say it's a miracle I didn't die from loss of blood."

"What kind of bad dream is this?" proclaimed a man and at the same time producing a heavy pop sound as he clapped his cupped hands.

"The doctors kept me for about five days, after I regained consciousness, during which time they treated my arm with wonderful care. This morning I was flown into the premises of their head office here in Nju'nki with the doctors who reported all that had happened to the police. After recording all we could give them, we were asked to go. Outside the police station, I turned and faced the doctors, waiting to hear them give me this wonderful bill. All they wanted was my address to be able to forward me a device to wear over the arm. Before leaving, they promised to visit me, if they would be able to find the time, or else they would see me when the prosthetic arm arrived from Germany. I then took a taxi home. This is me before you all."

When Mungeu' stopped talking, for about a whole minute there was no movement. Not even a fly buzzed past; all was quiet. Then one woman clapped her hands and rubbed off the right palm against the left in a quick sudden movement towards and beyond the fingertips of the left palm. "Wa-a-nd-a-f-u-l!" she exclaimed.

Mungeu' was already sobbing and it drowned her last words as she tried to sum up with one or two more sentences. Ndomnjie rushed towards Mungeu' and took her in his arms and led her to her seat.

"What is the matter? What really is the matter? What has a child like this done to deserve this?" It was the same man who had called Mungeu's story a bad dream.

Ndomnjie turned and faced the visitors. "Well, we have all heard what our sister has gone through and no doubt, as Pa Ndeh has already pointed out, it sounds like a bad dream. We thank God for bringing her back to us after everything. The food and drinks our sister has offered us is her own way of gathering us to join her in thanking God, for He Himself is the one who told us that where two or three are gathered in His name, He is present. Let us rise in prayers."

As people rose to their feet, Nkang, a short skinny man with wrinkles always on his forehead, who believed in the curative powers of humour, saw his chance. In Nju'nki, Nkang is known as a man who makes light of even the burden of his own misfortune by transforming it into a joke. He claims that anyone who cannot crack a joke, or at least enjoy one, is dead. Nkang walks as if he is trying to keep his thighs from having any contact. He tells all who ask him why he always has on a loincloth instead of a pair of trousers like other men and why he walks as if his scrotum had been operated upon, to go find out from his ex-wife. Nkang had realised it would be difficult transforming the solemn atmosphere conjured by Mungeu's affliction into one for drinking and eating without a joke and so went to work.

"Ndomnjie, are you a businessman or a pastor?"

"What is your concern?' asked Ndomnjie with a smile.

"My concern is simple. If you are the rich businessman I know you are, then I know why you are fighting so hard to please God. You know God does not like rich people so now you are trying to bribe Him. You are only wasting your time. If you want to go to heaven, hand over all your wealth to poor people like myself. Only then can you enter heaven, for God said he would rather have a camel enter a needle than a rich man enter heaven."

"It is not enter a needle, Nkang, it is pass through the eye of a needle," said another guest as they roared with laughter. More so even, you have turned the whole thing round. God does not hate rich people. He ..."

"What is the difference?" Nkang cut in. "Did you comprehend me or not?

"Break the grammar, Nkang!" somebody exclaimed, reacting to Nkang's use of the high sounding word, "comprehend."

"It's not my fault if you are not schooled," Nkang answered back laughing. "You see the kind of people who spoil this world? What is the difference between a woman and a girl? Stupid!" He went on firing back at the man who accused him of distorting the biblical passage on the camel and the eye of a needle, and the rich and heaven.

"Okay, okay," Ndomnjie tried hushing the guests, some of whom had laughed themselves to tears. "I am very sure Nkang would like to put something between his molars before anything else."

"Yes, it is always Nkang! You would not like anything between yours? No doubt you are not as fat as I am," Nkang retorted jokingly. "Tell people you want to eat and leave my name alone."

It was late in the night when an old man sensed it was time many of the guests would like to leave. He called for quiet as he stood up. "My daughter, I know you as a neighbour who sews my daughters' clothes and the mistress to my house girl who is one of your apprentices. Whatever the case, I thank you for bringing us here together. Before I go, I just want to say one thing: do not give up, do not feel defeated. The good Lord permitted you to live, for as you have pointed out, those with whom you were, died. Accept this challenge and work hard. We will always be behind you. Thank you. Please kindly stand up and let us thank God for this day."

"This quarter seems to be getting many new priests," it was Nkang again.

## Chapter Seven

A couple of years had gone by quietly. Ndolo-Mabel was now five and in primary school. Mungeu' and Yefon had done so well in managing Mungeu's business to the point of adding a third arm—a giant provision store—to the tailoring and knitting units. They had named the entire business Mungeu' Ventures (MV). Mungeu' Ventures had besides the numerous apprentices, eight workers on its payroll. Back in Batemba, Mabel had done well at her job and had been promoted to the rank of assistant manager of African Progressive Bank, Batemba branch. Her husband, Leke, to whom she got married without Mungeu'—her only regret—a very calm man with an understanding look always in his eyes, was a practising lawyer. Leke and Mabel, after several years in marriage, however, were yet to have any children. Angwi was her very self, but some silvery strands of hair were now decorating her head. Pa Anye was himself quite grey and, ever since Mabel's return and the scene she created over Mungeu's disappearance, had observed more and said little. His rheumy eyes now emphasized a stern countenance.

It was a beautiful Monday morning and places were cool and smelled fresh. It had stopped raining during the early murky hours of the day, but the ground was still damp. The rising sun sprinkled its golden rays onto the fresh green leaves and the roofs of houses as well dressed civil servants hurried along to their places of work side-by-side young and old women with large baskets carefully balanced on their heads, on their way to market. The whole environment was busy but strangely calm. Whenever in Batemba, Mungeu' lived with her friend, Loretta, in her family home in a part of town far removed from her own father's neighbourhood. She had been friends with Loretta since elementary school, but unlike Mungeu', Loretta had gone on with her education, first to secondary school and then to some of the best institutions of higher learning in the country. Being the first day of the week, Mungeu' decided to spend a few more days before returning to Nju'nki where Yefon was in total control of her business. It was always difficult for them to leave each time she visited Batemba with Ndolo-Mabel. Even though it was colder, Ndolo-Mabel seemed to like it better and always enjoyed playing around with the other young kids who normally lined up by the door into Pa Ebot's compound as if they were in mourning when it was time for Ndolo-Mabel and her mother to leave. With her days in Batemba numbered, Mungeu' decided she would tape some records to which she enjoyed listening whenever she was relaxing or even when busy working. She took a taxi into town to "Discothèque Denver," the most popular recording kiosk in Batemba.

At the threshold of "Discothèque Denver," Mungeu' knocked on the door, but there was no answer, then she knocked again and louder. Nsung, the sale's clerk and apprentice, for fear it was his master, rushed towards the door after dipping his fingers into machine oil and picking up an old screwdriver which, in his haste, he gripped firmly after the manner of a dagger. With much humility, Nsung opened the door while Adey, his friend, looked on from behind the door, waiting to hear Agbor shout at Nsung. The shout did not come. Instead, Adey saw Nsung's lips part.

"Ye-y-e-e-s, can I help you?" Nsung babbled.

"Please, I hear you tape records here, is that true?" Mungeu's voice was calm and steady.

"You mean to tape records?" Nsung asked, repeating Mungeu's words with a shaky voice, his eyes full of admiration.

"Yes."

"Yes, we do," answered Nsung.

"Okay, please record some *makossa* in these two cassettes... just the very recent ones," Mungeu' added

"When do you need them?" Nsung asked with the hope of hearing that voice once more.

"When do you think I can have them?"

Nsung told her later on that evening, then delayed a little to see this strange girl walk off before hurrying into the inner room of the workshop to talk to Adey about the beauty of the girl who called.

Adey sprang up and hurried to the door to see for himself this girl upon whom even Nsung, who has nothing but derogatory remarks for young girls, lavished so much praise. At a distance, Adey saw the girl he had so much wanted to meet for the past weeks disappear into a waiting car and it drove off into the heart of the town. Adey could neither move nor speak but stood gazing in the direction where the car had disappeared leaving behind a trail of dust. Then suddenly he turned and shouted at Nsung: "You, can't you use your common sense?"

"*Hei-eh*!" Nsung stammered.

"*Hei-eh* what? Couldn't you come and tell that this was the girl standing outside?"

"Is that not what I've just done? Do I even know her? How was I to know that you wanted to see her?"

Even before Nsung could finish his sentence, Adey interrupted, "Ge-t o-ut!" he said dragging his words.

"Tr-o-uble!" Nsung murmured, enjoying the scene.

★★★

About two weeks had slowly gone by since Adey first saw her. Mungeu' was just getting up from sleep after the tedious and long walk back home from Pa Ebot's farm in the village where they had gone the day before to help when through the glass window occupying the back wall of her large and comfortable guest room, her eyes caught the enraged movements of the trees. Then came the "wo-o-o-oh" sound from outside, coupled with the drumming on the newly installed zinc roof—the first heavy drops of rainfall.

Mungeu' stepped out of her room into the opening behind the building to enjoy the breeze in her face. She could smell the dust in the air as the wind blew past, causing her clothing to flap against her body. Thud! thud! thud! came the muted sounds of the heavy raindrops falling into the thick layers of dust surrounding the house.

The banging of unlocked doors and windows was heard at the same time with the screams of dusty little children who dashed out of their houses, defying the threats from their mothers, to play under the refreshing drops of the first rains. The dry season had been harsh, with the tropical sun seemingly standing directly overhead for hours on end. The rain drummed harder on the roofs, and then the hitherto dusty surroundings were transformed into a pool of dirty water. The water flowed violently round and round the meshed buildings as if waging a war against the houses and their occupants for lack of effective drainage. Mungeu' was about going into her room when the laughter from the veranda in front caused her to change her direction.

Pa Ebot's house was U-shaped. His adult children occupied the wings of the "U," while he, his wife and guests occupied that part of the structure linking up both wings. Mungeu' was like a child to the Ebots, and so although she should normally occupy one of the guestrooms by Pa Ebot and his wife, she preferred one of the rooms in the wings of the "U" which had a door leading directly to the exterior. It gave a certain sense of freedom as she could come and go without disturbing anybody if that was what she wanted. In front of Pa Ebot's own section, which had a parlour and three different bedrooms, there was a huge veranda on which Pa and Ma Ebot always spent their time relaxing. The heavy rainfall had caused passers-by to gather on this veranda. There were those going to the farm early in the morning; those on their way to the old Presbyterian Hospital perched on a knoll about half a kilometre in the distance, which, but for the continuous movement of white jacketed men and women to and fro could be mistaken for abandoned; and those hurrying to market, some to buy, others to sell. They were talking and laughing, anticipating a lull in the downpour.

In this group was a smart looking young man all in black. Had there been anyone watching Mungeu' keenly, the slight delay of her eyes as she scanned the group would have been noticed. But whereas the women went on talking about the sudden rise in the prices of goods as compared to the days when white-francs were the lowest denomination of the Caramenju Franc, the men, like the young man in black, were suddenly captured by the beauty of a young woman. Mungeu' had emerged from the side of the building, stared at them for a moment and turned and disappeared back through the gate of the fence that hemmed in the back of the compound, giving it some kind of privacy.

Pa Ebot's compound is situated down a valley, off the Batemba-Mbuli supposed trunk "A" road, the quality of which changed as the seasons came and went. During the rains the road is decorated by potholes full of muddy water, which dry up to give way to dust come the scorching heat of the dry season. This accounts for the dried up trickles and the prints of people's hands on the white painted walls of the buildings close to the road. Their strategic position gave them a constant supply of uninvited guests whenever it rained: market women, teenagers, and kids who stand in front of these buildings on the broad verandas whiling away time looking at passers-by. It was the appearance of one such uninvited guest, trapped by the rain, which caught Mungeu's attention. She felt the warm air from her lungs escape through her unconsciously parted lips and decided she had to leave before she made a fool of herself. As she walked back to the back of the building, she heard someone call after her, "Excuse me," but she kept walking and did not turn to look behind. She felt her heart swell though, as she thought of the young man in the group, and wondered what it was about him that caught her attention.

About thirty minutes had gone by before the downpour subsided to a light drizzle under which pedestrians could walk without getting drenched. Gradually, and as if without any intention, Mungeu' approached that face of the building where she had stumbled on those sheltering from the rain. The rain had completely subsided. With every step taking Mungeu' nearer to the spot, she could feel her heart pounding through her thoughts. It was obvious she felt something for this stranger, but she was unsure of what it was.

Before taking the last steps that would bring her face to face with the group, Mungeu' thought of what she could do in front of the building that would be an excuse for her having to come there again. However, even before she could come up with an idea, the extreme silence from the veranda carried a dreaded message—it was already deserted. The best she could do was stand and gaze into the now flooded road, with the boy's face floating like a soap bubble on her mind. Mungeu' sighed in disappointment before looking around her with a start to ensure nobody was watching her. She wondered why for absolutely no reason, this young man had caught her attention. She wondered if she would ever see him again. She was sure he was the one who had come after her, but she could not find the courage to answer his rather general call. She sighed as she walked back inside.

"Why did I do that?"

"Maybe you love him."

"Don't be silly," she heard another voice coming alive, "how can you just see a man for the first time and claim you love him?"

"Then maybe it's 'like,'" Mungeu' concluded, as voices in her head convinced her she could not love a man at first sight. True, her patience has been short with men ever since she had Ndolo-Mabel, but she was convinced things could change with the right person coming into her life.

She was brought out of this battle of opinions by Ndolo-Mabel who ran to her munching groundnuts with her right hand darting in and out of the source—the bulging right pocket of her pair of girl's shorts.

"Mommy, what are you doing here all alone?" She asked staring into her mother's eyes with a smile on her lips."

"Hey!" Mungeu' exclaimed in mock surprise at her question. "What are you now, my mother?"

"Y-e-s-s!" Ndolo-Mabel teased giggling just as she was scooped off the ground by Mungeu' and her face covered with kisses.

"I was just whiling time looking at places and counting the cars," Mungeu' answered with a pale smile. "And you, what are you eating hungrily as if I don't give you food."

Ndolo-Mabel laughed aloud. She loved hearing her mother say this about her whenever she ate something with relish. She knew her mother loved it when she ate well for she always thanked her for eating well and told her often that it made her healthy. "Groundnuts Mommy," she answered.

"Groundnuts? Who gave you groundnuts, and you put it in the pockets of your beautiful shorts like some little rascal of a boy?"

The both laughed as they walked back to the back of the building. "Aunty Loretta gave me," Ndolo-Mabel pointed out as she walked with her hand in her mother's.

Ever since the day Mungeu' saw the group of people standing in front of Pa Ebot's house, she had spent her time, as usual, shopping by day for items for her business and reading novels at night whenever Ndolo-Mabel left her alone. Usually, she read until she was carried off by sleep during which, most of the nights, she dreamt of the young man she had seen on that day. Once, Mungeu' saw the young man in a dream all in white, with a big wooden cross on his chest, waving her goodbye. Not having been acquainted with the young man, Mungeu' pushed the dream from her mind with little or no second thoughts. Neither the dream nor the passing days discouraged Mungeu' in any way. She was positive that some day she would be lucky to meet him, again. "Did I not see him in front of Pa Ebot's house?" Mungeu' asked herself. "Then he must have some relatives around here, which means he is bound to come this way again," she concluded.

★★★

It was, therefore, like a cup of water to a thirsty man when Nsung told Adey that the girl was to come back later on in the evening for her cassettes. Adey dropped into an armchair, striking a very relaxed pose. He was going to spend the rest of the afternoon chatting with his friend. They talked about Nsung's rapid progress as an "Electronics Engineer," the title Nsung now preferred. Nsung was the son of an old night watchman who had spent his last days drinking and offering drinks to anyone willing to join him in condemning the nature of society nowadays. Pa Nsung vented his anger only when drunk, and it was directed at anyone who seemed to be forgetting those good old days when his many wives looked up to him as their husband, until the coming of the white man with his strange and confusing ideas, forcing people to marry only one woman.

It was the chiming of an old wall clock, with "American" written on the glass through which the pendulum could be seen, that drew the young men out of their talking. They realised that darkness was almost engulfing the last rays of daylight. A good number of houses had already switched on their lights, and a few lanterns with their flames twitching inside the globes could be seen in other compounds as their bearers crossed from one building to another. It was that time of the year when darkness rushed in even before the sun had finished setting. Through a small window in the outer section of the workshop facing the Co-operative Roundabout, Adey saw the night watchman completing one of the numerous tours he had to make round the Co-operative Union building for the night. The roundabout took its name from the gigantic co-operative union building standing close by, a union that pooled the efforts of many local farmers and helped with the marketing of their crops. It was a very successful venture until the government changed hands and French-speaking Caramenjuans flooded the West occupied by English-speaking Caramenjuans. With accountability as a strange phenomenon to the new government, their French-speaking representatives whom they enforced on the union stole and stacked away the Union's money in foreign banks leaving the farmers penniless. The night watchman was chewing at something in his hand. It was then it dawned on Adey that he had not taken his lunch and he was again already late for supper, for it was now past the hour his mother locked up her kitchen. "Strange!" he thought of the fact that he had not even felt hungry.

The roof of the workshop cracked in response to the first few drops of rain. Adey sighed and looked at his friend like a frightened child.

"Well?"

"Well what?" Adey questioned impatiently.

"What do you expect me to say, that she must come?" asked Nsung shrugging.

The knock came at the same time with Nsung's last words and went unnoticed. The second knock startled Adey out of his thoughts, his eyes staring at Nsung questioningly, to know if that was indeed a knock. Then he voiced his thought: "Was that a knock?"

"What did you hear?" asked Nsung, feigning lack of interest, although unable to hide his excitement. His fingers shook as he moved towards the door, then they grabbed the knob. There was a slight delay before he swung open the door. It was an old tailor from nearby who wanted to borrow a screwdriver. The two friends sighed disappointed and then Adey flopped into an old barber's chair that was no longer serving its purpose since Agbor took up the profession of a radio repairer. A move made after a young woman refused getting married to him because, as she put it, "He is an old man who earns a living by picking lice from the heads of people."

Nsung and Adey began closing up the workshop for the day. Nsung was carrying in those loudspeakers reputed for blasting old tunes to the public when he felt rather than saw that there was someone behind him. Nsung turned round with the speakers weighing down his torso. He caught his breath as if he had received a jab, and then hurriedly placed the speakers on one of the unpolished tables in the outer room of the workshop. Nsung was still searching for what to say when that voice he liked so much because of its slightly deep and coarse quality rescued him. The girl spoke first:

"I'm sorry to be late...."

"No don't worry it's all right," Nsung cut in.

"Thank you," she said with a voice barely audible.

Adey, all nervous, brought the cassettes to the girl. He thought he saw recognition in her eyes, but he could not be sure. In any case, it was now left for him to take the initiative, yet there he stood, like one enchanted.

"Thank you very much," said Mungeu' handing over a thousand francs note to Adey. As he fingered the note, he could hear his late grandfather's voice reverberating in his head as he recounted the beauties of the days of old, when everything was so simple and natural, those days when people even used cowries for payments. "Things have changed," grandpa would conclude, shaking his head.

As Adey turned to hand over the money to Nsung, he saw his friend at a safe distance looking back at him with a suppressed smile. Just then, Mungeu' turned to go and Adey, a little tense, called out. "Excuse me!" The voice was unlike his. Adey was almost choking as he spoke.

She had expected this for she had felt on that first day that there was a kind of mutual attraction between them, although she pretended not to have heard him when he called out after her the first time. She knew she had been thinking of him, but there was nothing she could do other than wait and hope she would run into him someday. Even then, she pretended again as if she did not hear the call, but with burning hopes in her breast that it would be repeated.

"Excuse me, please," the request came, and this time louder.

She turned slowly around to face Adey.

Adey could see the well shaped teeth that lined her mouth but could not tell whether this was a smile to encourage or mock him for being so daring. He heard a voice saying within him, "It is now or never." With unsteady legs and hot air oozing from his lungs and out between his slightly parted lips, Adey moved forward.

"I wanted to see you ...," Adey spoke with his voice dying down towards the end.

"Here am I," answered Mungeu'. "Anything?" she asked, having waited in vain, for a few seconds, for Adey to continue.

Nsung felt sweat running down his neck and left armpit.

"Ye-e-s!" answered Adey, unable to hide the quiver in his voice.

This situation was not new to Mungeu'. It was obvious from the way she was composed, but most unlike her in previous cases, she wanted very much to help Adey out, so she stayed calm but staring directly at the young man she had hoped to meet again.

Seeing some encouragement in those calm white eyes, Adey heard himself talking in a voice almost diminishing into a whisper.

"I believe I admire and respect you a lot," he said, "and would like us to be friends."

There was silence.

Adey prayed inside him that she might give in. The moments that followed were gruelling to Adey. Nsung crossed his left arm over his face in an attempt to wipe off sweat gliding down his forehead in a serpentine movement.

The girl stared on and so did Adey. He could hear his heart banging against his chest. He fought against the temptation to pull out his handkerchief and wipe his face. He felt he was sweating, but it was only a feeling. To Adey, it was hours before she spoke, but only seconds had gone by.

Nsung's fears for his friend had risen to the peak. They had been good friends from his primary school days and were always together until Nsung's father died in an accident that foiled his plans to go ahead into secondary school and the university subsequently, like his friend Adey. They were still as close to one another as in the days of old, in any case, and Adey spent most of his leisure hours watching Nsung scatter and reassemble radios and turntables.

"But I don't know you. Have we met before?" asked Mungeu' enjoying the control she had over the situation.

"Well, I have seen you before, and that's exactly what I am trying to do. I am trying to get to know you better since I have only seen you from a distance."

Mungeu' was enjoying the courage that seemed to have crept back into Adey. "Okay, I have heard you," she whispered at last.

"I don't quite get you," said Adey after a slight delay, unable to believe.

"I mean it's alright, what you've said."

Adey's lips parted. He wanted to say, "Thank you," but his voice was gone. He heard her talking.

"Okay, it is very late and I have to go back home, so see you next time."

Before Adey could gather himself to ask when really "next time" would be, she glided off leaving behind a young man who felt on top of the world. Adey did not move. He sensed joy invading him and drowning him. He struggled to keep afloat in his sea of pleasure, but it submerged him. Yes, he was ecstatic, but he could not stop wondering why of all the girls he had known he felt tense in front of this one. And she had simply walked away with a "see you next time," as if taunting him.

Nsung brushed past Adey in an unsuccessful attempt to show he was ignorant of all that had happened, but Adey could not be deceived. He was sure Nsung had been watching from start to finish.

"Where do you think you are off to?" Adey asked faking anger but with his lips curving into a smile.

"Won't you celebrate your victory?"

"What victory?"

"Look man, I must taste some *mbuh* before it's late. You see what you are, you people of today? Nobody, in fact nobody, according to tradition goes to ask for a lady's hand without at least a calabash of very good palm wine, so what you have done today goes against the ways of the land. In addition, as if that was not enough abomination, you made a ceremony that lasts at least a month last just minutes. One would think you were buying just kola nuts. It is time you bring your wine, so forward march Mr Mungeu'."

"What? Mr. what?"

"Oho, you see!" Nsung exclaimed with obvious pride, "He doesn't even know the name of his woman."

"How did you know her name Nsung?"

"Are all the fingers on your hand the same? Her name is Mungeu' period!"

While Nsung emptied mug after mug of *mbuh,* Adey struggled with a bottle of Export 33, the notorious beer reputed for starting arguments. Mammy Mbuh is a well known woman in her late forties, who always has in store all qualities of palm wine from new wine to "overnight." It is not surprising therefore to hear a regular customer of hers asking for "overnight," which is believed to be the stuff for manly men because of the alcoholic content that increases as fermentation intensifies.

The friends staggered out of Mammy Mbuh's in very high spirits. While Adey walked ahead with the airs of a chief newly installed, Nsung grazed his heels, like a griot, with songs of praise. Nsung continued straight up from the Co-operative Union roundabout where Mammy Mbuh's bar is, to Nta'kom, the next quarter immediately further on, where he had a single room all to himself. He could feel his head reeling as he moved. He seemed to be floating as he walked on elated, no longer conscious of his own weight. As a young apprentice Nsung had struggled and succeeded in augmenting the status of his room by changing his creaking bamboo bed, which was just barely big and strong enough to accommodate him provided he did not move around much in his sleep, to a bigger wooden bed that was now the craze in town. On this newly installed bed was a foam mattress with pillows, all covered in blue sheets and cases that matched the sky blue paint on his wall.

A few minutes' walk brought Adey staggering into his room. He ate his supper of pounded cocoyam and bitter leaf soup, which had been placed on the lone table in his room, pulled off his trousers and shirt and climbed into bed. His breathing came on hard and in a moment, he was asleep.

## Chapter Eight

It was 10:00 am when Mungeu' opened her eyes and sighed long and deep. She had overslept, tired from her sudden trip to and from Nju'nki in just two days. It was all a dream. She had been in the arms of that young man for whom she had worried herself so much. She felt those gentle yet penetrating eyes roll over her body soothingly. His touch brought to life many pricking sensations under her flesh. Mungeu' heard herself moaning, "I love you," all through when suddenly she jerked into reality and immediately opened her eyes. She felt disappointment surging through her body, coupled with the desire to see Adey again. The talking outside brought a smile to her lips as she heard her friend, Loretta, and her siblings complaining to their mother that she had overslept and that surely, something was the matter.

"We shall get the news," Loretta continued.

It was the last statement she made before Mungeu' came out of her room into the opening between both wings of the U-shaped back yard. "What's all that talking about?" asked Mungeu".

"Did you hear your name?" questioned Loretta smiling.

"I thought I overheard someone complaining of someone having overslept?"

"Since when did 'someone' become your name?"

"Stop that noise behind there," commanded Pa Ebot from inside his parlour where he was trying unsuccessfully to focus on the weekly newspaper the vendor had just brought.

Silence prevailed as they all ran back into their rooms laughing at their father's occasional display of authority.

★★★

The third term holiday was just a week away from the end. In another part of town, Adey sat on his bed with his head weighing in front of him. He wished the holidays were much longer. He felt the pain of having to part from his new girlfriend, whom he had not seen since the day he won her affection. He felt like going to find Mungeu' but decided against it because he had not been told he could do so. There was an underlying fright which checked Adey's anxiousness to go in search of Mungeu' where he first saw her—the thought of being humiliatingly chased out of a compound. "With what society is today, some parents still cannot bear the thought of their daughters being visited by young men," thought Adey, "and I do not know whether or not Mungeu's parents are honorary members of this group." He finally decided not to risk it.

As Adey sat thinking, ideas flashed through his head. He sighed to relieve his anger against this escapist manner of parents who just say "no" to their daughters having male guests without explaining why. "We are classmates," Adey imagined himself saying humbly to Mungeu's father. "No, it was Mungeu's place to make use of this advantage and present me to her parents as a friend who helps her very much in school," he thought.

Four days had gone by and Mungeu' was nowhere to be found. The holidays were virtually at an end. How he was going to see Mungeu' remained Adey's greatest problem.

It was just two days more to the end of the holidays when Nsung jumped into Adey's room, and before Adey could gather his wits about him, he was already being led out of the house like a five-year-old.

"What's it? What's happening?" asked Adey completely at a loss.

"That girl... that girl with the cassettes ...Mungeu'"

"What has she done?" Adey cut in, with a troubled look on his face.

"She was asking of you, so I told her to wait in the workshop for..."

Before Nsung could finish his sentence, Adey had already gone past him. The hot sun was burning up the last hours of the morning. Primary school children could be seen hurrying back to school after a well spent break, some dancing as they hurried along to the tunes from the ever present loudspeakers that blared music into the atmosphere. Their uniforms ranged from green, brown, to sky blue, deep blue, and so on, some clean, some dusty and, worse still, others torn. As they hurried along the main road leading up to Nta'kom and Bari further off, Nsung and Adey were no longer talking. Adey once more could sense the pride of belonging to a higher institution of learning as their calendar required them to return to school two weeks after all the other schools had reopened. Nsung tailed Adey, as the rusty hinges of the workshop door protested against the latter's weight. They could hear themselves breathing hard as strangely the tunes blaring forth from the loudspeakers around died down. Neither taxis nor any other vehicles could be heard plying the street at this moment. All was suddenly quiet as if in response to some supernatural command. Some Christians would joke that an angel had just gone by.

Her back was towards the door, her eyes on the wall where Nsung had carefully arranged musical albums of various indigenous as well as foreign musicians. The mostly coloured pictures at the back of these albums amounted to an interesting scene. Mungeu' was slim with thick black hair falling over the base of her neck. In a brief but sweeping move, Adey's hungry eyes engulfed her body from the back of her head and the shoulders, down to her heels. His slight delay about her hips extracted a snort from Nsung. It was the first time Adey had seen Mungeu' from behind from such close quarters. "Beautiful!" he thought.

He was just about to say something when slowly Mungeu' turned around until she was facing him and staring directly into his eyes. Adey stood transfixed. The dull white of her eyes contrasted with the thick black lashes that accented her eyelids. The well shaped blunt nose and slightly thin lips accented the beauty of her face. Her fairly pronounced bust line narrowed down to an extremely flat stomach which gently sloped out into provoking hips bulging slightly at the sides as if to announce her maturity. Yes, there she stood at last, in her prime, revealing more of her qualities in a delicate black gown that gripped the contours of her body almost like a second skin. The contrast in colour between the black gown and her fair complexion was a tantalizing blend overwhelmingly in her favour.

Adey was confused. He had never touched Mungeu' before and was contemplating whether to use this as an opportunity. Nsung cleared his throat.

"Good evening Adey," she greeted with a broad smile.

"Good evening Munny," Adey answered as he turned to look at Nsung who pretended not to realize the double pair of eyes searching his face. His role as a mediator had surfaced. As well as telling his friend Mungeu's name, and how friends called her, he had also revealed his friend's name to her.

Adey apologized, saying he had been so tense and confused that he forgot to ask her name. Mungeu' brushed aside his excuse with her right hand and blamed herself instead, saying the error was more hers than his. "If you stopped me, then I should have been bold enough to ask your name."

Adey smiled. He was beginning to feel relaxed in Mungeu's presence. "Strange how you make me feel like a kid."

"Isn't it a good thing?"

"I don't know. It's just that it has never happened before."

"Well, lucky me I guess? In fact, Adey, I know you must have been worried, but I couldn't help the situation. Just as I left you people that evening, I had to travel out of town urgently the next day. I really couldn't help the situation. There are things I have to tell you about myself. I guess only then would you be able to understand."

"It's alright. Whatever it was that took you out of town, the fact is that I'm glad to be with you once more. When did you come back?" Adey asked, looking indifferent but barely succeeding in hiding his joy at hearing Mungeu' apologize. He had been used to some girls who prided themselves with the inability to condescend to the point of apologizing to a man.

"I came back just last night," answered Mungeu'.

"Well, you know I'm going back to school in two days' time...." There was a brief pause as Adey searched Mungeu's face before continuing, "But I don't think that's any problem, because I'll always write to you," he added when he noticed a slight change in her countenance. "You'll at times, if you can help it, visit me, right?"

"Yes of course," answered Mungeu' whispering. "But there is a lot we must talk about before anything else."

The kiss would have been much longer than they made it, but for the groaning of an old Land Rover as it gasped and jerked to a halt in front of the workshop. Adey needed no one to announce to him who that was. Agbor almost bumped into Mungeu' as he leisurely walked in. Mungeu' curtsied slightly and was out into the street.

A couple minutes later on, Adey joined Mungeu' in the street and together they boarded a taxi. It was still a new car. The driver twisted his right hand below the steering wheel and the car's engine came alive. They were on their way to Nekwa. As the car hummed along, occasionally bumping against the inconsistencies of the road, Mungeu' curled up inside Adey's embrace as if to say she had really missed him for so long. They were fondling one another, and the driver, being conscious of this, was caught a number of times stealing looks into his driving mirror. It was surely their last time together until during the next holidays or when Mungeu' could visit as she had earlier promised.

It was about a hundred metres to Mungeu's residence when Adey felt his shirt abnormally clinging to his chest. His shirt was wet. Adey was still trying to figure out the cause of his shirt being wet when Mungeu' sobbed and it dawned on Adey that Mungeu' had wept and was still weeping—she would miss him a lot.

"Darling!" Adey heard himself calling, but the voice was most unlike his: it was coarse as if unaccustomed to those syllables. He was not used to addressing girls as such, yet Adey knew that this time it was different. He knew how much he felt for this girl now leaning against his chest shedding her emotions.

The driver had long expected to hear them tell him to stop for he was already driving past the point where Adey had told him they would drop. He wondered if his passengers had forgotten about the rest of the world around them. "Do I go ahead *patron*?" asked the driver blending English and French as is typical in Caramenju.

"No, you can leave us here," answered Adey lifting his face away from Mungeu's. He paid off the driver and thanked him for his patience.

The young man drove off with a smile and a promise to see Adey next time. As the driver disappeared round the nearest curve, Adey returned his attention to Mungeu'. "Munny," he whispered, "what's wrong?"

There was no answer. Mungeu' bent her head as tears flooded her eyes once more, grasped Adey's right hand in hers and pressed it against her bosom. Adey could feel her heart beating and her chest rising and falling. It was then that she spoke: "I will miss you badly and I fear this whole thing cannot work for I don't think you understand yet what love is all about."

"Munny!" Adey called, "What are you talking about?"

She looked up in response with a smile as she got the impact of Adey's use of her pet name. Her lashes were wet and clinging together. Mungeu' looked like a four-year-old girl, but no, she was a young woman, with a daughter and a successful business of her own.

"It is just a feeling ... a fear I have," she answered.

"I thought actions speak louder than words," he spoke with his head slightly bowed as if to gratify an audience.

"I don't deny that."

"Then why should you have doubts? Anyway," he continued, "I know I love you with all my being. I can't explain it, but ever since the first day I saw you, do you remember, I just found my thoughts always about you."

Adey felt the tears once more on his chest as Mungeu' leaned against him in an attempt to shield her face from those passing by. Adey found this strange. He had known girls but had never gone through this experience before. He wondered what Mungeu' could be thinking that brought tears gliding gently down her cheeks. He could not guess at Mungeu's worries. She knew, however, Adey was yet to realize that what looked like her left hand was only a prosthetic limb. She wondered if this would shock Adey and bring her down in his esteem. These doubts and knowledge about how her life had suddenly changed kept tears welling to Mungeu's eyes. She had never bothered about the consequences of her accident before, but now she was beginning to nurse a secret fear that it might amount to the end of her hopes for the future: a husband and a happy home. For how many men would want to get married to a woman with just one hand she wondered.

It was already dark. The cars that sped by had on their headlamps but dimmed them as they splashed a young couple standing just a few metres from the edge of the tarmac in each other's arms.

"Good appetite," one of the taxi drivers called out as he sped by.

With all the tears, Adey felt himself softening. He could cry too, but that would be ridiculous, he thought.

Then came the rumbling sound of thunder—the harbinger of rainfall—causing the atmosphere to vibrate from horizon to horizon. Adey raised his eyes to the sky and not a star was visible. All had been swallowed up by the thick rain clouds through which the light of the moon was barely visible, as the rain clouds glided to an unknown destination. The atmosphere was damp and cold as the wind blew by. Adey's eyes dropped to his left wrist and he announced the time: some minutes after seven. He heard his stomach rumbling in protest. He had neither taken lunch nor supper.

"Munny!" Adey called, "It's late and I won't want anyone scolding you for being late. Let me see you off."

Mungeu' smiled at the idea of somebody scolding her. Adey was yet to know she was her own mistress.

They walked back slowly, hand in hand, towards the Nekwa taxi park. Just before the taxi park, a dirt road meandered directly to their right, but Adey could not see the end where according to his imagination stood a beautiful compound. Contrary to his expectations, Mungeu' turned right with him, off the paved road, and there it was. A lovely compound stood down in the valley, defying darkness, under light from powerful electric bulbs. But for a number of buildings on both sides of the road as Adey and Mungeu' slowly descended the slope, the compound was all on its own. Adey could see different flowers at the front of the building, almost to the walls, and a garage standing away from the building with the green wooden doors barred. A path snaked through the nearby raffia palm bush—a short cut to the Presbyterian hospital in the distance.

Halfway to the building, Adey stopped and turned to Mungeu'.

"Munny!" he called gently.

"M-mm!" she answered.

"You very well know that I care a lot about you, not so?"

Mungeu' did not answer but kept on staring at Adey's face with a gentle smile hovering around her lips. She was sure there was a lot more coming.

"Okay," continued Adey, "when you go back to school, promise me to work hard so as to please your parents in particular and of course me."

"I'll do my best," answered Mungeu' with a smile.

"Why all these smiles which I can't understand? Am I ridiculous or what?"

"No, that's not the point. I smile at some of your comments which make it obvious to me that you don't know me yet and can hardly guess who I am."

"So who are you? Why don't you tell me who you are instead of making me appear stupid?"

"Not today, Adey, not today. There's so much to tell, but it's late and you must go home. Next time will do."

Adey stared at Mungeu' with drooping lips. He did not know what to make of the situation in which he now found himself.

They reluctantly parted from one another after a breathtaking kiss. Mungeu' ran down the slope and round to the back of the compound and Adey saw her no more. It was then he felt the pinch. He realised he was going to miss Mungeu' very much. He suddenly felt a powerful urge to see her face once more but turned and walked away towards the main road, knowing this was impossible now that Mungeu' was indoors already.

"I'll see her whenever I like," he said to himself as he waited for a taxi.

When Adey was through with his meal and his evening prayers, which he remembered to say occasionally, it was already late and he could hear some cocks in the distance crowing as they mistook the bright moonlight for the approach of dawn.

★★★

Another tedious day had gone by since Mungeu' and Adey last met. She had spent time shopping for more items needed in her business spot and she hoped today would be the last day for her to shop. She wanted to get done with it earlier on in the day before meeting with Adey since she hoped to leave the next day for Nju'nki.

The sun, as usual during the rainy season, was directly overhead, preparing the earth's surface to absorb more water during the rainfall in the afternoon. During this season, people in Batemba realize nature's programmed diversity: the sun shines almost with impunity until about midday or 2:00 pm, and then comes the downpour as if to draw a contrast between the early hours of the day and the second half. This was almost routine in Batemba. Mungeu' who loved walking would have trekked to the market in spite of the distance of the main market from Pa Ebot's compound, but the burning heat of the sun's rays coupled with the fear of the inevitable advent of rainfall later on in the day posed a threat. She hailed a taxi and was soon on her way to the Batemba Main Market. As she toiled along, Mungeu' saw many young men and women about her age, shopping for their needs in preparation to return to school. Together, in groups of threes and fours, they chatted as they walked on, young men looking out for young women and vice versa. Mungeu' smiled to herself. They may be age mates, but she knew she was way ahead of them because of all she had been through in life. She was not only a mother, but she had her own business and people working for her. She went on with her shopping.

"How much is your soap?" Mungeu' would ask a trader.

"Sister, na thirty-five!'

"For one?"

"Sister, na so i dey," the trader would coax.

"Take twenty," she would urge.

"E no dey so sister. Bring thirty."

"Twenty-five!"

The trader would sigh before saying: "Bring money."

This would continue from place to place and from item to item until all that was needed was finally bought.

Hours had slowly gone by, and the bag Mungeu' was carrying had become quite heavy, when she decided it was time to go back home. She got a young man—there were always many idling around waiting for such opportunities—to help her with her bag. With her tired legs carrying her towards the market exit, Mungeu' raised up her eyes to the sky and was about to praise the rain for having behaved itself when a thick layer of dark clouds, as if to oppose her thoughts, gradually shaded the bright afternoon sun. The brightness of the atmosphere faded. The thick dark clouds were spreading fast across the blue face of the troubled sky, and then the tears came. From the Station Hill the heavy drops could be seen as they showered down, increasing to a downpour as they approached the centre of the town. People jumped from cars to nearby shops and others from shops into cars. The boughs of very tall trees skirting the town dipped violently from north to south and south to north, involuntarily obeying the wind. The young man with Mungeu's bag hailed a taxi, and as the yellow painted car skidded to a halt in front of them, Mungeu' collapsed into the seat behind. The car sped off, Mungeu' sitting with her bag by her as water dripped from her body.

Back at home, Mungeu' walked into her room, closely followed by Ndolo-Mabel.

"Hey!" She greeted her daughter. How have you been?"

There was no answer. Ndolo-Mabel was still pouting.

"Com'on now, see how wet I am. If I had taken you to market with me you would be wet now and shivering like a chicken."

Ndolo-Mabel smiled at her mother's demonstration of her shivering.

Mungeu' took out a packet of biscuits she brought from the market, ripped it open and gave the whole packet to Ndolo-Mabel.

Ndolo-Mabel beamed. She showed the packet to her mother to take some for herself before she sped out with the packet to join her friends with whom she had been playing when her mother retuned from market. But she immediately returned as if she had forgotten something.

"Have you bought all the things we need?" she asked.

"Yes, I think so!" replied Mungeu'.

"Are they enough?" continued Ndolo-Mabel.

"At least for now," Mungeu' answered smiling as she wondered at the maturity of Ndolo-Mabel's questions.

"Then why did you do this--," she sighed as Mungeu' had done.

"No, I sighed because I'm tired," Mungeu' lied.

"Okay!" Ndolo-Mabel confirmed before running back to her friends.

After eating her late lunch, Mungeu' picked up a broomstick, broke off a frail end and started picking her teeth as she lay back in her bed partially satisfied. She smiled at this bad habit she had picked up from her father who always used a broom stick to pick his teeth after a satisfactory meal. Her mind jolted back into the past as her toothpick searched the tiny crevices between one tooth and the other, occasionally bringing out battered pieces of white muscle fibres from the bush meat she had just eaten. This action of hers brought to mind a picture of her late grandparents sitting on a bamboo bed in their smoke-filled kitchen, with the red hot coal smouldering in the hearth, complaining about what the coming of the white man had done to our people. The old man, at other times, would sit down quietly on a stool with a calabash of palm wine beside his left ankle and his right hand delicately holding the well shaped horn of a buffalo. From time to time, the horn paid brief visits to his mouth, after which he would smack his lips and wipe the white liquid from them with the back of his left hand. Then he would question: "Why do you think you children of today are dead even before a strand of hair can grow below your navel?"

Mungeu' would sit quietly during these visits to her grandparents, only smiling from time to time as the questions and answers flowed.

"It is because you are very weak. Children can no longer walk for just a kilometre without asking for a ride."

Then it would be her grandmother's turn: "And as if this is not enough abuse to the system of upbringing in this village of ours, I now see children sitting with their legs the one on the other in the presence of their elders. Women, not a fraction of my age," she said pointing at Mungeu', "smoke tobacco and end up with black smelling fingers and stinking breaths. Virginity before marriage is now outdated. What is it that these people tell you in their schools when those of us who did not even go there have by far more respect for our elders and society as a whole?"

Mungeu' would try to console her grandparents who normally complained themselves into anger by telling them she was sure with time things would change for good, but all she got was her grandparents waving away her words as meaningless.

"How can there be this change for good my daughter, when you people are today strangers to the ways of your forefathers?" Nnemue would shake her head from side to side, "Very few of you can even attempt your native tongue nowadays. I even see young women today going to funerals in tight fitting pairs of trousers to tempt men instead of to mourn. Slowly, I can see the ways of the white man turning you all into strangers in your own homeland."

Mungeu' could see the pain and disappointment in her grandmother's face as she lamented the overthrow of order. She could still hear Nnemue's voice as she narrated events of the great days of old, when "we were ourselves," as Nnemue always put it.

Mungeu' was still picking her teeth when she became conscious of her surroundings again and made up her mind she had to go see Adey.

About twenty minutes had gone by when Adey heard a faint rap on his door. Before he had time to find out who it was, Mungeu' walked in with a smile. "Am I rude?"

"Is that what you're trying to play? Rude? At your worst, you can hardly be mistaken for rude. Instead, I saw it as the confidence of an owner who had knocked just in case she had someone in her room. Nsung did a good job with giving you directions." It was more of a statement.

"Yes he did" replied Mungeu' smiling.

"Did you see anyone outside?"

"No!"

"Well then, come and meet my family.

Adey stepped out of his small, but well furnished room into the square opening between the houses. The square was formed by the structure of the buildings in Pa Adey's compound. There was an L-shaped building of about eighteen rooms, which was leased and so had tenants ranging from professional school students to young families with a limited number of children. To come into the compound from the road in front, which led into the neighbouring town of Mbeta, one had to climb a short flight of stairs and then go through a corridor in the tenanted building to come to the space behind. It looked like a square patio because Pa Adey's own building fits in at an angle as if to complete a rough square structure started by the L-shaped building occupied by tenants. Adey knocked on the door and walked in leading Mungeu' by her hand as his father looked up.

"This is my friend, Mungeu'" Adey announced to his father.

"Hello! How are you young woman?"

"I am fine Pa."

"Good, you are welcome."

"Thanks Pa."

Pa Adey was a retired civil servant whose understanding nature had won for him so much respect from his children and friends. Although somewhere in his sixties, Pa Adey had the build of an athlete. Because of his height, one got the impression when he was standing that he was slightly bent forward around the shoulders. A thick and almost completely grey moustache gave him a very stern look that belied the friendly person he was. Pa Adey lived and changed with the times: a father, who, although he did not read much, knew what changes the white man with his book, religion, and insatiable appetite, had brought into today's society. He was conscious of the fact that those good old days, when only men were privileged to eat the gizzards of fowls at meals, were almost gone. At this point as he recollected, Pa Adey always shook his head in disagreement but never said a word. Not seeing his mother with his father, Adey led Mungeu' out to the kitchen where he knew his mother would be busy preparing the family's lunch, and there he went through introducing Mungeu' to his mother and some of his siblings before retiring to his room.

Once back inside Adey's room, it was Mungeu who spoke first: "So how are you preparing to go back to school?"

"As you can see, I am as ready as I could ever be."

"You are very happy to go, right?"

"Munny! What are you trying to say? You are wrong. Why don't you sit well? Why are you hanging on the edge of the bed like that?"

"I'm sorry, but I've come for us to talk and I must hurry since you should be leaving any second now."

"You are ready to tell me why you always laugh at me?"

"On the contrary," Mungeu' spoke smiling gently, "I'm always laughing at myself and maybe my foolish hopes."

"What do you mean?"

"Yes, I always laugh at myself. I laugh at my foolishness in thinking I could have you as mine some day, in spite of all the forces working against me."

"What are you talking about? What forces?"

Mungeu' was staring at Adey confidently. "Adey, there are things about me you must know before this joke continues."

"What are you talking about? You call my love for you a joke?" Adey sounded hurt.

"*S-s-s-h*!" Mungeu' hushed him. "Listen! It may not be a joke to you but would be to others. There are things about me I want you to know. One thing you've not noticed, Adey, is the fact that I'm disabled."

"Disabled? You are? How? Where?" Adey asked in disbelief.

"Yes I am."

"How? I can't see what you mean."

"Yes I am. I'm telling you. You've not noticed because all you see is my face."

"No, it's not just your face. It's your voice and the look in your eyes when you listen or are talking to someone."

"It doesn't matter; are you ready to see for yourself or ...."

"I am," Adey cut in.

"Well, I had an accident and lost my left arm, from my elbow down."

"You had ... you mean ... you ... let me see."

Mungeu' stretched out her left arm.

"O my God! I'm sorry."

"It's alright. I'm kind of used to it now."

"What happened?"

Mungeu' ignored the questioned for the time being. "That's what I wanted you to know, and much else, before anything. I'm saying this because I take life seriously. I want you to be fully aware of who you are dealing with. You see, my mother was the last of four wives. It took quite a while for her to get a baby, but she never saw that child for she died shortly after having her baby—me. My life ever after that has been very difficult and gloomy because of my step-mother—the first wife—whose only daughter, until I got my own baby, was the best thing that ever happened to me."

Adey found himself in a very strange world as he listened to Mungeu's life history while trying to make sense of everything she was saying. "Oh, I'm so sorry," he exclaimed when after a while it occurred to him that Mungeu' had stopped talking. Her last words were still echoing in his head. "So that is my story and now you can see the forces working against my having anything to do with you: my education is technical instead of the popular grammar like yours, I have a baby, and I am disabled. Do you see?"

"Yes I see, I see," Adey answered absentmindedly. "No! No! It's alright, it's alright," he said coming to himself. "My goodness. I'm really sorry Munny. All that is too much for one person. I am indeed very sorry. So you are at Nju'nki?" Adey did not wait for an answer. "I got it all wrong. To me you looked so young I thought you must also belong to Batemba University. When are you going back?"

"I'm leaving tomorrow. That's why we had to talk today. Now, at least, you can say you know who I am."

"Yes, I now know," Adey answered. He was yet to recover from the shock of Mungeu's revelations.

"I must go now." Mungeu' wanted to run away from the fact that Adey had been stunned by her story.

"Okay! Okay! But you know I'm returning to school this evening. Now that I have your address, I'll write to you and I do hope you'll be able to find time to write back. I know you are busy but try to write."

"That's up to you." Mungeu' gave Adey a peck on the jaw at the door and glided out of Adey's room quietly.

The creaking of the door as Mungeu' shut it brought Adey out of his stupor. He tried jerking himself up to rush and say goodbye to Mungeu' but failed. His body felt too heavy. He crumbled back on his bed as a gush of air escaped from his lungs. "Oh God!" he exclaimed, how could all this happen to such a girl while I'm here enjoying the warmth of my parents' protection—financially and otherwise? "How unfair nature can be," Adey wondered, "and she can still afford to smile and be happy? Yes, it is as our elders say: The Almighty does not send anyone a burden he cannot carry."

As the evening drew on, on September 17th, the campus of Batemba University was dotted here and there by scanty groups of students walking around fearfully, wondering at the bush now surrounding the buildings. "It is good the government has labourers to mow the lawns with our occasional assistance in the name of Green Revolution, else to keep this yard clean again would be hell," thought Adey. The cars sped along the main street into the campus, loaded to capacity with students and their belongings. The rain, as usual, had just ceased and some students were trekking back to campus from the surrounding villages. They darted in and out of nearby bushes as vehicles—taxis in most cases, a few private cars, and overloaded Land Rovers with state colours obscurely painted behind—sped by splashing in and out of potholes and sending muddy water flying in every direction. The rebirth of life on campus was rapid as the cars pregnant with students returned empty.

Once more the buildings sparkled with lights. Students ran around locating their friends and sharing stories. Adey was in his room, ensconced on his bed and taking in the activities of his fellow students. From time to time, he relapsed in and out of a reverie. Mungeu' was on his mind. "Where exactly could she be now, and doing what?" Adey wondered.

Mungeu' had also returned to Nju'nki. Ndolo-Mabel had to go back to school too. Her school, expensive and elite, and privately owned, ran a program completely different from the mission and public schools. The students, accordingly, outperformed the others in every way. As the days went by, Mungeu' felt a little better with only sporadic attacks from her affection for Adey. She was helped by the beautiful and reassuring words that came in from him, through letters brought her by the driver of Caramfish, the company that supplied Batemba University with fresh fish from Nju'nki. The driver knew Mungeu' and her business. This was a postal system much preferred by the students from the coast because besides the fact that the school needed only to buy this supplier's fish for him to render the service, the letters spent a maximum time of just one day to get to their recipients. How effective! It was unlike the official postal system in which letters took a week to move from one end of town to the other. In his letters, he wished her well and hoped her business was prospering. He had hurriedly written to Mungeu' a few days after he went back to school. Although he could hardly remember the contents of his letter, he knew he had felt a powerful urge to write and comfort Mungeu' after she told him of her experiences in life. Mungeu' urged Adey to work hard and be of good conduct until when next they were on holidays.

# Chapter Nine

With time, Mungeu' had been to Batemba on two separate occasions during which time Adey was also on holidays—Christmas and Easter, each of which was two weeks long. She was now looking forward to the third term holiday which was the longest—three months. She felt herself longing to get to know Adey intimately. Adey was a young man unlike any other she had met. He was very confident, honest, and respectful of her. He did not seem to want to rush her with anything. They had been getting along very well, exchanging postcards, pictures and greeting cards as events and significant dates came and went, especially Valentine's day. He had told her that although he was yet to get over her divulgence to him, even after all this while, he was now convinced, more than ever, that what he admired in Mungeu' was far beyond the physical plane. "Maybe it's the way you express yourself confidently, maybe it's your hidden strength of character which I am only just discovering, that strength which has kept you going ever since you were a baby, or maybe it's your ability to manage the scale of your business at your age—twenty-one—I am not sure." Mungeu' smiled calmly as her mind replayed his words and the sober look of disbelief on his face. What had amazed him the most was that he was two years older than Mungeu' and still depended on his parents for everything, unlike Mungeu' who had people working for her. But he will be earning his Bachelor's degree in a year and that's great for his age,' thought Mungeu'.

During the last two holidays—Christmas and Easter—Mungeu' had visited Adey, and they had spent time playing games, listening to records, strolling around at night, talking and just getting to know each other well. On such occasions, Mungeu' always took time off her business to spend with Loretta and her family, so as to be able to meet Adey. She always left Yefon in charge of her business and even little Ndolo-Mabel whom she no longer took on all her trips to Batemba as was the case before. Her presence left her no time to spend with Adey. Mungeu' could hardly believe what she was doing each time she travelled all the way from Nju'nki to Batemba—a seven hour drive—to see Adey, a much younger man when compared to all the men she had known, albeit briefly. She would sit quietly in the taxi transporting her to Batemba and suddenly burst into a broad smile at the thought of what she was doing. The fact that she liked him seemed to be all that mattered. After all, the older men she had barely known turned out to be after her for personal gains only.

The school year had ended well for Adey, who later that evening discussed how school was coming with his father. His parents were always happy when their children did well at school; they claimed it gave them the strength to work harder to provide for them.

That evening, as Adey prepared to go out, he heard those familiar sounds on the roofs once more—tac! tac! tac! Adey took his brown overall from inside the small wooden wardrobe standing beside his table and stepped out of the room, locking the door behind him. He walked into the parlour where he found his parents relaxing over a bottle of Gordon's Dry Gin and two other tonic bottles with their contents halfway gone.

The sight of the gin bottle brought to mind Adey's grandmother's voice as she sat some years ago in a smoke-clouded kitchen, telling him stories of the days before the white man came, when all was good. "In those days that were long gone by," Mapah would begin, "long, long ago, even before those people with their shoes reaching their knees, the *Dzamans* came, when I was still like your second follower, life was good, beautiful. There was order, and whatever happened, be it farming, hunting, or fishing, was done by the villagers for the good of the village and the citizens. But when I attained your present age," she would stop to poke at a smoking brand that caused Adey to choke and shift his head from side to side in an attempt to elude the gently rising smoke which wafted itself towards the soot-covered bed he occupied, "we had visitors, visitors whose arrival was as furtive as that of pregnancy. They were uninvited. At first, they were friends—although the colour of their skin frightened the women and children. Then they started talking of a god who is up beyond the clouds. They claimed he had all the powers in the world. They asked us to stop talking to our own gods and to talk only to this strange god they had brought. They claimed he was everywhere yet we had to go to his house to talk to him. I can remember my own grandmother then warning us about these strangers, comparing them to medicine men that went about looking for patients to treat for free. Yet some of our people listened to them, and their numbers increased until just a few were left out. This village, which until then had been one, was torn apart because of the arrival of these uninvited guests with large appetites. Before long, thanks to their influence, our elders no longer spoke like themselves: their words were like those of children. Our men of wisdom and respect lost their heads because of funny games these visitors played with them. Adey!" Mapah would call out, thinking him asleep as he listened attentively to her.

"Grandma!" Adey would answer.

"Are you sleeping?" his grandmother would question.

"No grandma, I'm listening."

"Good, my son," she would answer back. "Take your time with him who was not invited yet came offering his services freely, for if there is nothing he will gain from you, then he will not fail to ruin everything about you. Is that clear?"

"I have heard grandma."

"Yes, that has been the meaning of the coming of *acara* to us—the death of that true society of ours. Today, our men are no longer themselves. Because of the white man and his strange ways, our men no longer have dignity and respect even for themselves and their own people. They now tell lies even to their own sons. The market, the stream, and the forest are no longer the same. Even our women are today not themselves for they say `yes' even to strangers they've never met before. In the market the fresh palm wine is no longer available and when one is fortunate to come by it, it is as expensive as the white man's clothes. In its place we now have some strange liquids which these white people call *dzin* and other liquids which fry our throats as we drink them. All these changes in this village where I was born, and where I gave birth to your father, and he to you, have been gradual. Today, we no longer know ourselves for our present ways are strange and confusing."

Having obtained permission from his parents to go out, Adey wondered at all these changes his grandmother had identified long ago. Before her death, his grandmother had complained bitterly about them, but then the changes had not reached his father's compound. Today he had witnessed the changes, from the frothing palm wine in brown calabashes to bottles with "blood" in them. Others contained some kind of strong smelling liquid much like the locally brewed liquor, *afo-fop*.

He thought along the lines of most old men and women now disillusioned about the trend of events. He pictured his late grandfather as he had seen him for the last time, seated in his beautiful bamboo chair which was brown with age, with a calabash of palm wine by his ankle, a black buffalo horn in his grip, instead of the transparent glasses which he saw everywhere today, and wondered where these changes were leading people.

In front of his father's compound Adey hailed a taxi. It was a Renault 12, and on the door the word "DESTINY" was neatly written in block letters.

"Nekwa!" he called out.

Without a word from the driver, the car shot off leaving him standing there.

"Nekwa!" Adey called out to the next car that stopped in front of him.

The driver nodded and pushed open the front door of the car for Adey.

After about thirty minutes of meandering around town, the taxi slowed down to a stop and Adey stepped out. He found himself standing, perplexed, a few blocks away from the junction to Pa Ebot's house. As always, Mungeu' spent time with Loretta and her family each time she was in Batemba. His problem now was how to get Mungeu' out of the house. He hoped she had arrived according to her last letter. The children playing around, as he found out while questioning them, could not give him any assistance. They had progressed well during the initial stages of the interview until Loretta's name was mentioned then they stood staring at Adey as if he was a statue. Not yet giving up, Adey approached the compound whistling to himself, but all to no avail.

Adey had just made up his mind to go home when, from the side of his eyes, he saw the front door of the building open. He hid himself behind a nearby hedge. The girl who emerged from the house was beautifully dressed in a black skirt which ended just below her knees, over which she had on a blue blouse that betrayed its contents as they stood out provocatively like two knolls on a slope. She held a blue jacket over her left shoulder, which was already laden with a black handbag hanging from a strap. Her smooth and well shaped legs looked tantalizing in a pair of black high-heeled shoes. Smiling to himself, Adey tailed Mungeu' as she headed for the Nekwa taxi park.

Where could she be going? Adey wondered. He was undecided as he hurried along looking for a means to get to the park before Mungeu'.

Mungeu' slowed down as she spoke to a taxi driver through a side window. Just then Adey hurried past, got into another taxi and sat in it waiting. She opened the back door and sank into the seat. As the car drove past, Adey saw Mungeu' comfortably seated behind. "Let's follow that car," he told the driver. "I'll pay."

Adey breathed in deeply about fifteen minutes later on when Mungeu' alighted from the taxi some ten metres to his father's compound along the Batemba-Mbeta road. Mungeu' slammed shut the door of the taxi and walked slowly up the three or four steps into the corridor of the rented building, ignoring the hissing sounds that pierced the air as she entered the building.

Adey waited outside for a few minutes before entering their compound. His younger sister ran out to inform him that "Sister Munny" was in his room. Adey smiled knowingly at her as he gave her his hand.

"It's alright," he said. "Is papa in the house?"

"They've gone out." Susan answered.

In front of his room, Adey let go of his sister's hand and knocked twice on the door before entering. There was Mungeu' lying down on his bed, with dreamy eyes staring at Adey now in the doorway. Slowly, trying to hide his excitement and the wish to rush to Mungeu', Adey shut the door behind him, took off his overall and walked to the side of the bed.

"Where are you from?" asked Mungeu' calmly, yet feigning being upset.

Instead of answering her question, Adey made for a kiss, but Mungeu' rolled further away into the bed and kept on staring at Adey as if to say "My question has not been answered yet."

"I suppose I'm the one to ask you that question because I've been to your place, but you were not at home."

"Don't tell lies Adey," Mungeu' sneered, struggling to suppress a smile. She loved Adey so dearly that she found it strange and even funny frowning at him.

"Okay, listen to more lies." Adey spoke with a clear voice and his right hand moving up and down to support the precision of his facts. "At about 3:00 pm ..." Adey went on to narrate all that happened that afternoon since he left his room to find out from Loretta if Mungeu' was around, including how he stood outside until he had the opportunity to tail her back to his room.

"Adey!" She exclaimed, much surprised.

"Mm!"

"Did you do all that?" asked Mungeu', finding it hard to believe.

"I sure did."

"Then I'm sorry I was hard on you, but why did you have to go spying on me?"

"I don't know why. I just felt like doing it when I saw you come out through that door looking so gorgeously dressed."

"So what have you gained from that?"

"A lot. Above all, it makes me feel you may be true to me after all, that's it."

"Naughty boy to go ..."

Before she could finish her sentence, Adey who was perched on the edge of the bed, sealed her lips with a kiss.

"Mm-m," Mungeu' moaned as waves of pleasure surged through her body, causing her to shudder.

Still in bed, Adey heard the wall clock in his father's parlour strike seven. He struggled to excite Mungeu' but met with fierce resistance, so much so that he wondered if indeed he was with a girl. Mungeu', with legs interwoven, turned and faced the wall, giving her back to Adey. Adey tried to talk but could not. His tongue felt too large for his mouth. He felt himself shivering, and then he swallowed a lump that had lodged in his throat. His chest felt heavy with excitement, but he was so tensed up he could only stare at the girl lying there in front of him. His eyes moved from her heels upwards, delayed a little at the now exposed thighs that looked delicate, softer, and welcoming to the touch, before continuing on their course to the back of her neck, which was covered by a mesh of thick black hair. For the time being, all was quiet. Adey could hear cars humming past on the main road in front of their compound.

"Munny!" he whispered.

"Ehen!" she answered with a clear voice.

"What's wrong?"

"What have you seen?"

"I hope you are not here for a fight?"

"Is that what I have said?"

"Then don't disturb me," said Adey with an air of finality.

Mungeu' did not speak. Adey cautiously went for her thighs. She did not move. His hands snaked upwards from her thighs and yet the expected resistance did not come. With much skill and caution Adey proceeded, then suddenly Mungeu' turned right round and was facing Adey. They were both breathing hard.

"Adey!" she whispered, "what do you want?"

There was silence.

"Tell me," she urged.

Adey choked himself with his own spittle from trying too hard to speak and ended up coughing and spluttering without uttering a single word. He decided to act instead of talking.

Their lips met. They could feel their warm breath powdering each other's face. The screams from the crickets and other insects in the darkness carried their protest into Adey's ears, but he brushed them aside. He had waited for too long. Days, weeks, and months had come and gone. Then they were both moaning. Adey, after a long and difficult struggle, felt her warmth at last. It was not that of the tropical sun at noon, nor was it that of the smoke-filled room with the smouldering hearth, but the warmth of contact, contact between two body temperatures, the one slightly warmer and engulfing. Then Adey was saying something, but no reply could be heard.

A rush of air gushed out of his lungs as Adey lay back on the bed, his body slightly wet, savouring the feeling of victory. Mungeu' was sobbing gently.

"Munny!"

Silence.

Adey stole his right arm round her shoulders and forced her round. Her face was wet, with strands of hair trapped all over.

"I'm sorry Munny."

"Why?" She asked the question with her eyes still shut.

"I feel I've hurt you and that wasn't my intention. I didn't know ... I mean ... I just couldn't help myself." Adey sounded confused. Mungeu' did not say a word, but slept off with her hand encircling Adey's waist.

The clock was chiming ten when Adey jerked out of his dozing state.

"Munny!"

"Mm," she answered.

"It's late, get up, let's go."

Mungeu' sighed. Slowly she got out of bed and stretched herself before getting dressed. With Adey, she walked out into the dark yard. Sport growled but went back into its kennel when it heard Adey's voice.

A few blocks away from Pa Ebot's house, Mungeu' kissed Adey good night and stepped out of the taxi. She hurried down the slope leading to the compound and disappeared within without looking behind to wave, as was always the case. Adey smiled to himself as the driver reversed the car and headed off to town.

Mungeu' met her friend's parents all relaxed and entertaining themselves with stories of the past. She curtsied and passed straight into her room, took her bath, and climbed into bed. She was thinking about all that happened to her earlier that evening when she slept off. She did not hear Loretta open her door to find out if all was well with her for never before had she come back home and gone straight to bed without even wishing them a good night's rest.

Back in town, Adey was undressed and in bed already, with eyes staring blankly at the roof as he savoured the refreshing feeling of victory in which he had been floating of late. He could not bring himself to believe that all that had happened that evening was true.

## Chapter Ten

In the morning, Adey awoke dreamily. His eyes strayed round the room. He saw his comb on the table, stuffed with hair strands far longer than his. He smelled the comb, "Yes, it's Munny's," he confirmed. "So it was not a dream. She was here, and it all happened." He was frightened when he re-enacted the scene all over again in his mind for he had not asked Mungeu' if she was safe. "If she gets pregnant, what will I do?" he wondered. "With a baby, she should by now know how to take care of herself," thought Adey.

"What do you mean? Couldn't you tell she didn't seem to know much?" The voice in his head went on.

Mungeu' had a terrible night: tossing from one side of her bed to the other, sighing and talking in her sleep. She had not succeeded in falling deeply asleep.

As the old alarm clock she had extracted from her late mother's belongings disturbed the early hours of the morning ringing six, Mungeu' crept out of bed. It was time to begin her ménage. She moved to the mirrored section of the visitor's room she was occupying, lifted her nightgown and scrutinized the lower section of her abdomen. She believed it was slightly swollen. She applied the same inspection to her dark and well formed nipples, convincing herself she was pregnant. She slouched in and out of the house with this fear as she helped Loretta with her morning chores. However, she was sure she had permitted Adey to do it just before her menses. "If what Mabel told me is true, then I might survive this time." Her mind went to the talks Mabel had begun giving her about when a woman could easily get pregnant, before she was terribly interrupted by the accident. She wondered in vain, because she could not talk about it to anyone else, how she could arrive at the knowledge Mabel was going to share with her. Many times over, she had made up her mind to discuss this with Ndolo, but wondered what Ndolo would think of her. She would consider her a certain type, and so would anyone else, to think sex was her preoccupation. Yet one can never tell when one, with all the intentions to abstain for fear of getting pregnant, would find oneself involved. Mungeu' could neither eat nor sleep well and suddenly dreaded the sight of a pregnant woman since it took her mind back to her own worrisome state.

Adey now out of bed was more disturbed, but he tried hard to hide how worried he was from the vigilant eyes of his mother. The only effective solution was for him to stay indoors, pretending to study. He was relieved when later on that morning his elder cousin Acongne, working with the Fosamou branch of the Asconi Construction Company, stopped by. He had come to tell him that he was almost ready for his return trip to Fosamou and that he was expecting his stepbrother, Wumboro, and Adey to come along since they had applied for holiday jobs. Adey's joy was without limits. He believed if he was out of sight for some time and did not see Mungeu', he would no longer be haunted by the fear of having impregnated her. Having agreed with his parents and cousins to leave for Fosamou the next day, Adey knew the next person to tell of his decision was Mungeu'.

With Acongne and Wumboro, Adey made his trip to Nekwa once more. There again at the junction they stood, watching as Mungeu' darted in empty-handed and out of the house with a box and next with some jute bags. All three of them could make nothing of these back and forth movements. Adey was completely at a loss. He heard his heart pounding within as he argued with himself: "Is it that she is really pregnant and it has been found out and she has been asked by Loretta's family to leave? But if that were the case, she would not be as happy as she appears with her packing." Adey consoled himself. He kept his fears to himself.

Together they walked down the slope to about the middle of the distance between the junction and Pa Ebot's compound since they could easily pretend to be going to the last house down the slope just before Pa Ebot's, should the situation call for this.

Mungeu' was about to hurry into the house once more when that hissing sound served its purpose. She stopped, undecided whether to look towards the direction of the sound or not. Then she made up her mind to answer the call. Mungeu' turned her head left and saw Adey standing with two others whom she did not immediately recognize. She ran up towards the smiling trio.

"Hey!" she called out as she drew nearer.

"How are you?" the three greeted.

"Fine, thank you."

"Are your friend's parents in?" asked Adey urgently.

"They left for Bongola yesterday."

"So why all this moving of bags?" asked Adey with a dark cloud spreading across his face.

"I am also going back to Nju'nki. At least Pa Ebot's driver will drop me off at Bongola. From there I will take a taxi and in under an hour, I will be at Nju'nki."

Adey stared at Mungeu' in disbelief.

"Why Adey, why are you looking at me like that?"

"So if we hadn't come you just would have left like that, not so?" asked Adey appearing hurt.

"No Adey, and why must you rush to a conclusion you know is wrong?" Mungeu' paused with a worried look. "I was to ask the driver to pass by your place before leaving. You see," Mungeu' continued, realizing that Adey was hurt, "it's just this morning that the driver came up from Bongola with the news that Loretta's father had sent for her and there are things she has to take down which her father needs today. Please Adey, I had no choice but to leave also. Of course they can't leave me, a guest, in charge of this entire compound. It is not Loretta's fault either that her father has asked her to come to Bongola. Unless you are telling me you would like her to disobey her parents?" Mungeu' knew she would get Adey to see her point with this question for she knew how loyal he was to his parents.

As hurt as Adey was, he knew what Mungeu' had just said was true, moreover, he had to go to Fosamou himself. He went on to tell her of his plans for his holiday job at Fosamou.

"Come into the house," Mungeu' urged.

They walked down the last few metres into Pa Ebot's compound and for the first time, Adey entered the house he had for so long wanted to visit. It was a beautiful neighbourhood with several well painted buildings dotting the valley. The parlour was big and well furnished. There were four sofas, each heading a group of three different sets of chairs of the same model but slightly smaller in size. They were red and complemented the thick red rug that covered the floor, branching off into the rooms and other passages. On the walls were pictures of Loretta's parents and of Loretta herself at different stages of her childhood. Soft music filled the air when Mungeu' pushed the "play" button of a musical system arranged on a shelf that covered most of one of the parlour walls.

"Hey! I was wondering what had kept you so long."

"Yes, I have visitors. Loretta, come closer. Meet my friends: Adey."

"Oh!" Loretta exclaimed. It was her first time to meet Adey. "You're welcome."

"This is Acongne and Wumboro," she concluded holding Wumboro by the arm.

"You're all welcome."

"Thanks," they chorused.

"Loretta, I was trying to explain to Adey, who wouldn't listen to me, why I have to leave suddenly."

"Hey Munny, that's not true. I understood, didn't I?"

Mungeu' looked at him from the corners of her eyes. "Did you believe me?"

"It's alright! It's alright! I wouldn't accept any explanations myself if I were the one. So I can understand," Loretta put in.

"You see," Adey teased, stealing a look at Mungeu' who jokingly looked lost at the fact that Loretta was taking sides with Adey.

Adey nodded as the sombre nature of his grandfather's hut flashed in and out of his mind. The rough walls plastered with thick red mud, the un-cemented and slightly undulating floor of his parlour, punctuated by a single table where, before the coming of Reverend Father Anthony of the local parish to which he belonged, stood the ever-lighted fireside. "What a contrast," thought Adey, as he recalled the refrigerator and the gas cooker he saw in the kitchen, and the electric heater standing under the chimney on top of which chimneybreast stood an enlarged picture of Loretta when she was ten. "No longer the shallow pits dug under shades for keeping things cold, no longer the flexible hearth used for both cooking and heating. Those good old days are almost gone," he thought." The clinking of a bottle against a glass in front of Adey brought him back to the present. They were all three comfortably sipping drinks before Mungeu' and Loretta went to complete their packing. Acongne licked his lips noisily tailing Mungeu' with his eyes as, with gentle strides that caused her hips to vibrate with each step, she walked out into the open. They all laughed at Acongne's display of admiration.

"Now I understand why you can no longer stay for just a week in Nju'nki before running back, pretending you are coming to see me." Loretta queried jokingly.

"You see, isn't he good looking?"

"Yes, he is very handsome and very polite too. See how easygoing he is."

"What's killing me is the way his family has accepted me, and come and see how they love NM," she said referring to Ndolo-Mabel.

"And nothing is more important than that, Munny; if he loves NM, then that's remarkable.

"He adores her, Loretta; he does, and queries me each time I come up without her."

"May be you've found your man after all."

"I don't even think about that; I just want to enjoy every minute of it while it lasts, for it is too good to be true. They are my other family, Loretta, and I love his siblings as well."

"Hurry up let's join them before they start wondering."

With the parking done, Mungeu' glided back into the parlour carrying along a fragrance of her deodorant which slapped her visitors in the face, causing Wumboro to sniff about as if doubting the source.

Adey was secretly proud that this girl was his, but he was still worried and dreaded the problem on his mind.

"Munny!" Adey's voice was low. "Do you know I've been very worried?"

"About what?" she asked.

"Come closer," urged Adey. "Have you seen your menses?"

Mungeu' hesitated, and then she smiled before speaking. "It came this morning," she whispered.

Adey could not help showing his relief. He gave her a long hug before asking the next question— "When are you coming back?"

"I can't say Adey, but I'll try to be back after about two or three weeks at most. Hope that's not bad, hmm?"

"Just be good to yourself by being true to me, you know, and bring NM this time or forget it."

"Yes sir!" She joked. "Hey, do you know what you did to me?"

Adey stared at her, completely at a loss. They were in a world for the two of them only. Acongne was standing by the turntable with a pile of records in his hands while Wumboro was stuffed with very large photo albums.

"Okay, let me tell you this, you are the first man to have gone that far after the traumatic experiences I went through before having my baby."

"That's obvious, but what has that got to do with anything?"

"It's just to make you know that I've known men but that love is different and I believe I love you. You make me feel alive. I'll be true to you, I promise."

"Stop all that grumbling over there," ordered Wumboro, trying to look offended. "Is this the only time you two can discuss your things? I came here to meet Munny and not for you to come and monopolize her." He directed his last words at Adey.

"I'm sorry Wumboro, but it was really necessary you know. Can we go now? I think it's time to start moving if we have to get to Bongola early enough. Do we go together and then drop you people off or ..." Mungeu' was saying.

"Never mind," Wumboro broke in, "just take off and we'll find our way home."

With everything ready and the driver relaxed behind the steering wheel, Mungeu' walked up to the three. First to Acongne, then to Wumboro; she hugged them goodbye and then walked up to Adey. Her eyes were flooded but not a drop overflowed. "Adey!" she whispered, "I can't stay without you. It's because my business and those down there need me so I have to keep shuttling to and fro. I had planned before now to go back to Nju'nki, but I couldn't bring myself to break away from you. Now the situation is different. Just be calm and good to me and I'll be back as soon as I can." Not caring about the driver's presence Adey engulfed Mungeu' with his powerful arms and promised to be true to her. Adey could feel her heart thumping against his chest.

"Go now," urged Adey.

She turned to go then stopped. She turned round, dipped her right hand into the pocket of her black leather jacket, brought out an envelope and handed it over to Adey. "If I had a brother I would have done the same to him," she said before running off to the car, a sky blue Peugeot 504, which before long was out of sight.

Adey sighed and walked up to his companions. Together they walked towards the taxi park, hoping to catch any taxi they could find even before reaching there. They walked along, looking at girls and making comments on things they found pleasing or displeasing about them. "Beautiful body! Wow, great eyes! Can't seem to walk well," and so on.

At the Co-operative roundabout, some three hundred metres away from Pa Adey's compound, Acongne, Wumboro and Adey parted, having agreed to meet early the next morning at Pa Adey's compound from where they would move to the park for a vehicle to Fosamou.

In his room, now alone, Adey tore open Mungeu's envelope from which he pulled out some bank notes and a letter. "My goodness!" Adey exclaimed, overwhelmed by this very generous quality present in a girl gifted with all the attributes—brains, wealth, and beauty—to make her arrogant, snobbish, and demanding. Mungeu' was the reverse, so calm and down to earth, neat rather than extravagant in her wears, and always giving instead of demanding. Adey read through the last lines of her letter repeatedly— "Darling, I don't know how to describe the way I feel. I'm afraid for I believe we are still too young, but I know how I feel. It is love..." —and was sure he had never met a girl like Mungeu' before. He was hoping someday to find faults with her, but until then he had failed, for even when he had intentionally been hard and indeed commanding, Mungeu' had quietly performed the task required by the boy she secretly considered hers with a short look of surprise, for she knew Adey was not the imposing type.

Adey believed he was lucky to have this girl as his, especially when he looked at the other girls around him. He could remember hearing his grandmother's voice echoing with that tropical respect for a husband as she answered to Grand Pa's call: "*Ba*, I've heard you." This he believed was the sign of genuine love the wife had for her spouse. The happiness and peace that always reigned between them further emphasised his conviction. Adey shook his head from side to side as the truth, like daylight, dawned on him. "It is true," he said out loud, "that many things are no longer what they were with us. We had our religions, courts, leaders, marital norms, everything, but when that arrow from abroad landed home, then began the piecemeal disintegration of our identity."

With a packet of biscuits from which he was munching, Ivan, Adey's baby brother, ran in breaking Adey's line of thought.

"Where have you been?" he questioned.

"I went to Sister Munny's place."

"How's she?"

"She is well but gone back to Nju'nki."

"When will she come back?"

"In about two, or three weeks."

"How long is two or three weeks?" asked Ivan looking up at Adey.

"Not very long, but quite a while."

"Have some biscuits," offered Ivan, stretching out his hand.

Adey was munching some biscuits when Ivan finally left. He then ate his supper, put a few things to be used in Fosamou into a bag, placed the bag on the table in his room and then lay on his bed listening to records by different artists.

# Chapter Eleven

Adey had hardly slept that night. He had never been to Fosamou before, although he had gone through the town many times on his way down to the Forest Province. He was excited by the idea of staying away from his parents for the first time and working too.

The morning was fresh and calm. Birds sang in nearby trees, and a gentle breeze fluttered through the curtains of his bedroom window. Adey heard voices greeting his parents. Acongne had a black suitcase and Wumboro a blue leather traveller's bag.

After their breakfast of fried plantains, fried eggs, and tea prepared by his mother, Adey and the others emerged from his room and made known their intention to leave. Pa Adey advised them to behave themselves well and to work hard.

They took off on foot and stopped at the market just next to the park, to buy a few things Acongne thought they would need in his house. They then spent time with a friend in his stall while it drizzled.

It was 5:00 pm when Acongne, Wumboro, and Adey approached the park, an area of about 150 square metres, surrounded by small unkempt restaurants with healthy bluish flies buzzing about paying routine visits to freshly used dishes. Potholes adorned the place and old motor tyres were strewn among the taxis standing nearby signboards announcing their destinations.

On entering the park, it was difficult for the boys to keep themselves and their bags together. Desperate taxi drivers dragged them here and there unceremoniously, while others went for their loads but to no avail. Together the boys got into a small red and smart-looking car that without wasting time was on its way.

It was already dark when they got to Fosamou, having been delayed on several different occasions by police and gendarme officers all along the road, thirstily asking for the same papers after about every ten kilometres. At each roadblock, the officers sat like gods waiting for the trembling and fawning taxi drivers to run up to them with their documents.

Their apartment was small for three of them but all right for Acongne alone. The most outstanding piece of furniture was a large bed, which ate up much of the space in the room. On a table stood a turntable, with its transparent plastic cover housing over fifty different LPs. The middle of the room was bare, but the right side as one walked in was occupied by a small, green kerosene stove, cartons containing raw foodstuff, dishes, and pots. A small window, which when opened exposed the upper half of the room to passers-by in the street directly in front, punctuated this very wall. The rest of the building was occupied by Adey's future interim boss—Pa Ngwa—a man with three noisy children who always appeared coated in dust, and a wife with a hard look for a woman but with a gentle heart open to all.

After having prepared and eaten their supper, all three, tired to the core, tumbled into bed: Acongne in front, Adey next to the wall, and Wumboro sandwiched. They were talking about the sudden and heart rending departures from their girlfriends then Wumboro became quiet, Acongne spoke as if from afar, and then his voice came no more. Adey lay thinking.

★★★

Acongne was awake and Adey too, but neither spoke. The pickup trucks could be heard outside, speeding up the steep street on the edge of that part of town called Famnah as they came in loaded full with corn from the farms. Acongne switched on the lights, stretched out his right arm and pressed the "on" button of the turntable, fidgeted for some seconds and Sunny Okosun's *Papa's Land* vibrated the small twin speakers hanging from nails on the wall. One after the other they sighed out of bed.

It was barely a few minutes to seven as the boys hurried along the streets of Ndifi, the central part of the town of Fosamou, towards their workplace. Adey and Wumboro, being unskilled labour, were to join the rest in that category to remove old nails from used planks, ferry cement blocks to the construction site, and generally make themselves available wherever unskilled jobs predominated. It was going to be hard work especially when they considered the revenge meted out by cement to the palms of the workers. The first two days were, however, interesting since Adey and Wumboro looked at their endeavour as an adventure into the unknown.

Acongne's job, on the other hand, was on paper and his sudden appearance sent eye-servants diving at their tasks with seeming characteristic enthusiasm. He spent most of his idle moments chatting with his younger brother and cousin as they struggled to earn their first salaries in life. They worked from 7:00 am to 12:00 midday and, after a thirty minutes break, until 5:00 pm. Back at home they cooked, ate, slept, and went to work the next morning. This was to be the monotonous rhythm of their lives at Fosamou for quite some time.

Mungeu', at last, was back at Nju'nki. She was very glad to be with Ndolo-Mabel and the Ndomnjies again. But her mind, as soon as she was idle, wafted itself back to Batemba, before trailing to Fosamou. She would spend her time dreaming of Adey and the rest at work. In her mind, she had painted a construction site, perched on the side of a hill, following Acongne's description of his place of work, and she spent her time imagining Adey there at work, breaking stones and digging holes and trenches. She was missing Adey so much that she sulked. Yefon was disappointed at her inability to satisfy Mungeu' with all the innovations she had introduced at the workshop, such as the need for their apprentices to put on uniforms and work in shifts. Yefon had broken the sewing apprentices up into two groups. For this week, group "A" came to work from 7:30 am to 12:00 noon and group "B" from 1:00 pm to 6:00 pm and for the following week, while group "B" came in the morning hours, group "A" came in the afternoon. She had introduced this while Mungeu' was away, but knowing her mistress well, she was sure Mungeu would simply be elated. How she looked forward to the day Mungeu' would be around and how she would jump for joy at her creativeness. She tried convincing herself with the arguments she hoped to put before Mungeu' as to why she had to introduce these changes and found them convincing enough. Instead of keeping the apprentices around from 7:30 am to 6:00 pm everyday, some of whom were mothers, Yefon was positive her shift system gave them more time to spend with their families. Secondly, she now had a smaller number to manage during each shift, along with those knitting, and she did this conveniently. How sad she was when Mungeu's joy was short lived. She felt she had hurt her mistress. Even when Mungeu' tried telling her that something else was on her mind, she failed to convince her. Yefon only felt better when Mungeu' opened up her mind to her about Adey, telling her how she could hardly get him off her mind.

"Is he handsome?" asked Yefon excitedly.

"Not only handsome, but honest, understanding, and very caring. Yefon, you know I have known a few men, right?"

Yefon nodded.

"Adey is great. Just wait until you can meet him. Yes, he is about my age, just two years older, very young when compared to some of the men who have wanted to go out with me, but he makes me come alive like none of the others could. I feel like being a part of that life which I was denied when things turned sour because I got pregnant with NM. I matured rapidly as you know, but now I know, for certain, that I don't mind feeling as young as my age again Yefon, in spite of all I have been through. I love the way Adey makes me feel. We are like the same person. Above all, he is true, I mean honest… I can feel it… I know he loves and respects me for who I am and nothing else."

"I think that is what is most important, Munny." Yefon was convinced Adey had to be extraordinary to sweep Mungeu' off the ground like this, for she had seen Mungeu' turn down marriage offers—claiming they just did not click—from all kinds of men: rich, handsome, well educated and more. Yefon was ecstatic for Mungeu', and how she longed to meet this Adey. "I hope he loves children?"

"You know what, he adores children. I have seen him with his baby brother and with NM. In fact, he told me not to show up in Batemba next time without NM or I should forget the trip."

"O my goodness. How strange men can be. The father of the child does not care, but here is another man dying because of her. I am so glad for you Munny. I wish I could come with you to see him."

"Don't worry, someday you will meet him. Thank you for everything you have been doing for our business Yefon."

"That is okay. You have yourself done everything for me. We are one now Munny."

"That is so true."

The month of July was on its deathbed and on this particular day, the 22nd, Adey, having worked all morning, was secretly resting when Acongne called him to his office, a sort of kiosk made of zinc and pieces of contorted plywood, which swayed in the direction of the wind. As Adey stepped into Acongne's office wiping his hands on his trousers, Acongne was smiling and holding out a white envelope—the long awaited letter. Mungeu' was informing Adey that she had succeeded in making time for another trip to Batemba and would be in Batemba the following Friday. She extended her regards to Acongne and Wumboro as usual. Adey passed the letter to Acongne who went through it before handing it over to Wumboro who was just entering the office after waiting in vain for Adey's immediate return. It was a relief to the boys who now saw a chance to visit Batemba after two weeks away. It was now left for them to do all that needed to be done and pay the workers their salaries early on Friday so they could be in Batemba by late afternoon.

The few days before the said Friday were busy ones. As Adey and Wumboro busied themselves running behind wheelbarrow loads of blocks, Acongne worked on the taxes and salaries. Before Thursday evening, everything was in order. The money for the salaries was to be cashed at the bank the following morning.

It was midday on Friday when the green Land Rover driven by the white overseer—Mr Pendergreen—groaned to a halt at the construction site. He daintily carried a black briefcase into the small kiosk where, together with Acongne and the foreman, the money was counted all over again.

"If you are satisfied, then start payin'," said Mr. Pendergreen as he tumbled down the slope to his van and drove off to his ever-phoning wife. The workers felt Mr. Pendergreen's French wife was spoilt as she did not seem to be able to stay away from her husband for just a few hours. He would leave his house, and even before he could get to work, his wife would already be on the phone asking for him. She called so often workers believed she was a nag, yet they could not understand how Mr. Pendergreen kept rushing to the phone on each occasion. "What a wife," they wondered "who seemed to want to be in control of her man, to know where he was at all times, and what he was doing," they thought.

"It is not like she is sick even," André added during one of such discussions, "as we always run into her at nightclubs dancing her head off while draining so many bottles of Champagne."

By 2:30 pm, Acongne had finished paying the workers. The foreman then gave them permission to leave.

Three hours later on in Batemba, little notes went to different quarters to confirm their arrival.

★★★

The sun's rays during the early hours of Saturday morning filtered through the curtains into the room. Noise from the busy housewives could be heard faintly as Acongne, who as the eldest, was always lying in front, stretched out his right hand from under the blanket to set the turntable spinning. He then lay back softly on his pillow to listen to the music as it played away the early morning dizziness he was experiencing. They had agreed to spend all their time together. During the week, they stayed together in Acongne's room in Fosamou and for the weekends, they were again together at Pa Adey's compound where they occupied Adey's room. It was much bigger than their room in Fosamou and had been rearranged to accommodate the three of them.

Wumboro got up a few minutes after the record sounded, looked at his wristwatch and whistled a note of surprise before heading for the bathroom.

After their breakfast of bread and tea which Susan brought, there was nothing left to do but to wait for the hours to tick by.

"What's wrong?" Acongne asked, looking at Adey and smiling to himself knowingly.

Adey looked up, then realising that the question was directed at him, answered: "Nothing exactly, I was just considering the changes taking place in our community. You remember last time Pa was telling us how their parents used to trek for days from here to the Forest Province? Just think of the distance we covered between Fosamou and here in just slightly above an hour."

Acongne only sighed and was quiet.

It was not long before drumming on the roof started. The three expectant boys looked at each other. Wumboro spoke first.

"This is why I hate the rainy season. How will Yvonne get here under this rain?"

"If she is serious, she will come," answered Acongne, "so be calm."

Wumboro was worried. He sighed, went to the door, came back and fell on the bed. He was just about getting completely relaxed when sounds of approaching footsteps tensed up everyone in the room. A knock was anticipated, but it did not come. Then they heard the steps go by as the person walked further away from their door. It took a few seconds more before Wumboro was really convinced the knock was not coming at all. He jumped out of bed and swung open the door. There was nobody in sight. He sighed and banged the door shut. Midway between the door and the bed, he changed his mind and decided on leaving the door ajar despite the heavy rains and the powerful wind.

The downpour was still torrential and had the effects of a lullaby. Wumboro had worried himself to sleep when the door creaked slightly as it gradually gave way to the gentle force from without, letting in a fresh gust of air. Nobody moved. The fresh breeze that invaded the room was perfumed. Acongne raised his head to determine the source of the scent. Yvonne was already sitting next to Wumboro on the opposite bed, with her body looming over him as she lowered herself to give him a peck.

"I was wondering where that smell came from," said Acongne, as he smiled at Yvonne who was already crossing the room to where Adey lay, still asleep. She ended up by Acongne, whom she hugged before going back to Wumboro who was still in bed.

Wumboro was all smiles as he moved further into the bed to accommodate Yvonne. Adey, who had been roused by Yvonne as she kissed him on the forehead while he was still asleep, was now wide awake. He looked around the room, still a little disoriented, and then smiled knowingly as Acongne stepped into a pair of his trousers.

Twenty minutes later, Adey and Acongne walked out of the room together with no particular destination in mind.

Everyone was now busy carrying in buckets filled with clear rainwater. Adey helped his mother carry in theirs before joining Acongne. He could not explain why Mungeu' was not yet around. Ideas darted in and out of his head as he suggested reasons to himself for this delay. The duo decided to keep themselves busy inside a nearby Off-License liquor store just a few blocks away from Nsung's workshop. Quietly they sipped their drinks, talking at intervals only to exchange reassuring suggestions about this terrible delay on the part of their girlfriends, hoping it was not going to turn out an outright failure.

It was 6:00 pm; Acongne and Adey had given up all hopes as they walked back home disappointed.

"Acongne!" Mungeu' called out from behind, pretending not to notice Adey who was now confused, not knowing exactly how to react: whether to protest or just stay calm.

"Munny! What happened?" asked Acongne.

"*Tse-e-u*!" she sighed, "We had visitors all through the day. I just couldn't find any excuse for wanting to leave the house when everybody else was cooking and entertaining the guest. I'm sorry." She spoke as she stole a glance at Adey from the corner of her eyes. "It's alright anyway, since I'm here after all, I hope."

Acongne turned and looked at Adey who until then had been quiet. "I hope!" he repeated.

Adey smiled and snaked his right arm round Mungeu's slim waist. "I have been very worried," he confessed, "but as you said, it's alright."

As they approached Pa Adey's compound, they saw trapped in the rays from a car's headlamp, Yvonne and Wumboro, hand in hand, as they emerged from the corridor down the steps on to the road. Yvonne told them she was leaving but promised to call the following day. She then walked on with Wumboro and Acongne, the latter having just turned right round.

Now together alone in his room, Adey realised how much he had missed Mungeu'.

"How did you enjoy your stay at Nju'nki and how is everybody at home, Ndolo-Mabel especially, since obviously you didn't bring her?" He asked.

"It was good to see them after so long. They were all fine, but Ndolo-Mabel is beginning to complain about my being away too often. I am sorry I decided not to bring her. She is a lot of work Adey and these trips are meant for me to take a kind of break from all that I do at Nju'nki. When NM is by me, there is no resting, and I want her to focus on her school right now instead of her growing up thinking she has to be with me all the time."

"I understand; believe me I do, just from dealing with Ivan."

Mungeu' smiled, wondering at Adey's relaxed way of listening to her and his reassuring manner. "I also missed you Adey," she whispered, leaning on Adey's firm chest.

"Are you sure you missed me Munny?" Adey teased her.

"Indeed Adey, else I should still be at Nju'nki now because there is a lot of work. The business is expanding very much and of course Ndolo-Mabel's complaints concern me. But here I am instead of being with her."

Unconsciously they had gradually lowered their voices until they were both whispering. Mungeu' was standing on her toes as Adey brought down his head, crushing her lips with his. The touch was silky and Munny's breath escaped in gasps. Once more, Adey, with his fingers exploring Mungeu's body, engulfed her in a powerful embrace. Mungeu' moaned and curved backwards as she tried in vain to control herself. Carefully, Adey lifted her off the floor and placed her on that same bed on which he had lamented her absence earlier on in the day. With Mungeu' flat on her back, Adey lowered his torso on her as his lips crawled all over her body while she wriggled from side to side, floating in a pool of pleasure. Adey felt the warm air gushing from her lungs, and felt it was time. He slipped his left hand between their bodies and Mungeu' squeaked. Adey heard himself breathing hard, with all his muscles tensed. He was shivering all over.

"Munny!" he called, "are you alright?"

"No!" she whispered.

"So what do you expect me to do?"

Silence.

Adey tried hard not to commit himself, but his brains reminded him of the pleasures of being wrapped up in the limbs of a beautiful woman. Their clothes were heaped on the floor next to the bed and then all was quiet. Adey could hear the sound of extreme silence in his ears like the tolling of a bell. He heard the insects, their shrill calls emphasizing the sound of silence in his ears. They seemed to be protesting angrily.

"What have I done?" he asked himself lamentably, barely a few minutes afterwards.

Mungeu' was lying motionless.

Adey was engrossed in his thoughts. He knew, according to all the explanations she had given him as she pleaded against the step, that this was the most unguarded moment to meet Mungeu', but he could not help himself.

About fifteen minutes had gone by when sluggishly Adey pulled himself out of bed and got dressed. He was followed by Mungeu' and quietly they walked out through the rented building onto the main road. Neither Acongne nor Wumboro was in sight. Mungeu' stopped a taxi and begged Adey to let her go alone.

Adey was fast asleep when Acongne stumbled at the threshold and crashed into the room dead drunk. As he landed on his stomach, the half-empty bottle of beer in his hand exploded as it hit the floor. Beer, he believed, was the most effective sedative to an emotionally troubled lover. Nelly had failed him and the next day they were to leave for Fosamou.

When the wall clock chimed five, Acongne was already wide awake and staring at the ceiling. He was trying to figure out why Nelly had failed him the day before. "This is strange," he said aloud as he fidgeted under the blanket. Wumboro, who was also awake, laughed at the comment.

"What's wrong?" asked Acongne pretending to be angry.

"Won't you even go to sleep?"

"Can't you mind your business?"

"It's my business. All these movements of yours disturb me. Why don't you jump out now and race to their house?" Wumboro teased.

Acongne sighed.

"Anyway, let's hope you will see her today, *hm*?"

Later on, still during the early hours of the morning, Acongne, Wumboro, and Adey were all taking their breakfast with Pa Adey at the head of the table when there came a knock on the door.

"Come in," they answered in chorus. "If you are beautiful," added Wumboro jokingly as he stuffed food into his mouth.

The knob twisted and the door creaked open. Acongne's hand stopped midway between the plate and his mouth. Adey tried to say something but failed. The sight was lovely. Hand in hand at the threshold, with the door now open, stood Mungeu' and Nelly. The smiles they wore were gentle and exposed a background of alluring white teeth.

"Good morning Pa," they greeted.

"Good morning. You are welcome. Come in, and how are you?" Asked Pa Adey.

"Fine, thank you," they chorused as they walked gently into the dining section of the parlour which was separated from the rest by a long, high cupboard containing glasses, dishes and plates.

"Are you just coming back from church?" Adey who had just regained his breath, asked with flooded eyes.

"Yes," Mungeu' answered, "What of you people, no church?"

Adey did not answer back, and instead renewed the war with his plate which was still half full, stealing a glance at his father who always told them that no reason was good enough to keep anybody from church on a Sunday. In fact, he often got dreadfully angry whenever he heard that somebody had stayed away from church on a Sunday. In silence they all ate. Ma Adey who had been in her room ever since she returned from the 6:00 am, or better still the "Blanket Mass" as Christians preferred calling it, entered the parlour and greeted everyone cheerfully before going into the kitchen to see what her household would have for lunch.

After breakfast, every other person except Pa Adey left the parlour to go into Adey's small room, with its sole entrance from outside. The five of them made the room appear crowded.

Nelly spoke first: "I'm sorry Acongne. I couldn't make it yesterday because of Bih's baptism. There were so many visitors celebrating, and I was even expecting you there. I just couldn't leave all the work to my older sister alone."

"Why didn't you send Nji to tell us you were busy? You know we were expecting you and you left us waiting all day?"

"It didn't occur to me." Nelly spoke with an apologetic smile. "I'm really sorry," she added in a whisper.

"It's alright, but next time don't keep people waiting all day like that."

Nelly went on to tell how Mungeu' had been to their house to explain how disappointed Acongne was the day before. Together they had left for church before visiting them. Acongne was all smiles. It was now obvious that the idea of leaving for Fosamou that Sunday evening was out of the question.

"Can't you even say thank you to Munny?" Adey teased Acongne.

"Oh, I'm sorry. Thanks Munny, before they kill me."

"The pleasure is mine," Mungeu' replied with traces of a smile on the edges of her lips.

It was completely dark outside, with stars faintly lighting the sky, when the group left Adey's room. They went first to Nelly's compound where before parting they promised to be back in town the following weekend. It was the same procedure at Loretta's place, where as usual Mungeu' always spent her time when in Batemba. She stayed behind to stare until the silhouettes of the three young men faded into the misty darkness. Mungeu' turned and dreamily climbed up the stairs into the parlour where she found Loretta's parents listening to traditional music from Radio Buemba, the oldest of the only two radio stations in the whole of the Savannah and Forest Provinces of Caramenju. After a brief talk with her friend's parents about her visit to town, she reminded them that she would be leaving very early in the morning for Nju'nki. Mungeu' bade them goodnight and walked into solitude. She always felt lonely when she was away from her daughter and Yefon. After Mabel, Yefon was the closest person to her, and then Ndolo-Mabel had come. Mungeu's mind went to the trip during which armed robbers attacked them. The entire experience made her shudder. She remembered the pain she felt and the horror that surged through her when she saw her arm without the hand just after the amputation. And how the young doctor had gathered her in his arms to explain why they had to remove the hand, in spite of how it would affect her life after that. "The bone is completely battered and so is the flesh. In fact, if we were not giving you blood, you would have died long ago. We, the medical team on this rig, agreed we had no alternative if you were to live."

"So be it," Mungeu' had answered before tears rolled down her cheeks. She felt the same way now and her tears flowed again. Mungeu' thought of what her life would have been had she both her hands. The fact that her body was incomplete troubled her and she was convinced it made her less the person she ought to have been. Mungeu' wondered if her relationship with Adey would have been different. She sat alone on her bed and dreamt of how different life could have been had she brothers and sisters, or even just a brother from the same womb. She was fond of taking along Ivan, Adey's younger brother, to spend some weekends with her for in him she saw Adey in miniature. Ivan was fond of her too. "Is sister Munny not coming here again?" Ivan would ask should just two days go by without his seeing her, until he was told she had gone back to Nju'nki. At times Ivan threatened to follow her to Nju'nki if she did not promise to be back soon. Mungeu' had told him it was possible provided he could live without his mother for a while. That was the ruse, for Mungeu' knew Ivan could not part with his mother.

Mungeu' sat thinking about Adey and his family. She loved the family so much and could see they loved her too, especially Adey's parents. She remembered that before leaving her, Adey had wanted to ask her something, but changed his mind. She kept on wondering what the matter could be. Mungeu' cried as she considered how lonely, in spite of her daughter's love, her life had been until she met Adey, then said her evening prayers and climbed in between her sheets.

As the boys walked back hoping to catch a taxi, they talked about their weekend, making fun most of the time of Acongne's sleepless night. The ride back home was smooth, as the driver sped by avoiding those streets highly infested with healthy potholes. The streets were almost deserted, except for a few couples here and there either going back home or to nightclubs.

Cuddled under their blankets, they decided on a very early trip the following morning so they would be on time for work. It was Acongne, this time, who gave irrelevant answers to questions he was asked. He was already falling asleep. The faint ticking of a wristwatch on the table could be heard as the seconds fled by, then it was heard no more.

## Chapter Twelve

At Fosamou, Acongne, who had the keys of the office and the storeroom with him, went straight to work, while Adey and Wumboro went home to drop their bags off first. It was just the beginning of another tedious week, a boring contrast to their weekend.

Four days had quietly gone by since Adey, Wumboro and Acongne left Batemba after their first and very successful weekend. They had enjoyed themselves very much and had had a nice time talking over the events that marked their stay at home, but Adey had a secret fear whenever he talked of the weekend. He had made love to Mungeu' even after she had warned him of her not being safe. He could not help himself and so had ignored all her pleas. He needed her very badly and it was obvious she needed him too. The more Adey thought it over the more frightened he became, for he was sure Mungeu' would get pregnant. All the same, he had hopes the reverse might turn out to be true. God might spare him just one more time. With this fear continuously nudging his mind, he delved into Acongne's books, reading about the female anatomy and the reproductive system. He went forward to master the section on women's menstrual cycles, but the more he read, the more the facts made almost certain his fear. Even where the facts gave him some hopes, the authors specified that their explanation held, with a greater degree of certainty, only for women with regular cycles. Mungeu' was not a member of this set.

Acongne was surprised at this sudden interest displayed by Adey in anatomy books. However, he satisfied himself with the explanation that Adey just wanted to acquaint himself with facts on birth control measures. Adey's mind kept on floating back to his weekend activities with Mungeu', and whenever this happened, he was sure that Mungeu' was going to be pregnant. He thought of what the consequences might be but consoled himself by hoping that nothing would happen to her. Another weekend had come and gone; he had not been to Batemba as planned. He hoped for, yet dreaded the arrival of the next weekend when he would go to Batemba, for what would he do should Mungeu' really turn out pregnant? Adey was no longer himself. He was less jovial than before and got offended easily.

Every dying second brought that much wanted yet equally dreaded weekend nearer. It was inevitable. The weekend had to come and it came.

★★★

Back at Batemba, a young lady carried out her ménage with a calm face but at war within. Mungeu' was ten days to two weeks away from her menses just before she met with Adey, but days had crept by since the deadline she had given herself, and nothing had happened. Even Adey had not been around for the weekend as he had promised. There was nobody to whom she could expose her fears. She thought of Loretta... no! Mungeu' decided she had to talk to Adey first and then together they would decide on what next. Accordingly, she had decided not to go back to Nju'nki until she had discussed the matter with Adey. Very disturbed, Mungeu' went about her affairs. She thought of how the members of her host family would feel—much less the Ndomnjies—if they should find out she was pregnant. She did her cooking on time but would no longer eat with appetite. There was fright and strain written all over her face. "Could I really be pregnant?" she occasionally wondered aloud when alone. She normally laughed off her fright, but it was short-lived for another question still haunted her: "Why did Adey not come for the weekend as he had promised? Did Adey know of her situation?" followed another question. She trusted him so much and felt hurt to think anything against him, but a voice kept on shouting inside her head: "He knows you are pregnant and has deserted you. He never loved you."

"No-o-oh!" Mungeu' cried out as she fell on her bed, digging into her pillow with her face and nails. "He can't do that," she cried. The pillow, like the thirsty tropical earth during the first rains of the season, absorbed her tears. Mungeu' had slept as she wept. The tear marks on her cheeks were like the paths of a painter's brush along a virgin wall. She was no longer crying but was thinking hard whether to tell Loretta the truth, when next they were together, or not. "No!" she once more decided against the marauding thought. "Then go to Fosamou and find Adey out," suggested another inner voice.

"I can't do that. How will I find him? Where will I begin my search?" Thus Mungeu' argued with the voices from within and disqualified their suggestions.

Just then, Loretta knocked on the door of her room.

"Come in," answered Mungeu'.

"Munny are you alright? You are very late in getting up and you don't look like you've slept at all."

"No I'm fine Loretta, just one or two little worries, but I'm fine."

"Hope nothing is wrong?"

"No! No!"

"In that case, I have good news for you."

"What's it?" Mungeu' was full of expectation.

"Remember I told you I've been trying to convince my parents to let me live on my own?"

"Yes."

"They gave in yesterday. Now you can bring your man home when next you are around for I would have moved by then."

Ultimately worn out from thinking, Mungeu' resigned herself to fate and made up her mind to bear the albatross alone if indeed Adey had deserted her. She would tell nobody her accomplice's name. Once more, Mungeu' found herself wishing she had a sister or a brother even, to discuss her problem with. Nature had been unkind to her, she believed. She was all alone in the hands of loving friends and a foster family that did not expect this from her. She wished she had been on good terms with her family. She might have been able to talk with her father. She laughed at the thought for she knew their reaction this time would be worse than before. To them, she was always a baby. Having made up her mind, Mungeu' wrote it down in her diary, kept among her clothes. She no longer went out but spent all her spare hours in her room thinking and crying. At times she cried out "Adey! Adey!" unable to believe Adey could treat her like this, and at the same time hoping he would hear her sad and mournful voice and come to her. Mungeu' prayed and hoped a miracle would happen and let her fears turn out untrue, yet time passed and nothing happened. How she dreaded going back to Nju'nki, to face her daughter and the rest with her fears.

It was a sombre Thursday afternoon, her second week away from Nju'nki, and Mungeu' was sitting at the entrance into the garage. The heavy rain clouds, as usual, sailed across the sky shielding the sun's rays. The wind was violent, carrying dust particles and bits of papers and pieces of clothing high up in the air. Mungeu' felt herself strangely happy. She admired the beauty of nature as heavy raindrops landed on the roof, playing a tune she had heard so many times before. She remembered the day Adey was trapped in front of Pa Ebot's compound on his way back from saying goodbye to his friend, Mbela, whose parents were leaving Batemba for their hometown—Buemba. "That day," she thought, "the rain's music had given me so much joy, but now it seemed to be compensating her with an equal amount of sorrow."

When Mungeu' sighed out of her thoughts, she saw the driver sitting in the car staring at her.

"I wanted to park the car inside, but when I came, I realised you didn't even notice me so I decided to hold on. Is there anything wrong Sister?" He asked with so much concern.

"Nothing Achidi," she answered uneasily, with an awkward smile hovering on her lips as she carried her chair out of the entrance."

"Here is a letter for you Sister. I stopped by Sister Loretta's office and she asked me to bring it to you."

Achidi was a young man of about nineteen, so humble and full of respect for any that came his way. Beneath his respect for Mungeu', who was a regular visitor at the house, lay a burning admiration he struggled to suppress. Achidi knew nothing could ever take place between them, mindful of their age difference, his humble background, and the fact that he never went beyond primary six. As a result, he tried looking at Mungeu' as a sister instead. He would spend most of his time chatting with Mungeu' who had always been very good to him whenever she was around.

Mungeu's hands were shaking as she studied the stamp on the envelope even before looking at the handwriting. Adey! It struck her, and then the writing confirmed it. With her hand still trembling, Mungeu' eyed the letter as if reading the contents through the envelope. She tore open the envelope and rushed through the letter the first time in search of anything unpleasant. Finding Adey still professing his love for her, Mungeu' then calmly read over the letter again. Adey had painfully gone through the details accounting for their absence from Batemba during the last weekend. With Wumboro, he had gone out in charge of a whole truck to buy plank for the company. Because of the unforeseen increase in the number of persons looking for sawed plank to buy, they had to stay longer in the forest than expected. Adey promised to be in Batemba the next weekend, which was now just a day away since they always came in on Fridays.

At the end of the letter, Mungeu' wept. She very much wanted to be in Adey's arms and hear him reassure her of his love for her, to hear him promise to be by her forever. She could run into the next day, had she a time machine. But painfully she waited as the clock, which appeared so slow, laboured at its task of pulling the cord of night and day to bring forth Friday.

Back in Fosamou, Acongne, Wumboro and Adey tiredly walked back home after work, making plans for the next day's trip.

Having gone through their after work routine of cooking, bathing, and eating, they packed their bags and went to bed. For Adey, the night was too long. Moreover, since the last time he met with Mungeu' he had hardly had any rest at all. His nights were turbulent, tortured by nightmares of a funeral at a female friend's compound, the death of his own elder sister or a whole clan carrying a corpse and pointing accusing fingers at him. In most cases, he stood planted to the spot unable to defend himself.

Adey remembered the early days of his youth, how his father made him aware of his maturity, when at fifteen his voice became deeper after a slight attack of cough, and when at seventeen premature hair dotted his chin. Yes, his father had spoken to him during the ups and downs in the dawn of his life. He knew very well his father loved him and made him understand the need of confiding in him whenever he faced problems. "But how could a trusted son come up with such a case as this, if indeed it was true that Mungeu' was pregnant," he wondered. Adey hoped it was not too late for him to heed his father's words. He begged God not to let what he dreaded turn out true, yet a voice in him seemed to shout out in his head with a combined note of anger and mockery: "Too-o-o late!"

Adey jumped up in bed. He had fallen asleep while thinking and had dreamt, yet it seemed so real. He could remember his dream. Yes, his father had often warned him and now a voice in his dream told him it was too late.

After a long night's rest during which it threatened to rain but never did, the morning was calm. The breeze that blew was wet and fresh as it dampened the faces of those out of doors, lifting dresses almost above the hips and threatening to rip off women's loincloths. Fruit trees and plantain plants dipped their heads in the direction of the hissing wind. Children and women, some barefooted, went out to fetch water with long green rubber tubes in their hands or big wide buckets and enamel basins balanced on folded loincloths on their heads. The children and women struggled together as they pulled hard at the rubber tubes (fitted into the protruding pipes from one main stainless steel pipe) spitting out mouthfuls of water and at the same time hurryingly directing the part of the rubber from their mouths into their containers.

The work that morning was hard, because Adey and the rest had to vie to finish a day's work in a shorter time. It was just a few minutes after their thirty-minute break when the foreman, satisfied with their work, permitted the three of them to leave a little earlier as was always the case when they had plans to travel to Batemba.

Acongne looked at his wristwatch as the taxi sped out of the park, before falling asleep. It was 2:00 pm.

Later on that evening, Adey was all set to visit Mungeu'. Together, with Acongne and Wumboro, they left the house but parted ways as they got to the Co-operative roundabout. Adey took a taxi for Nekwa; Acongne walked the short distance to Nta'kom while Wumboro headed towards the *Brasseries* depot junction along the hospital street which is part of the Batemba-Bachiri road.

Adey stumbled down the slope to Pa Ebot's compound as he battled with the stones, which were reinforced by the darkness. Cautiously he climbed up the steps leading to the front door. He did not want Loretta's parents to see him, but, again, he had no alternative. If he had to see Mungeu' then there was no way out but to knock and go into the house, since the family appeared settled for the evening. Adey strained as he listened. Soft music came from within. There were neither voices nor movements. He stretched out his right hand, but it stopped midway between his body and the bell. What would he say was his problem should the bell be answered by Pa Ebot himself? Adey could not answer the questions that swarmed his mind as he stood there under the security light, like an escaping convict under a searchlight in some

American movie. He looked around him. All was calm but for the soft music that sounded in his ears as if from afar. He wondered if the old night watchman had suddenly retired. Carefully he retraced his steps back to the junction deviating into the neighbouring compound, where he stood contemplating. At this point, he could tell anyone questioning him from one compound that he was on his way to the other.

With a story ready for whoever would turn out to be the bellman, Adey walked boldly back to the door and immediately thumbed the doorbell thrice before he could change his mind. Seconds passed and nobody answered his call. Again, he thumbed the bell, this time lengthening the sounds. In the room on his left, from which floated the soft music, Adey discerned a figure disturbing the rays from the bed lamp. From the silhouette seen through the window curtains, he decided it was a woman approaching. He heard the woman hurriedly shuffling along as she forced her feet into her slippers in the process of taking her first few steps. With a thumping heart, Adey waited for the door to open. He was sure it was Loretta's mother. As his face searched for an expression he thought would suit the woman, he heard the key turn inside the lock and the bolts being pulled back seconds before the door gave way. There at last stood the girl of his dreams, in a beautiful transparent nightgown, lovely as ever, but a little worn out. She did not move or speak. She just stood there with a faraway look in her eyes. Then she called out calmly: "Adey!"

Adey did not answer but walked into the house and shut the door after him before turning to face Mungeu' who stood gazing with hands clasped on her breast. As if pushed by unseen hands, Mungeu' fell into Adey's arms and held him tightly round the waist like a child would hold her mother after a long time apart. They stood quietly in each other's arms. Adey could feel both hearts banging away as they held each other tightly.

"Munny," he whispered, "I'm sorry I couldn't make it last weekend. I'm sure you've seen my letter."

Mungeu' fought hard but in vain against a spasm of tears. She succeeded in nodding.

"It's alright darling. I'm here now m-m?"

Her sobs were ebbing.

"Did you understand the letter?"

Mungeu' nodded.

"So you are not angry with me?" asked Adey.

"No! Why?" Mungeu' managed to ask. "When I did not see you, I knew something was wrong somewhere although one can never be too sure and so I was sometimes scared all the same."

"Why?"

"I thought you had deserted me," she whispered.

"Don't be ridiculous Munny, why should I want to do such a thing? By the way, where are Loretta and her parents?"

Mungeu' just stared at Adey's apparent naivety but did not feel like answering back to his first question. She smiled as she answered the second. "They have been invited out by friends. They have an all night dance at Moonshine hotel. Somebody is celebrating a wedding anniversary. Come let's sit down," she urged.

Mungeu' led the way into a room conspicuously occupied by a large bed covered with rose print bed sheets. Adey looked around, accustoming himself to the space, before joining Mungeu' who was sitting on the edge of the bed with her hands clasped between her thighs. Adey's eyes fell on the lamp standing by the bed. It illuminated a photo of him lying on the bedside cupboard.

"I think I like this room so much that I'd like to stay in it all the time."

"It's all yours, at least for as long as I'm a visitor here." Mungeu' answered with a smile as she pressed the "play" button on a tape recorder at the other end of her bed. They sang along with the voices of the group *Dark City Sisters*, stirring slightly the peaceful night air. Mungeu' heard Adey laughing to himself and turned to face him with raised eyebrows.

"I was laughing at that musical instrument."

"Why?" asked Mungeu' still unable to make any sense out of his words.

"Have you ever seen a gramophone?"

"Why?" questioned Mungeu' again, still unable to get Adey's point.

"It is one of those old machines from the days of the Germans," he said, using his grandfather's favourite expression when he was referring to the faraway past, "on which," he continued, "one spent a lot of energy, comparatively, winding so as to enable it to play for a brief moment. I was just comparing it with your automatic set, which requires just that slight push on a button, and imagining the changes the gramophone has undergone before reaching this point."

Mungeu' smiled as she understood Adey's words. "Adey!" she called softly. Adey tensed. "I've not been very well all this while, and I've been so worried. I very much wanted to talk to you."

"For how long have you been sick?" Adey asked, with renewed interest and seriousness, as Mungeu's words struck home.

"Since the last time you left me, I've experienced a sudden increase in temperature. Although the illness has not been terrible, I just don't feel like myself."

"What do you mean by that?" asked Adey, with an inner hope that her explanation might turn out different from what he feared.

"I'm abnormally weak, yet I know I'm physically well. As a result, all this makes me worried," she answered avoiding Adey's looks by gazing at the floor.

Quietly Adey considered all that she had said. It was clear, as clear as daylight. Mungeu', he was certain, was pregnant. However, Adey did not just want to put the question to her directly, for if she were not already aware of it, Adey thought, the effect would then be horrible mindful of the nature of her first experience.

"Have you told anyone about all these changes you are experiencing?"

Mungeu' cowered.

Adey pretended not to have noticed it. "Mm-m?' he insisted.

"No!" she answered with a voice barely audible.

"Why didn't you tell them?"

"I don't know. I... I thought it was wise to tell you first." Mungeu' was becoming restless. She wrung her fingers, and Adey could see her almost scaly lips trembling.

The silence that followed was piercing. Adey had been careless. He now felt sorry for this poor girl whom his recklessness had put into trouble. All what Mungeu' had said, which culminated in a sort of new awareness of herself, were obvious symptoms to Adey. Adey's fright of the idea of pregnancy turned into a stabbing pain near his heart, but he treated this fear, and the idea of pregnancy with scorn. He turned to face Mungeu' and saw in her face, for the first time ever, a strange brightness. Mungeu' had also been looking deeply into the features that contorted Adey's face and trying to decipher his thoughts, but she failed. Instead, looking at Adey's face, she was so carried away by her own thoughts that she did not realize that Adey was no longer thinking but only staring at her. Completely convinced that Mungeu' was deeply in thought, Adey called out her name. His voice broke through her thoughts and she started.

"Oh! I'm sorry," she pleaded, "I didn't realize what I was doing."

"There is no harm in thinking," answered Adey, "but should you go on in that manner, it would be terrible."

Adey was very aware of all that Mungeu' went through when she was pregnant with Ndolo-Mabel, so he knew how terribly scared she ought to be about the idea of being pregnant again. What would she tell her friends? What would her family say of her if they should find out, and they were sure to? Who would she say is responsible? These questions fell in Adey's mind in cascades as he sat there next to her on the bed. Although Adey was sure from all the changes Mungeu' had undergone that she was pregnant, he still felt he should approach the problem more directly. He wanted to ask her if all that she had said was to support the fact that she had not seen her menses.

"Munny!" he called.

Mungeu' looked into his eyes in response, but just then they heard the sound of a car as it pulled up to a halt in front of Pa Ebot's compound.

"That was a car. It could be your host family returning," hinted Adey. "Was that the sound of their vehicle?"

"I don't know, I didn't get the sound of the engine clearly," answered Mungeu' as she rose to answer the doorbell. "Just stay where you are," she said to Adey as she left the room.

Adey was surprised at how calm he was—not the least frightened by the idea of being found not only in the house but also inside Mungeu's room with her. Yes, Adey now cared less. He was already in a desperate situation. "When it rains, it pours," he thought. The fear of a bigger problem reduces that of a smaller one to almost nothing. It would mean less to find him with Mungeu' in her room, without her ultimately complaining of pregnancy.

About three minutes had ticked by before Mungeu' slouched back into the room heaving a protracted sigh.

"Who was it?" Adey questioned with relief as he heard the car drive off.

"Pa's friend," she said referring to Pa Ebot.

"What did he want?"

"He called to say hello, but I told him the Ebots had gone out."

"So why did that take you so long?"

"Don't bother yourself about that now Adey. Well, he also wanted to know if he could join me in the house when I told him the Ebots had gone out."

"And what did you tell him?"

"Of course I refused. I told him I was with a friend. He still wanted to come in so I threatened him with reporting him to Pa Ebot if he pushed me any further. He smiled and then walked back to his car."

They were both quiet for some minutes before she spoke. "You were about to say something before I went out."

"I remember."

Mungeu' let her eyes linger all over Adey's face before letting them drop.

"There is something troubling me, Munny, and I'll be glad if you help me solve it."

"Adey," she called and waited for Adey to lift up his eyes into hers before she continued, "you very well know I'll only be too glad to help you if it's within my reach," she answered, unaware of the trend of Adey's thoughts.

"Promise me you won't let it worry or hurt you."

"You have my word," she promised without the slightest hesitation.

"Have you seen your menses since I last left Batemba?"

Without any change in expression, Mungeu' pierced his heart. "No!" she answered. She searched Adey's face but it was blank.

"I see," said Adey plainly, "and do you find this strange or just normal?"

"What do you mean?"

"What I mean is, have you ever before experienced such a prolonged delay?"

"I don't think so. This is the first time it has taken this long."

With his questions at an end, and his mind firmly made up about Mungeu's situation, Adey decided to let her know how he felt about it, but this, he thought, should be on the next day—a Sunday. He looked at his wristwatch and rose with hands akimbo before speaking.

"It's very dark and late already. I must be going."

Mungeu' tailed Adey to the door where they exchanged a gentle and brief goodnight kiss.

"Goodnight Adey," she whispered.

"You will come to the house tomorrow, won't you?"

Mungeu' nodded.

As Adey walked up the slope, Mungeu' shut and quietly bolted the door then walked back into her bedroom.

Adey was much consumed by his thoughts as he followed the main road to the Nekwa township taxi park. For quite a while he did not realize how the nearby compounds were dotted with young couples. They looked engrossed in various topics of conversation. Some were sitting on boulders and others on verandas of neglected mud-walled buildings. Although in pain, Adey smiled knowingly to himself as in a glance he captured the scene before him. It brought to mind his earlier days with Mungeu', how they had, like these replicas of themselves, spent long hours outside, their bodies drinking the refreshing cold air of the Batemba Highlands. Adey had counted himself lucky and was happy when Mungeu' gave in to him as a lover, but now he was a bitter beginner in another dimension of this strange dish which begins so appetizingly only to suddenly turn sour. He felt pity for these fledglings as they sat in almost foetal pairs, lapping the dish from the edges of the plate with relish. "Just let them wait, one false step and they will know everything has two sides," he thought.

Adey had been like them but was now in the heart of this dish—the very sour part. Adey thought of telling these successors what was in store for them come the slightest error. "It is the duty of their parents," he countered, "or are they, too, disobeying?" Loud and piercing, the honk sliced its way through Adey's thoughts and he jumped into a nearby bush at the side of the road. The car was long gone. He stole furtive glances around to see if anyone had noticed his little drama on absentmindedness, but all was still.

"Co-operative Roundabout!" Adey called as he slid into a taxi.

The driver stepped on his accelerator. As the car moved forward, Adey took a sweeping glance at the delinquents and shook his head. "They don't know what the end of that road holds for them," he thought as the car carried him home.

As Adey tiptoed towards his room, he heard voices singing along with the tune *Fly Robin Fly*. Confidently he pushed open the door and fell into the hands of the ghost that was now haunting him all around the place. Both beds carried a couple each: Wumboro and Yvonne on his left hand, Acongne and Nelly on the right. They were listening to music as they relaxed in each other's company.

"What happened?" questioned Acongne, "I thought you were no longer coming back today."

"Thanks for caring so much," Adey answered with sarcasm.

"Anyway, hope you've enjoyed your stay with her."

"Very well, thank you," Adey said formally, forcing a smile. He sat down on the edge of the bed to remove his shoe and the depression he caused at the edge of the mattress made Wumboro wake up with a start.

"Hello nightjar," called Wumboro, "back at last?"

"It is true I'm late, but I'm home already," answered Adey. "What about ...," he finished the sentence by indicating, with pouted lips and raised eyebrows, Yvonne who was still asleep. The presence of the girls hurt him much for it took his mind to Mungeu', and he could picture a disturbed girl all alone in a deserted building. His heart ached. He wanted Mungeu' to be in his arms so that, like their love, they could share their grief together. Yvonne and Wumboro, and a few minutes later on, Acongne and Nelly all went out leaving Adey behind. He struggled for quite some time before falling asleep.

Meanwhile a troubled Mungeu' went into Ma Ebot's bath, took a tablet of Valium10 from a bottle, and returned to her room with a glass of water. Mungeu', suffocating with the frightening conviction that she was pregnant, crossed over to the life-size mirror she had consulted before. She looked at her abdomen with her nightgown held up high above her breast. If at all there was any change, she did not detect it, yet the month of August was completely past without her menses and now September was ten days old. She smiled to herself, but it brought no sense of relief. She was still scared and confused. There was one more test to run. Mungeu' completely pulled off her nightgown and then standing very close to the mirror with her right breast in her hand, she peered at the nipple. It appeared to her slightly larger and darker. She thought her breast felt thicker. Mungeu' had heard friends mentioning these signs when amongst themselves and discussing pregnancy and the symptoms that accompany it. Still confused, Mungeu' swallowed the tablet.

# Chapter Thirteen

Having fidgeted all night, Adey got up to face a bright morning. The sun promised to be out sooner than usual. The children were busy with their routine morning chores in Pa Adey's compound and in the apartment occupied by tenants. The older ones swept the rooms and the surroundings, the younger ones washed the dishes used the night before, while the youngest went around just looking on like white overseers during a forced labour session.

It was a bright new day and full of promises, yet Adey was gloomy. His forehead was hot. Since the night before, he had been considering what to do about his situation. Now and again, the question echoed in his head. He wondered if he should open his heart to his father, and in fact, he walked up to the door of the parlour before deciding against it. How would he begin? How would he say it all happened? When did he discover sex, and how? He would not be able to face the look of surprise and disbelief in those old and deeply searching eyes, which had always been friendly and full of hopes for him. No, he would wait for Mungeu' and together they would talk it over. Adey knew he loved her very much and so should it come to the worst, they could get married.

"You?" questioned a voice, "Getting married now? Ha! ha! ha!" It seemed to mock.

"Yes I will ..."

The argument continued within him.

Adey remembered Mungeu's stories about her parents and their terrible reactions the first time she was pregnant. Deep down in him, after listening to Mungeu's stories, Adey was convinced that in spite of Pa Anye's apparent indifference after Mungeu's disappearance, the man loved his child. Adey was sure were Pa Anye the only hurdle in their path, they would be able to handle him after a while. But with Angwi present to paint the error in a most hideous light, they had no way out. It would be terrible. As Adey's already fatigued brain toiled along the thorny and undulating landscape of thought, he realized the situation was going to be the same no matter from which perspective it was attacked. Chaos was sure to prevail, either temporarily or forever after. Once is enough and considered a mistake, but the same error twice, is something else.

Adey had to go to church. Together after their hurried breakfast, Acongne, Wumboro, and Adey rushed to St Raphael's Church situated on a knoll at one end of town, where they hoped to catch up with the 9:00 am Mass. Mass had indeed already started by the time all three stole in, placing themselves just near the door. The church was half full with children who made their presence felt by slowing down the choir and once in a while singing out of tune, with others shouting here and there and ultimately crying if reprimanded by any of the church wardens. The wardens' red bands with the white cross standing out made the children look at them with a feeling somewhere between awe and fright.

While Acongne and Wumboro superficially floated along with the current of the Mass, occasionally stealing glances around to see what beauties the 9:00 am Mass could boast of, Adey knelt down deeply in prayers. He could not remember how long ago it was since he last prayed with such fervour. He prayed that his fears about Mungeu's state turn out false, but if already too late, that he receive the courage to fight. Adey alone was sure of the love he had for Mungeu'. He joined the rest as they stood up after the final blessing to wait until the priest and the servers had disappeared into the sacristy. There was disorder as the parishioners jostled against one another on their way out of the church.

Back at home, Adey felt a bit relaxed at having placed his problems into the hands of his God, the Architect of life. He strongly believed nothing could happen if God did not want it. After all, was that not what the catechist taught him in those days when he was struggling with the doctrine of the church in order to receive his first holy communion? Why had there to be rain on that fated day? Why had he to be out on that particular day? Why had he to shelter himself only under Pa Ebot's roof, for him to see her and later win Mungeu's love? He was certain the forces controlling the events of life were above his powers. Being a Sunday, there was nothing else to do but eat and go out dancing, but Adey recoiled into his room where he sat listening to records with the others, as well as deciphering the direction of approaching footsteps. Acongne was the first to leave the house.

It was a few minutes past midday when Wumboro left Adey in the house as he hurried out. He had a rendezvous with Yvonne at their compound where, like Mungeu', she had a comfortable room all to herself; a second door led directly to the exterior behind. Her parents had realised how self-ridiculing it is to restrict a daughter of theirs from going out or receiving respectable visitors of the opposite sex. Bih, their eldest daughter, who was always obedient and at home, had ended up with tubes connected into her body as doctors struggled, in vain, to save her life after she attempted an abortion. They now preferred to point out to their younger daughters like Yvonne the dangers of premarital affairs and, worse still, pleasure seeking youths who take to their heels with the slightest problem, as in Bih's case.

"That is as far as I can go these days, when schooling take them away from my eyes," Yvonne's father was always heard warning his friends. Yvonne's mother, on her part, kept on lamenting, "When we were children, a man would run after a woman for months without being able to touch the woman. But what is it like today ...," she would open her palms and show them to the sky—a sign of frustration. Ma Yvonne was a woman calm in appearance and brilliantly dark in complexion, with too slim a body given her age and the number of children she had brought forth.

The relic of a wall clock had just chimed 1:00 pm from the parlour when Adey heard them. They were short and rapid. He smiled to himself. Adey had heard those footfalls so many times that they seemed to be shouting "Mungeu'" as they approached. She pushed in the door without knocking. Those fingers again, slim and long, topped by long and carefully trimmed red-coated nails. She was all in red, but for a black bag strapped to her shoulder and black shoes. She stood there at the threshold with a smile behind which Adey could discern a disturbed mind.

"I can't regret having this girl for a wife," thought Adey. He got out of bed as Mungeu' shut the door behind her. There was a clash of thighs, groins, chests and lips as they merged to express their feelings.

"How are you?" Adey asked whispering, with a smile parting his lips.

"Just like that," Mungeu' answered shrugging gently.

Adey took her handbag from her, which he placed neatly on the side of the table. The high heel shoes Mungeu' wore added grace and a certain sexy quality to her slim but fleshy legs, making them appear longer. Adey felt himself drowning in pride as he looked admiringly down at this girl sitting on the edge of his bed.

"I love those shoes," said Adey.

Mungeu' did not say a word but smiled at him as he fidgeted in his wardrobe to bring out a pair of slippers. He stooped and unbuckled her shoes. That done, Mungeu' ignored the pair of slippers he gave her and immediately rolled further into the bed. Adey smiled as he arranged the pair of slippers by the side of the bed before leaving the room.

Mungeu', now alone, looked around the room. She sighed with pleasure for she enjoyed it whenever she was in this cosy room, the walls spotted with pictures of movie stars, footballers, musicians and practitioners of the fighting art. She stretched her left hand out and pressed "play" on the turntable. A record dropped and the speakers came to life, blaring forth Jean Dikoto Mandengue's *Sunday Afternoon*.

When Adey entered the room, he was carrying a small wooden tray with two bottles of orange drinks, some sweets, biscuits, and two glasses. He sat down on the edge of the bed before serving Mungeu'. She took a sip then placed the glass on the table.

Adey, with his own glass in hand, struck a very relaxed pose with his back on a pillow and his head against the wall. But his heart was now beating faster as he thought of a suitable opening sentence for the inevitable discussion that afternoon.

With his mind made up, Adey questioned, "How are you Munny, any changes?"

"Not as yet," she answered without looking at him.

"But are you expecting any?"

"Adey please spare me the pains. I've worried myself about this delay long enough."

"She still calls it a delay," Adey noted mentally, "yet this is about the middle of the second month and never before had she had such an extended delay." He asked her out loud, "Why don't you visit a doctor?"

"What for?" Mungeu' asked wild eyed.

"This is strange," thought Adey. Never before had Mungeu' been obstinate to him. He made up his mind to put off, until later, any discussion relevant to their problem. The afternoon progressed. Fun and laughter unceremoniously snatched them from their worries.

Later that evening when they left the house, Mungeu' was glad Adey would be coming back from Fosamou finally the next weekend. She had missed him so much. With her mind on Adey who sat quietly beside her, she took no note of the numerous stops and diversions the driver made to pick up and drop passengers off. The driver reversed at the junction leading down to Pa Ebot's compound.

"I am also going down tomorrow."

"How long do you intend to be away this time?" asked Adey.

"Just a week. While here, I have made some contacts with traders dealing in the kind of threads and yarns I use in sewing and knitting. I guess I will rush up next weekend or so to collect the supply."

Loretta's parents were all in. Mungeu' stopped for a while to greet them before continuing straight to her own room. She could not bear anybody's eyes on her body, for any slight delay in the movement of their eyes made her think they had detected a change.

Back in town, as Adey climbed in between his sheets, he was thinking. He could hear the clock going tic-tac, tic-tac. The sound faded away until it was heard no more.

## Chapter Fourteen

As their taxi rolled into the Fosamou taxi park, Acongne, Wumboro, and Adey saw workers hurrying to their offices. Some were in township taxis or private cars, and others were trekking. Acongne once more removed the office keys from his briefcase and ran all the way to work, while Adey and Wumboro hurried home to leave their bags. Acongne was a few minutes late by the time he opened the store for the bricklayers, carpenters and unskilled labourers to take out their tools.

With minds full of thoughts about Batemba, Adey and Wumboro toiled through the last week of their holiday job happily. Acongne was already feeling the pinch of their impending departure. He spent most of his time complaining about the problems he had staying all alone at Fosamou, yet days unfolded into nights and nights into days. The end of the week was fast approaching.

It was the last Friday of the month. Acongne struggled out of bed, more worn out than relaxed. The impending departure of his younger companions was turning into something else. He was feeling sick already. Although it was still a day to payday, Acongne worked hard and all the departing students were given their salaries, calculated according to the number of hours put in.

Later on that afternoon, Adey and the rest were in a taxi for Batemba. It was going to be Acongne's last trip to Batemba in the company of the others.

★★★

When Mungeu' entered his room on Sunday morning, Adey had returned from church and was lying down.

"So you are finally back." It was more of a statement than a question.

"What about Acongne and Wumboro?"

"They are all fine but now with their own family since we are no longer going back to Fosamou together."

"I see," she commented as she sat down by him in bed.

"Have you seen Mom?"

"I saw her in the kitchen, but she said Pa is still on the way back from church with Ivan."

"It's alright. Hope you had a nice trip, and everybody is well?"

"Yes, it was indeed a nice trip. I have a surprise for you – something you've always asked me to bring although I've never wanted to."

"Please, may I have the thing at once?"

With a smile, Mungeu' foraged her bag for a while and brought out a card which she gave to Adey.

Adey turned the card round to the other side. "Don't tell me this is NM!" Adey asked, excitedly referring to Ndolo-Mabel

"Yes, she is," answered Mungeu' with a pale smile before leaning forward to look at the picture of her daughter which Adey was studying."

"Only a few months since I haven't seen her and she is a big girl already."

"Yes she is."

"And as beautiful as her mother," declared Adey categorically.

"Thanks," said Mungeu' smiling. "Before I forget, Loretta now has a house along Alliance Street. She moved into it three days ago. It's big and comfortable: a parlour, two bedrooms, an internal kitchen and toilet facilities within."

"That's good."

"I guess you'll get to know it one of these days."

They had relaxed for over an hour after eating the food Susan brought to them when Adey made up his mind he had to talk then or never.

"Munny!" he called.

"*M-mm*!"

"Please pardon me if I hurt you, but I think I just can't do otherwise. I have been very worried and confused for so long now, so I think it is time we talk and seriously too, you know," Adey paused. "One cannot keep running away from one's problems because the problems will stay there and by the time one comes back to face them, it might be too late."

Mungeu' did not say a word, but felt her heart swell inside her chest. She had the feeling her chest was choked tight, making it difficult for her to breath. She swallowed a lump in her throat and air rushed out of her lungs like one suddenly relieved of a burden. The reverse was true. Mungeu' was all tensed up and frightened.

Beads of sweat played on her nose. She dreaded her state and was sure something was wrong with her, but she feared christening it pregnancy.

"Can you think of what my problem has been?" asked Adey.

Mungeu' stared at him like a frightened child, eyes wide open and betraying the clean white in the middle of which stood a black island.

"Munny!" whispered Adey urgently.

She tried to answer but faltered. Her voice was gone. She could only stare, with eyes full to the brim, and then they were flooded. A tear glided down her cheek, and she found her voice and cried. The sound of her voice as she cried aloud and moaned, completely letting herself go, stabbed Adey's heart which grew heavier and heavier. He wrapped his hands round the crying girl as he spoke.

"Munny, what's wrong? Why should you cry like this? I'm not talking of leaving you, or is it that you regret having ever known me?"

"N-n-no Adey, that's not the case," Mungeu' sobbed in a whisper.

"Then what?"

Silence.

"Munny, I think it's time we put our ideas together, I think it's time we put our ideas into words. Neither of us is still a kid, in fact, I want you, or rather us, to help ourselves."

"I know Adey." She spoke as she dabbed her face with his handkerchief. It was one of Adey's first presents from her.

"Thank you," he said relieved. Her tears had been sharp daggers piercing his heart. They seemed to be blaming him on her behalf, for all that had gone wrong. "Now Munny, don't let my questions hurt you, for what will be, will be, right?"

Mungeu' nodded.

"It's more than a month now since you started expecting your menses, I think?"

"It's exactly ...or let's say about two months," she answered with conviction.

"And what do you think about that?"

"I don't know what to say, I...I...I'm confused."

"Am I hurting you?" Adey asked with his eyes peering into hers.

"Adey!" she called, "I didn't cry because you hurt me. It's the other way round. You show so much concern for me and this makes my heart heavy with emotions, so I cry. You know, I just believe I'm lucky for I've had friends who found themselves where I'm convinced I am now, and they had to face the music alone because their boyfriends denied the fact that they were the ones involved. One ran away and worse still, another (and I know this boy very well and the relationship he had with my friend) claimed he never knew the girl. I have equally never seen NM's father after the first and only time he took me to bed. As much as I'm sad, so too am I glad. I just wish this will come to pass someday and then ...," she fell into Adey's arms and smiled sadly.

Adey could see how determined she was. "Munny!" he called and with a barely audible voice continued, "I'm strongly convinced you are pregnant." He then kept quiet as if to see the effect of his words on Mungeu', but she remained as calm as ever.

"Are you sure?" she asked as she bent her head and looked down at her mid-section.

"I'm very, very certain about this. Do you feel like anything is wrong with you?"

"Like I told you, I've not been feeling very well, not really sick but not quite myself, and I keep on having a nauseating feeling."

"Well, with all what you've said," Adey spoke calmly and with conviction in his voice, "there is no longer any doubt that you are pregnant. Will you go ahead then and tell your parents?"

"No I won't ..."

"Why?" Adey cut in.

"I can't, Adey. You won't understand, no matter how much I explain. I had considered all these things before now, after just assuming I was pregnant."

"Go ahead and tell me all."

Mungeu' cleared the tears from her voice. "First of all, Adey, how do you think I can face my parents, after so long that we've not met, with such a story? Don't forget that I left them because I was pregnant. Am I to return to them pregnant again?"

"Quite true, I understand the problems involved Munny, but I can't think of an alternative. I will also have to tell my parents, don't you think so? Everything aside, they will ultimately have to know with the inevitable physical changes bound to occur, and with people gossiping, so why don't you go ahead and tell them?"

Mungeu' had her own plans. She knew many things were at stake: her reputation after the first mistake, her mother's memory which she was sure would be cursed by her step-mother who just to hurt her would claim it is an inherited trait, and even worse, Adey's life. She smiled painfully as she felt pity for this boy who thought all parents were as understanding as his. Besides, he appeared unaware of the fact that whereas some parents might want to understand, relatives and customs might be vehement. "What you've said is true," she said, "but unfortunately, Adey, I just can't bring myself to tell my parents this story. It is simply impossible!"

"Then I'll meet them for you."

Smiling quietly, Mungeu' looked into Adey's face. "Poor you, Adey," she said, "you can't understand and it will be very difficult for you—"

"But this is something we cannot keep from them."

"That's true, but you've not seen my point."

"What point?"

"Why I can't tell my parents."

"Now Munny, be plain with me. Why?"

"I don't want my parents to know for our sake, and above all for yours. It will be shocking to both parents. I don't doubt this and you'll find yourself in problems, especially with my family."

"But we don't have any choice—"

Mungeu' went on without listening to Adey. "Let me explain this to you as it relates to my past. I didn't have the intention of bringing up the complexities of my life again, but circumstances are making it necessary for me to go down that route a second time. Adey, my mother died shortly after delivering me, as you already know. And this is a very difficult situation in a polygamous home because if one of the wives, the first especially, is not kind enough to shoulder the burden of bringing up such a child, then the child idles around the compound without any maternal guidance, eating only when the father is eating or...." Mungeu' went on to narrate her life's story in every detail. Adey could now see that as much as he thought he knew about

Mungeu's life, it was only the tip of the iceberg. "So you see Adey," she continued, "I got pregnant while still an ignorant teenager and my family members were going to kill me. My father and other relatives condemned me and did in fact repudiate me while the rest of society said all sorts of horrible things about me. It was as a result of this that I decided to leave the town ...." After going on for quite a while, Mungeu' concluded: "Now you can see why I sneak around in Batemba and have not been willing to visit my parents and my dear sister, Mabel. I don't want to complicate anyone's life, especially Mabel's. I have moved on, and whether it is for good or evil, nature has taken its course and I can't see myself going back to where I was years ago with all that pain and humiliation. For now, I just want to live my life as quietly as I can. The date of our reconciliation, it is my plan, will be the day I'll bring NM up to tell them she is going to college. I cannot damage the joys of this day for which I have worked so hard. I can't even think of what people would say of me if I should now emerge with a second pregnancy. Accepting this pregnancy would mean reliving a bad dream. It was too painful an ordeal for me to want to experience it again. I might not get through it alive this time."

"Pfo-o-o-oh," the air that had been damped in Adey's chest, for fear he would disturb Mungeu' with his breathing, now rushed out. "To tell you the truth, Munny, this is a lot more serious than I figured, I must confess, but to hell with what people say. As for your parents ... maybe we should get married, in this way we would not hurt them much."

"Very true," answered Mungeu', "had all been in our hands, but do you think my proud parents would consent to this? They had plans for my marriage, and what you've succeeded in doing, as they would see it, is foiling those plans, for with just one child, I still had a chance to get married to some established person. You'd no doubt be seen as an enemy, Adey, an enemy to whom they can't give their child happily. Adey, when a thief is caught in a house, he is not held responsible only for that which he stole, but for all else that had been stolen from that household and the entire quarter even. My father will hold you responsible for NM's pregnancy and so all the anger he has had in him, added to this, would be vented on you.

"To my father, Adey, permitting our marriage would mean accepting total defeat and he is not the man to accept such a deal.

The decision even, would not be his alone. His brothers must have a say and they all reason alike, no saving grace. Adey, my father can never give his permission for such a problem-oriented union as he would see it. I'm just too sure about this. My father is not that flexible. He won't say it is spilt milk and so dry it up. Lies! He would see it as a wound in his life, and instead of letting it heal, he would keep on needling it with questions as to why this had to happen to him. My father would fail to realize for how long I have struggled against men. He would consider me a whore and would no doubt scorn me even more. How then would I live with your child until you can take care of us? Adey, please, the odds are many. I have failed my parents and you yours and none of them would be willing to see how numerous and intense the temptations are that we face today. My uncle, for example, kept on saying, until his death, that he discovered sex at twenty-six, but what books had they then? He didn't even go to school, but today we have all sorts of pornographic literature and biological facts that make us aware of our bodies at an early age. Very few of us have struggled against and defeated today's temptations. But does it mean that those of us who fall, as I have, should be treated with scorn? Yet this is what my family would do and this is what other families have done and driven their daughters to their graves and some young men to neighbouring countries if not to jail." Mungeu', who all this while had appeared to be in a trance, turned to Adey: "How then can I plunge you and me into such a situation, being completely aware of myself? Adey please reason with me."

Adey looked pale. He realised painfully that he had ruined not only the life of the gentlest and most understanding girl he had ever met, but those of her parents, and there were chances of his life being ruined too.

As if reading Adey's thoughts, Mungeu' spoke: "I'm not blaming and would never blame you Adey, for I felt love burning like never before in me when I met you. I couldn't resist you and so I gave in. The fault is ours, not yours alone. I still, and I'm sure will continue to love you always. I don't want you dead, Adey, for I'm sure my father would kill us both should he find out. Moreover, it will be too much for those parents of yours who have all this while been so good to me. How cursed I would be to bring such pain into their lives." Mungeu' was crying this time bitterly as she struggled to suppress her voice.

"Don't cry Munny, please don't," begged Adey as tears rolled down his own cheeks. With Mungeu' in his arms, they both wept. Her words, her tears and the way she cried had touched Adey's heart more than anything before. He wept for the two of them and she wept too. He had never before considered this problem so profoundly. He saw her reasoning, yet he felt they should have their child. They had to look for a way out.

They had slept as they wept. Now Mungeu' used a wet handkerchief on Adey's face and then on hers.

"Munny, after all you've said, what then do you want us to do?" asked Adey bringing up their problem again.

"Adey, if I have to be very honest with you, I won't keep this child."

Adey had a suffocating feeling. Something seemed to be filling his chest. He could not tell whether it was anger or fright. Calmly, Adey got out of bed, opened the door and stood at the threshold staring unseeingly at the pale blue sky of a Sunday evening, while inhaling deeply the fresh air from outside. His brain was racing up and down. This is just what he had feared. With his mind made up, Adey turned and faced Mungeu' who was still lying in bed with her upper half held at an angle by two pillows.

"Munny, you can't do that to my child," said Adey shaking his head from side to side a number of times.

Mungeu' smiled bitterly before talking. "I see the way you are looking at it. It is your child only and not mine, not so? The child is ours," she whispered emphatically, "and I'd very much like to carry our child, but have you ever honestly considered the odds? Even after all we've just discussed? What have you to take care of a family? All this escapes you. My family, as I earlier said, won't welcome the child nor would they welcome me. Why then should I suffer an innocent child? Why should I consciously bring forth a child who would be stigmatized by its relatives or at the least, treated with suppressed scorn? Your father will take care of us all, is that what you are thinking? Don't you think my parents can cause him much trouble and thus hurt such a kind-hearted man by calling him an accomplice? I have a more serious problem even, Adey. My decision is against my religion, but then, what am I to do? I know you want our baby Adey, and I would love to see what would come out of me too, with you as the father. But I'll not survive giving birth to this child for I would die of scorn and torment. I can't accept to stay with your parents until my family gives their consent for us to get married, for this they would never do. What even, do you think, would happen to my business at Nju'nki?"

"Then we will run away from home and settle down at Nju'nki."

"We can't do that."

"What do you mean? We will elope to Nju'nki and I'll get just any job that would help us care for each other until our child is born."

"In reality Adey you wouldn't need a job that much for I have money to take care of all of us. But that is not the problem. Although I have not seen my parents and have been separated from them for so long, it doesn't mean I'll go into any marriage without their approval. I'm equally convinced my father cares about me but for the demonic influence his first wife has over him."

"That's very true, so what do we do, because we definitely have to keep the baby."

Mungeu' quietly gave thought to Adey's ideas. She admired his courage and love for her and their child, yet the odds, she was convinced, were against them.

Hours later, the clock in the parlour tolled nine and upon the last note, Mungeu' and Adey roused from their stupor. It was dark outside already. Ivan could be heard telling stories outside where they always gathered before going to bed.

Mungeu' sighed as she buckled on her shoes. Adey was standing ready with her handbag in his grip. Hand in hand, they walked out of the room.

"Ivan, will you come and see me off?"

Ivan, who loved Mungeu' so much, cut off his story in the middle, to the disappointment of his young audience, as Mungeu' took his hand. "He will be back just now to bring his story to an end," said Mungeu' to the others apologetically.

"Goodnight Sister," called Adey's younger brothers and sisters.

"Goodnight!" answered Mungeu' with a smile. "Tomorrow, okay?"

"Okay," they returned in chorus.

At the outer entrance into the rented building's corridor, Mungeu' twisted a five hundred francs note into Ivan's small hand as she sent him back into the courtyard with a promise to call the next day.

Before entering the taxi, Mungeu' stood on her toes and gave Adey a kiss. "I'm all yours, but Adey, please do understand," she said as she sank into the back seat of the car.

Adey banged shut the door and waved. "Tomorrow!" he called out. He walked back into the house with his hands in his pockets and his chin almost on his chest. Adey changed into his pyjamas and ate his supper before climbing between the sheets. He was tired. The day had been the most difficult one ever since he met Mungeu'. They had argued for hours on end, yet he was sure from her last words that Mungeu' meant what she had said. A little more pressure would change her mind, he hoped, so he made up his mind to tell his parents about their problem. He was frightened, though, for he did not know how his father would react. All the same, he had to tell his parents since he wanted their child.

When Mungeu' got back to Loretta's place, she bared her heart to Loretta without mincing words. Loretta was surprised because she knew how firm her friend was, especially after her first pregnancy. She knew about Adey and understood how intensely Mungeu' loved him, but she could not understand how they got themselves into their present plight.

"He wants the child and so expects me to tell my family about it," Mungeu' told Loretta.

"And what does he think would happen next?"

"He believes we can get married if it comes to the worst."

"Crazy! I'm sure he is just talking without giving a thought to the whole situation. Is he aware of all that can happen to you or worse still, to him?"

"He is so bent on having the child, no matter what I say he just seems to care less."

"So what are your plans?" asked Loretta.

"I will not keep the child."

"How old is it?"

"About two months and some weeks."

Loretta, aware of society's approach to such pregnancies, was not surprised by her friend's decision. Her only fear was the risk it all involved. She liked her friend so much and with all she had heard about girls attempting abortions, she feared for Mungeu's life. She wondered if any doctor would want to help her as that was the only safe way out. The act was illegal and as a result, to scare away girls, doctors asked for astronomical amounts. But money was not Mungeu's problem; it was finding a doctor who would be willing to go along with their plan. With a thumping heart, Loretta promised to help Mungeu' in any way she could.

Adey woke up when the cock, that spent its night on a young avocado pear tree behind his window, crowed. He had hardly slept. The price was a pair of red eyes and a terrible headache. He carried a bucket of water into the bathroom with his towel wrapped round his waist while his toothbrush darted in and out of his mouth, directed by his right hand.

As he buttoned his shirt, Adey smiled when his eyes fell on the voluminous medical book still lying on his table. He had spent part of the night going through the pages checking on the various symptoms of pregnancy. He no longer had even the faintest doubt that Mungeu' was pregnant. He was bent on having the child. Adey spent the rest of the morning working out a way of convincing Mungeu', when next they met, to keep the child. Thrice he jumped out of bed when he heard the tenants shouting and showing surprise at something outside. He was sure Mungeu's hosts had discovered her pregnancy and had brought the police. Cautiously he opened the door of his room and peeped outside, then finding nothing strange he emerged into the open, only to find a handful of women rejoicing over the early attempts of a child at standing erect. With a sigh of relief he retreated back into his room where the idea of being arrested at any moment kept on haunting him.

Adey was very relieved when he heard those steps approaching. His door was pushed inside after a faint rap.

"How are you today?" he asked after Mungeu' was comfortably seated on the bed.

Mungeu' smiled, but Adey was not deceived. He saw clearly the lines of tiredness below her eyes. She had not been sleeping well. "I can't really go to sleep," she confirmed, "I just keep on thinking and thinking," she said with a sigh.

"Have you made up your mind to tell your parents?"

"I've made up my mind not to tell them," she answered coldly.

"So what do you hope to do?"

"They will know when they will, but I'm not telling them anything. However, I told my friend, Loretta, about it."

"So you are keeping the child?"

Mungeu' nodded without looking at Adey. She knew for once she had lied to the boy she loved so much. Her heart was heavy. The tears flowed. Mungeu' wondered how he would feel, where he would place her when the truth came out. "Don't tell your parents yet," she pleaded and forced Adey to promise to keep quiet until she was psychologically prepared.

## Chapter Fifteen

Her days with Loretta were reassuring. After work, Loretta would spend her evenings consoling her friend. At times, with the optimistic view that their plans would work out well, they would joke about Mungeu's pregnancy and then examine her paunch, which they believed was bulging slightly when carefully scrutinized. When pessimism prevailed, they would cry together in each other's arms.

The next day was a Tuesday. Loretta had asked her friend to meet her up at the station where she worked, and together, so as not to attract the attention of gossips on Mungeu' alone, they would go together to the General Hospital on the edge of the centre of town.

The morning was bright as the sun slowly but confidently soared from the eastern horizon towards the centre of the sky. Mungeu' knocked once before pushing in the door on which was written *poussez*. She looked around for the English equivalent in vain, even with all the noise about Caramenju being a bilingual country. It occurred to Mungeu' that it was the English speaking Caramenjuan who, being the minority, had to learn to speak French and so be bilingual, not the other way round. She sighed knowingly as she crossed the threshold into Loretta's office. Loretta was ready and met her in the middle of the office and together they walked out, followed by the lascivious looks of two men whose tables were to the right and left of Loretta's.

A fresh breeze played with the loose bottoms of their dresses as Mungeu' and Loretta stood patiently waiting for a taxi to take them into town.

The taxi glided downtown slowly along the single tarred road meandering from the station into the town and branching off at intervals into other streets and sections of the township.

Together, along the wide veranda of the hospital outpatient block, they moved from one doctor's office to the next looking for help. The answers they got varied from unsure comments such as "too late, two months old already!" to outright refusals.

It was noon when the tired pair stumbled into Loretta's two-bedroom apartment along Alliance Street—the main trunk of that tree of a road, with a bough going up to the station, a few main branches, and fibrous roots branching off into different sections of the town. Although not as slim as Mungeu', Loretta was taller and had a very lively appearance. She always wore a smile that belied her integrity in the eyes of young men who always took her for an easy catch, until after their futile attempts. Her hair, bundled in a knot at the back of the head, with some strands left dangling by her right cheek, bared and brightened her forehead. Below well trimmed eyebrows, her long lashes were tactfully separated, the upper ones turned upwards and the lower downwards. Her strangely light brown pupils gave her an eerie appearance, one heightened by the almost upwards slanting nature of her eyelids, the darkened edges of which contrasted with the rest of her smiling face. She walked with a lithe grace, which caused men to turn and stare each time she walked past. Loretta entered her room on the left side of her parlour but immediately rushed out with only a loincloth wrapped round her body when she heard Mungeu' sobbing. Mungeu' would cry for minutes, which appeared too long to Loretta who sat there trying to calm her, then she would dry her eyes and continue with household chores like cooking.

The time was 3:00 pm and Loretta had gone back to work for that sleeping second half of the day in the office, when Mungeu' made up her mind to visit an acquaintance of hers who lived alone along Central Avenue. Clara had been a student in the Township Comprehensive School until she was determined pregnant by the school's authorities and sent away, although she never gave birth.

On the way, Mungeu' prayed to her stars that she may find her long time friend at home. Clara was in. As surprised as she was, she knew, however, that something must be wrong for it was a long time since they last exchanged visits. Their discussion was brief and Mungeu' was generous in giving her the details of her story but left out names, especially that of the boy concerned. She thought of Clara's flippant nature but decided it was needless fearing gossips at this point in her life. Clara could go ahead and talk, all she needed now was her help. After all, people had, many times before, given out that she was pregnant again simply because she had gained a little more weight, so what difference did it make?

It was cold and calm as darkness approached, with a soft breeze that caressed bushes and light tree branches and leaves making them bounce gracefully. The round setting sun splashed the Western horizon with burnished red. Mungeu' followed the directions from Clara, in search of the man she claimed had helped her. The tarmac gave way to a path which Mungeu' followed for about twenty minutes with her eyes searching along the right side of the path as she walked. Then she saw it: a path that was not worn but showed signs of frequent use. Mungeu' switched off her torchlight as she trailed the path which, like a serpent fleeing from civilization, led her along. She felt her heart banging away in protest, yet she continued, tired, and frightened but determined.

Suddenly, after a curve, the path entered an opening and there stood in the darkness a black mass punctuated by a faint glow from within. Mungeu' switched on her torchlight. The hut stood defiantly like an island in a sea of woods and grass. The two windows Mungeu' saw were firmly fastened, but to her surprise the door was ajar, betraying the partial darkness within. Mungeu' thought of running away, but the idea of being treated with scorn all over again by friends and foes alike nudged her on. Slowly she approached, ashamed of herself and bitter about this abuse to her pride. As she moved on, she thought she was dreaming, but she could feel the soft grass under her feet and then she saw a girl inside the hut, standing in front of a man. The man was sitting on a stool with his head engulfed by darkness since the only source of light was the hearth with two or three smouldering logs of wood. His hands were fidgeting round the girl's hips and abdomen. His actions brought to Mungeu's mind the actions of a medical doctor checking for strange symptoms from a patient who has complained of stomach problems. There was a rustling sound to her left and Mungeu' turned just in time to see another girl emerging from the nearby bushes.

Kock! Kock! Kock! Mungeu' knocked.

"Come in," answered the man with a voice Mungeu' thought too tiny to be his.

Mungeu's eyes moved from face to face. She had never seen any of them before.

"Sit down," urged the man.

Mungeu' sat down on a nearby stool, relieved to see she was not alone in her state. One after the other, girls were coming and going. It was at last her turn.

"Yes sister, can I help you?" asked the quack.

"I hope so," she answered before proceeding with her history.

"How old exactly do you think it is?"

"About two months and some weeks at least."

"*Tse! Tse! Tse*!" the man exclaimed moving his head from side to side. "Why did you have to waste all this time?"

"I wanted to be sure I was pregnant."

"But when you didn't see your time and you knew you had slept with a man, what did you think was happening? *Ts-s-seu*!" the man sighed at length with the airs of a healer being presented with a problem he thought was too small for his powers in spite of its seriousness. "This is a strong case, you know, and so you will have to pay more. Do you have money?"

How much is it?" Mungeu' asked in a manner which did not hide the fact that she did not like the quack whom she thought was assuming a lot of airs and just talking to her in any manner.

"Because yours is a strong case, you'll pay 8.000 francs instead of five.

Mungeu' walked out into the dark, after promising to call the next day with the money. She walked back home feeling as if a load had just been taken off her head. She wondered at how kind nature could be at times, to direct her to such a cheap solution to her problem.

Back in town, Adey paced his room, wondering about Mungeu's condition, after two whole days during which they had not met. He feared her pregnancy might have been discovered and the police would soon be coming for him. Adey rushed out of his room on every occasion when he heard a bang that he believed to be that of a car's door slammed shut. But neither the police nor Mungeu' arrived. It was now he saw why he had always been warned against any such relationships with a girl. The trouble was too much for whatever pleasure he had had. He vowed never to go to bed with any girl again, should this problem come to pass. All was now gloomy. Even that small room of his which carried mementos of his past and ephemeral pleasures had lost its glamour. Adey hoped this nightmare would come to an end eventually, but even as he slept, he dreamt: the secret was out and they were after him.

Adey was very happy when at 8:00 am the following day, a Wednesday, Mungeu' called to see him after two days. He ran his eyes over her and for once, within him, accepted that Mungeu' had cared less about her appearance. The red coating on her nails, without being replaced, was falling off and it made her fingers appear chapped. The thin layer of lipstick she normally wore, in keeping with the colour of her dress, was absent.

Mungeu' stayed with Adey only for an hour, during which she lied to him about her positive plans for the baby, yet she wept again in his arms and was unable to say why. Adey, thinking it was the thought of carrying the baby for nine months that worried her, decided to let the question about her tears go unanswered. For the second time since they first met, Mungeu' left the boy, for whom she cared so much and by whom she loved to stay, with doubts about the possibilities of her visiting him again for some time.

When Mungeu' left, Adey sat brooding over the changes she had undergone. He was, above all, troubled by the idea that she looked scared of something and got easily irritated. He was sure something was up, but he could not tell what. To relax a bit Adey decided on a walk towards Nsung's workshop, his mind racing as he strolled along, then it started raining. Nsung had gone through his apprenticeship and had had a workshop opened and fully equipped for him to start managing his own life. Now he could no longer steal a few minutes to visit Adey as he did when he was still with his master. The time was now all his and he had to make the best use of it. Adey spent an hour with Nsung, during which he was offered a bottle of Special beer and the latest stories in town.

From Nsung's workshop, Adey was still so worried that he decided to take a walk to Alliance Street to Loretta's house. He felt like staying by Mungeu' and comforting her. This was no problem as he found out, for young men around knew all about "that tall fair-in-complexion girl who works up at the station." Stories even went around that she was "one side man and one side woman" and this is why she is not interested in men. Loretta, however, was just one of those girls lucky enough to have learnt from the errors of friends.

Adey found the house deserted. "Where could Mungeu' have gone," he wondered. He felt sweat trickling down the furrow between the two broad ridges of his back, from his neck, between his shoulder blades to his waist. He was frightened but consoled himself that Mungeu' could have stopped somewhere to see a friend.

After waiting for an hour in vain for either Loretta or Mungeu' to return, Adey walked leisurely along the street hoping to catch a taxi back home.

★★★

From Adey's place earlier on, Mungeu' had alighted from her taxi in a deserted area a few hundred metres from where she had to leave the tarmac. Just then the thunder rumbled angrily and lightning flashed with a cracking sound from horizon to horizon. Then came the heavy raindrops tap-tapping on Mungeu' sporadically as she progressed. She turned round and saw the heavy shower spreading down from the Station Hill then it overtook her. Without faltering Mungeu' walked on, drenched with water dripping form her garments. She held the money tightly in her palm to prevent it from getting soaked. The path was flooded as she stepped off the tarmac into the pool of water. The raindrops that had gathered much weight from a brief stay on the green leaves of trees shading the path were heavier. With a thud the drops landed on her and plopped as they fell directly into the pool of water in which she walked. Mungeu' was shivering and her teeth chattering as she waded along. The rain was heavy and the rumbling and crackling of thunder and lightning were frightening.

There again it stood, the hut, with the door wide open like an entrance into hell. It was dark within, but for the faint glow from the smouldering hearth. As Mungeu' stepped on the veranda, she heard a bird chirping hard as if calling for help. The sound was from nearby. The bird was on the veranda too, with its reddish brown feathers all soaked. It was shivering violently with its head occasionally dropping into the water and then its tail dipping in as it brought up its head, only for its head to go back into the water as it struggled to maintain its balance, and then resurface again as its tail went back in. The bird laboured at this balancing ritual. Mungeu' stood transfixed. "All that rain fell on the poor thing," she thought, "and now it is going to die." Once more, the bird chirped before moving to the silent rhythm of its macabre dance. "There it goes again," said Mungeu' aloud to herself. Its head went first, but this time it did not resurface. Then the bird fell sideways and was immediately submerged.

Mungeu' sighed and, with very low spirits, entered the hut with the quack seated as if he had not moved since the day before. His hands were clasped and placed on his right knee, with his eyes facing the main path leading into his hideout. Mungeu' wondered if indeed he ever moved. "He is too young to lead a solitary life," Mungeu' thought, so she decided he must be coming there early each morning and leaving late in the evening. Many more girls besides those she met on her first trip to this quack were there, so Mungeu' had to sit and wait her turn.

"Sit down near the fire," advised the quack for whom Mungeu' had unconsciously cultivated a deep hatred.

"He gives orders, and most of the time like some god," thought Mungeu' angrily. "How can people take undue advantage of others at a particular time just because of their desperation," she wondered angrily. Mungeu' moved forward and sat on the chair in front of this mysterious character who sat looking at her like a watchdog at a captured intruder. "His hair," Mungeu' considered, "is too grey for his age; a possible disguise," she convinced herself.

"So what is your problem, Miss?" asked the quack, trying to give Mungeu' the impression of his being a very busy man, while at the same time his small, deep-set eyes darted suspicious glances at the path leading to the hut.

"Didn't I tell you everything yesterday, and was it not you who asked me to come today?" Mungeu' snapped back at him.

"Don't be angry with me Sister," pleaded the quack with a smile, "you can see for yourself that I meet very many people here every day. How old did you say it is?"

"Two months and some weeks," Mungeu' answered emphatically.

"Oho! Oho! Oho! It's you with that difficult case!" exclaimed the quack.

Mungeu' did not answer but looked straight into those young eyes in fictitiously old surroundings as they gazed back at her shiftily. There was something in those eyes she did not like. It looked like uncertainty. But Mungeu' had been directed by a friend who claimed to have consulted here with successful results. Mungeu' sighed. "Had I listened to and adhered to the values of our people, I would never have found myself in such a mess."

"I had prepared your own medicine okay, and I think I told you the price – ten thousand francs."

"No! You said eight and I have it here with me."

The man did not argue but twisted himself right round from the waist upwards on the stool on which he sat, as if to pick up something. In the process, he betrayed a small passage behind him, through the wall, which was partially covered by a fresh plantain leaf. The quack took a small, round object, brownish in colour, from an old goatskin bag hanging from a piece of bamboo drilled into the wall. It was not smooth all round, betraying the haste in which it was moulded. The object looked more like moulded incense, the size of a bolus a normal African, mature in years, would swallow during a meal of pounded cocoyam.

"When you get home, you'll have to put this inside your *lass* like this ..." The man followed his words by demonstrating how she had to hold the bolus before inserting it into her vagina. "After putting it," the quack continued, "you will go into a kitchen where there is a fireside like this one, where they have just finished cooking and warm yourself, sitting like this...." Once more, actions took the place of words to show how Mungeu' had to sit astride a hearth so as to channel a good dose of heat inside her. "If this is done this evening, by the morning it will be out just like that!" the quack assured her with a snap of his fingers.

Mungeu' wrapped the bolus inside a piece of toilet tissue given her by the quack. She gave him the 8.000 francs and walked out without a word. Like a somnambulist, Mungeu' retraced her steps, talking to nobody along the streets until she entered Loretta's house.

Loretta had been home for break, but had gone back to work. This was the message on a piece of paper lying on the dining table. In the same note, Loretta expressed hopes that there had been some progress.

Having read the note, Mungeu' looked for food to eat. She felt like crying when she found out that Loretta had spent her break time cooking instead of resting. Mungeu' prayed all should be fine soon so that she could show her how grateful she was for the trouble she was going through because of her.

Mungeu' had eaten after having a shower and was comfortably seated in a cushioned chair in the parlour. Her mind was racing through all that had happened to her in the last week. She thought of the small bird that died earlier on in the day under the rain, but she did not want to be superstitious. Adey floated into her mind. She blamed Adey for not realising the risk she had to undergo for his sake, yet her conscience shouted back at her that Adey had refused this step. She wiped her eyes and had just completed the act when she heard a knock on the door.

"Come in," she called out.

A boy of about ten walked in. "Sister," he called, "a man came here this afternoon, but nobody was in so he gave me this letter." He stretched out his tiny hand with the note.

"Thank you," said Mungeu'. She gave the child twenty-five francs for his *acara*. She wondered why the child did not give the note to Loretta when she was home for break. Mungeu' knew the hand very well; it was Adey's. His words made her feel like a queen. She was missing him too. He had felt a strong urge to see her again and could not help himself. Of course, he was expecting her the next day. Mungeu' was happy to think of Adey still missing her as ever, but she was confused. At one point in her pool of difficulties, she hated all boys, but now she was glad to have met Adey. He knew she was pregnant, but unlike most boys had accepted the responsibility and had struggled to keep up with her recent fluctuating temperament. She remembered how Bertha's boyfriend, albeit being much older in age, had refused, not only that he was responsible for their neighbour's pregnancy but that he even knew her. "Some boys can be wicked," thought Mungeu'.

Bang! The door of a car sounded outside, bringing Mungeu's thoughts to the present. Mungeu' met Loretta at the door and took her handbag from her just before she slumped into a chair. Mungeu' ran around a little and in a few minutes Loretta was eating and sitting with Mungeu'. She suffered along with Mungeu' as she listened to her story. Loretta's supper ended on the note that Mungeu' should take her treatment as soon as she got to Nju'nki for Mungeu' was bent on leaving early the next morning, even without seeing Adey. She had been away for too long and, moreover, needed to begin her treatment as soon as possible.

Pa Ebot always called to see if Loretta was alright. He did not want her lacking in anything at all so he came in often with food and at times with money for her, notwithstanding the fact that she was a worker herself. This was one of such evenings. They had spent the time talking, with Mungeu' sitting wrapped up in a loincloth as if keeping off cold. It was getting to past seven when Pa Ebot drove off towards Nekwa.

With Pa Ebot gone, Mungeu' entered her room and sat down on the bed with a heavy heart. She listened to the clock ticking, and then she looked at her wristwatch. It was 8:00 pm already. She heard the cars as they zoomed past along the tarmac in front of Loretta's house. "Life is going on normally," she thought, "but mine seems to have reached a point where it is standing still." Another car zoomed past and she could hear the passengers laughing as they sped by. An early drunkard was singing and whistling at intervals and like a moth to a flame, he staggered to the next Off-License liquor store.

# Chapter Sixteen

Mungeu's trip to Nju'nki had been long and tiring, but after her bath and meal, she was beginning to feel much better with Ndolo-Mabel hanging around and trying to tell her everything that happened in her absence. Ndolo and Ndomnjie had spent almost all their afternoon with her and were just about leaving.

"You are welcome Munny. We have to go now so that you can rest."

"No, why? What's the haste about? Please stay. You can stay on; I'm not really that tired."

"No Munny, you have to rest. These children's father is leaving for Batemba this night. He must also get some rest before it is 11:00 pm."

"Now that's a better story, instead of asking me to rest. Goodnight then."

"'Night!" answered the couple as they walked out laughing.

Mungeu' was now all alone in her parlour. Her mind replayed all that she had been through ever since she met Adey. She was still thinking when Yefon walked in.

"Munny," she called, "can I talk to you for a minute?"

"What's wrong Yefon?"

"If anything is wrong, it is with you and not me. For so many years now, I have served you, and faithfully too, to a point that I now consider you a sister. But I must tell you that I am beginning to hate the way you treat me. You give me the impression you are just using me."

"What? Yefon please ..." Mungeu' made to speak.

"No, excuse me Munny. You can entrust your entire business in my hands and even your daughter's life, yet you can't take me into confidence. For the last two months, at least, I have managed your business all alone, while strangely, you move back and forth to Batemba virtually every week. Your daughter has been bothering me, just like your customers who cannot understand why you are almost permanently absent these days. Now you have returned looking worn out and pensive. Yet you don't think you can tell me what is wrong. Please tell me. If I have done something wrong or have become a burden and you want me to leave, just say so without troubling yourself and I'll leave."

"Yefon please ...."

"Munny," Yefon cut in again, "there is no point my staying with you after all the changes I see you've undergone. You no longer care about us, nothing, and you want me to stay?"

"Yefon, will you listen! Please! You've got my moodiness all wrong. Truly, I've been worried, but it has nothing to do with you, or the business. Why do you think I'm in the parlour now? *Hm*?"

Yefon stared at her silently.

I'm trying to figure out how I can begin opening up without disappointing you. Yes, you've meant more to me than I've let you know, but my problem is in a strange area, strange to the two of us for we've hardly explored that dimension together. Please kindly sit down and listen."

Slowly, Yefon took the seat directly in front of Mungeu'.

"Yefon, I will be blunt with you. You know I am now always in Batemba. Besides the business deals I have there, I also met somebody and fell deeply in love with him. Yefon, I've been seeing him, each time I went to Batemba, and now we have a problem."

"But how did this happen, Munny? I have seen men here to whom you've been of so much help financially and otherwise while refusing to have anything to do with them. Why was this so extraordinary?"

"Yes, that is the point. I don't know what happened, other than to think it was destined to be. I have turned down men here because I was determined to succeed, while taking care of the business and my daughter. Yet somehow, when I met this boy, as young as he is, and as much as I had come to dread men after the way Ndolo-Mabel's father behaved, I felt like I have never felt before in the presence of a man. Whether you believe me or not Yefon, after all I went through with NM's pregnancy, I just could not help giving in to this boy with my whole being. Yes, there have been men who wanted me, but I was taking my time while trying to know them better. But they all failed, as you are aware. With Adey, it has been different. With how much I fell for him, one would have thought he would rush into bed with me, but no, he was in no hurry. I saw him more interested in knowing me first than anything. In this way, he made me trust him. I could relax in his company for I saw he was offering me real love. Even when he found out that I had a baby and that I am handicapped, he treated these things as if they didn't matter and gave me all his love and attention. It took a long time for us to meet, and when that time came, it was not forced; it had not been hurried; we both felt like it. Yefon, are you listening?"

Yefon nodded her head, stared at Mungeu' with a hollow look in her eyes and said, "I am."

"The problem now, Yefon," Mungeu' continued, "is that I got myself pregnant."

"No!" Yefon started, "No Munny, that's not true." Tears were already welling in her eyes.

"It's true. Now you see why I've been very worried."

"But you—you at least should have told me before now," Yefon sobbed.

"That's true, but I was afraid of how you would react to the news. You are all that I have besides NM, and I feared you would abandon me to the lonely life I have been condemned to ever since my step-mom deprived me of Mabel's company. I am sorry I caused you to worry when I was trying to save you from that. I didn't realize you had determined the fact that I am worried. I am really sorry. It's my fault. You know how confused one can be when one is in problems. In any case, I hope you will pardon me."

Yefon nodded vigorously before speaking: "But what do we do now?"

Mungeu' explained all she had tried to do in Batemba and failed.

"Even with the money, the doctors refused?"

"Money was never the issue, Yefon. They just seemed to be avoiding it. I was already contemplating doctors in Bongola when a friend of mine gave me a cheap and apparently easy way out." Mungeu' went on to give Yefon every detail of her impending procedure.

It was 8:30 pm when Mungeu' clicked open her handbag and took out the bolus the quack had given her in Batemba. She scrutinized it before placing it on a stool next to her bed. With shaky hands, she pulled off her underwear, parted her thighs and the bolus was home. A few minutes afterwards, she was so frightened that she crossed the parlour into Yefon's room to inform her that she had already inserted the bolus. Yefon consoled her with the optimistic view that all would soon be fine. Yefon went into the kitchen, lit a fire and stuffed it with wood before calling Mungeu'. Inside the kitchen, Mungeu' sat with her legs apart, her body, from the knee to the groin, taking the shape of a funnel to direct the heat into her bent up body. After thirty minutes she trudged back into her room.

Mungeu' had not been long in the room when the pain started. Initially, it was not much and was just around the groin, but as time passed, she could feel the pain slowly spreading and mounting further up into the lower region of her abdomen. She tried hard to bear the pain, but it was searing. She started moaning. Yefon, who was herself unable to go to sleep, heard Mungeu' crying. She jumped out of bed and, barefooted, ran through the parlour into Mungeu's room. She found her writhing in pain. Yefon's eyes bulged when she saw the blood. Mungeu' had bled and was still bleeding. Consumed by fright, but still alert, Yefon ran to the giant flask always standing on the dining table, poured out hot water into a bucket, diluted it with some cold water, and then returned to Mungeu' with a towel. Yefon was now sobbing.

"Munny!" she called out, "what exactly is wrong?"

"It's just the pain, it's just the pain. It's terrible," Mungeu' answered, her voice distorted.

"Did you realize you were bleeding?" Yefon asked as she went to work with the towel, moistening it, squeezing it and then cleaning up her mistress.

"I thought so," Mungeu' answered painfully, "but I couldn't call you."

That same evening back in Batemba, Adey had walked up to the Co-operative roundabout junction, some five hundred metres from his father's compound, but there was no taxi around to take him to Alliance Street. He kept on walking towards Alliance Street using the road by the fish pond, a brilliant experimental project started by the Local Council, but like much else belonging to the government, it was suddenly abandoned. It was by this fishpond that Adey met with a group of young men sprinting back from the heart of the town.

"What is it? What is it?" he questioned all tensed up.

"Police!" shouted one of the boys as he sped past.

"Identity card," shouted the next in line. It was Nsung.

"Nsung! Nsung!"

"Run!" was all Nsung said as he negotiated the Co-operative roundabout curve.

Adey heard the whistles and the screams as more people came running. He felt for his own identity card; it was not there. He was now running, running and cursing, in his mind, such irresponsible behaviour by the police. He was sure there was hardly any need for them to go on harassing citizens in the name of identity cards. What pained Adey most was the fact that although they claimed they were looking for citizens without identity cards, they heaped everyone they saw into their characteristically dilapidated trucks caring less whether one had his card or not. Adey wondered if the police force could deteriorate any further. How he longed for the day when he would be able to take a policeman to court for assaulting him, like it used to be before Caramenju West joined Caramenju East to become the Republic of Caramenju. He ran until he reached the corridor of the rented building before he turned round. The beam from the police man's torchlight was heading in the wrong direction. With a sigh he slouched into his room lamenting such poor behaviour from men who are supposed to be most disciplined. "What do you expect when any idiot who has another idiot in power is unexpectedly recruited into a unit that is supposed to belong to the most disciplined members of society? Fools!" Adey cursed as he entered his room.

Just then, Pa Adey emerged from his parlour. "Who was that running?"

"I was on my way out when I bumped into friends running away from policemen who claim they are looking for identity cards."

"Is that what they are taught in police colleges these days, to go chasing and harassing individuals who are walking in their own towns without having committed any crimes?"

"It is an opportunity for most of them to embarrass people, especially those they envy. After all, what do you expect when a born outlaw is suddenly given power?"

"How dare you call a policeman an outlaw?"

"As you very well know Pa, this is not the police of your days. Today, just anyone who can run and has a 'godfather' can become a policeman. After all, is there any point in the recruitment programme where they probe into the background of applicants? If at all there is, then something is wrong with those who do the probing, for it is common knowledge today that individuals with very terrible activities to their discredit are putting on uniforms and calling themselves officers of the peace. What a shame. What's more, any new commissioner comes to town with his own way of doing things. Look at this one now; his specialty is to mobilize the mobile wing unit and they go around harassing citizens for no reason. It is that nonsense from Caramenju East they call *Kalé-kalé*."

"Whatever that means," Pa Adey retorted.

"It is a notorious practice by which police officers, simply because they have the authority, invade citizens' homes at any time, but usually very early in the morning, while they are still asleep. They claim they are searching for citizens who disobey the law by not paying their taxes and the likes. The truth is that this is systematized intimidation and subjugation of English speaking Caramenjuans who are too rights conscious in an emerging nation that could care less about the rights of the people. Officers use the opportunity to harass and extort money from civilians for phoney reasons. Consider the case where a stupid police constable, *Gardien de la Paix*, threatens to seize a couple's radio, which was probably bought before the young constable was born, simply because they could no longer provide the receipt. In the process of this so-called *Kalé-kalé*, policemen go so far as to beat up those who dare to resist or question their actions. Can you imagine that? It is even believed that this idiotic practice helps those thieves parading as policemen to identify homes with valuables, which they can attack later on with their gangs.

"What a shame. Police force my foot!" lamented Pa Adey.

Yefon had been cleaning Mungeu' up for quite some time. The flow was slow but constant. She tore open Mungeu's bag and emptied a packet of pads and placed them between Mungeu's thighs. But she saw Mungeu' was wilting. "She must have lost too much blood," thought Yefon. Mungeu' could no longer cry; she was just lying there with her eyes shut.

"Munny!" called Yefon, "I should take you to hospital."

There was no answer. Mungeu' lay motionless, her beautiful face distorted by pain. Not a word escaped her lips.

Yefon, who was still sitting by her, glanced at the clock. It was 2:00 am. She snatched her loincloth and wrapped it round her waist. With her hair flowing in every direction and the lower end of her loincloth restricting her movements, she ran along the street that early morning with the air of a mad woman. There was not a single car in sight. Then as Yefon ran into Half Mile which sends out its various limbs into other parts of the town, one towards that section of the town called Chapel Avenue, the other to West Beach Avenue, another to the hospital, and yet another to Jardin Street from which direction Yefon was coming, she saw a taxi. The driver must have been out this late hoping to pick up passengers as they emerged from nightclubs.

"T-a-x-i-i-i!" Yefon screamed.

The driver slowed down, but seeing a figure most unlike the late dancers he expected to be out at this hour of the morning, shot off. Yefon saw the lights of another car approaching. She jumped into the road waving the driver to stop.

As the driver slowed down, a tired, shabby looking girl in her nightgown ran up to him. "Please, my sister is dying. Help me take her to the hospital."

The driver, in about his late forties, pushed open his front door and Yefon got in.

"Jardin Street," she whispered trembling.

With one fast and narrow U-turn the driver reversed the car.

"Thank you," said Yefon as she ran down into the house. The driver followed her but stopped at the door. Yefon found Mungeu' just as she had left her. She hurriedly put on her gown and staggered out into the parlour with Mungeu' in her arms. The driver jumped forward to help, and together they carried Mungeu' to the car. Yefon sat behind with Mungeu's head in her arms. She was breathing faintly.

"General Hospital," Yefon informed the driver.

As they shot off in the direction of the hospital, Yefon thought of Ndolo. She had completely forgotten about her. How easy it would have been for Ndomnjie to rush them to hospital. In her confusion, it just did not occur to her. Even then, she thought it wise to keep things to themselves until it became really necessary.

Adey lay in bed tired. He had been wondering about Mungeu' and her whereabouts. The day she promised calling had passed and already it was midday on Saturday. He had to go back to school the following Monday and Mungeu' to Nju'nki on Wednesday. Not to betray his state of mind, Adey had done his shopping in preparation to go back to school as usual. He looked exhausted, but everyone believed it was because of hard work in preparation for the fast approaching June exams.

With his mind made up, he walked out of his room to check on Mungeu' again, having been disturbed the day before. He spent his brief ride in the taxi dismissing and putting on probation ideas that haunted him about Mungeu's situation. He hoped after all that she would be well. All tensed up with expectation, Adey paid off the driver and took some hurried strides that landed him in front of Loretta's door, which to his greatest disappointment, was locked. Confused and feeling frustration wearing him down, Adey stepped off the veranda. As he looked up on the tarmac at the vehicles speeding past, he saw Loretta descending towards the house with a loaf of bread in her hand.

"Hey Adey, hope nothing is wrong."

"No, why? Anyway, I'm sorry to be so early."

"How did you find the house?"

"It was easy. Following Mungeu's description, there are no two brown houses down below as if in a valley, and, besides, who doesn't know you around here it seems."

"I see," answered Loretta avoiding Adey's eyes.

"Where's Munny?"

"Oh, she didn't tell you." It was a statement. "Something urgent came up yesterday and she left suddenly for Nju'nki."

"What?" Adey exclaimed, unable to believe his ears. "What did you say?"

"She went down yesterday, Adey."

Adey's looks frightened Loretta who knew Adey just didn't know what to say or do to her. "Okay, thank you," he said as he climbed up the short slope to the road hurriedly.

Loretta felt it wise to leave him alone and not utter a word.

As Adey walked off towards the Sunshine Chemist roundabout at the end of Alliance Street on his way home, he decided he was leaving as early as possible the next morning for Nju'nki. Mungeu's workshop, Home Craft Centre at Jardin Quarters, Nju'nki, would be easy to find, he thought. He would put up with his friend Samba, the cashier of Caramenju Bank, Nju'nki.

Eight hours later on, when Adey knocked on Samba's door, he had just come home on break. They had just enough time together for Adey to confide the reason of his sudden visit to his friend. Samba understood completely and felt sorry for his friend when Adey would neither eat nor bathe before rushing to find Mungeu'. Samba's thoughts went to some four girls who died in Nju'nki within the last two months from abortions clandestinely performed by quacks. He was surprised that the government was doing nothing to sensitize the youths about their actions as young men and women, and the potentially fatal complications that could result.

As he had thought, finding Yefon's workshop was easy. Just before he climbed up the steps, Adey read the bold letters on the big board hanging above the door: "Mungeu' Ventures: Tailoring and Knitting Experts. Come in for All Home Designs, Female and Baby Wears." Adey could not believe Mungeu' was in control of so many young women. He was about to knock on the door when one of the uniformed women said from behind the lace curtains:

"Yes, come in."

Adey stepped in and threw his eyes round the workshop without even looking at the lady in front of him. He had always had a wrong mental picture of the nature of Mungeu's business. It was bigger than his wildest imaginations could conjure. There were twelve girls sitting each at a sewing machine, which were all arranged in three columns. Their uniforms were a beautiful purple skirt topped by a white blouse. Leaning against the walls were quaint wardrobes with glass doors through which Adey could see assorted materials and well tailored female dresses.

"Can I help you, Sir?" The woman asked in a business tone.

"Oh, I'm sorry," said Adey apologetically. "I got carried away by the size of your business. Yes, I'm looking for Mungeu'."

"Okay, madam lives just next door."

"Thank you," said Adey, slightly amused at the epithet 'madam' being used in reference to Mungeu'.

Nobody answered to his knock. Then he noticed the door was in fact open. He knocked once more before pushing the curtain to one side. Things were scattered here and there. He entered Yefon's room. The bed appeared to have been slept in, but nobody was present. Adey rushed into the other room. The bed had also been slept in, but the room was, like the other, empty. Then he caught sight of the bucket by the bedside and the towel hanging there with an edge in the bloody water. Adey could no longer feel the pain as he knocked his head against the room door fighting with his senses to reach the parlour. He felt as if someone was tugging at his heart. The environment was suddenly strange. Adey thought it was a dream. He felt the drop of sweat crawling down the side of his nose. He looked around. He was alive and standing in Mungeu's house. There she stood smiling and looking into his black eyes. The picture was on the cupboard against the central wall of the parlour across from the dining table.

Adey had just closed the parlour door and was about leaving when a boy of about thirteen chased his ball that stopped rolling directly in front of Adey. Instead of picking up his ball and running to where they were playing, the boy stopped short of his ball and looked up with a sad and worried countenance at Adey.

"You are looking for aunty?" the child asked.

"Yes," answered Adey quickly bending low to the child's head with all attention.

"My mother says she is not well and they have taken her to the hospital."

Adey's heart sank. He stood there looking at the boy confused.

The child ran away without his ball. Adey feared, yet he did not want to think that Mungeu' could have tried anything funny with her pregnancy.

In no time, Adey was in a taxi heading for the General Hospital situated on the way out of Nju'nki. He felt the heavy blows of his frightened heart against his ribs and saw his shirt moving to the rhythm. What would I tell her parents happened to Munny if something is indeed wrong? Adey wondered.

As Adey stepped out of the taxi, he saw the crowd. There were men, women, and children, all struggling to catch a glimpse through a tiny window. The thought that Mungeu's problem could have caused such a crowd to gather weakened Adey's joints. He felt like crumbling to the ground, but he thought he saw too many eyes staring at him as he approached. "Yes, there he comes," was the accusing message he could read in so many eyes, although none of the faces was familiar. Adey stopped for a moment, too frightened to continue. Then he moved on, not feeling like himself. Something was pushing him along until he reached the crowd.

"What's happening here?" he dared to ask an old man who was struggling with the rest to catch a glimpse.

The man turned and looked at him blankly before continuing to fight his way to the window.

"What's wrong here?" he asked a girl who had satisfied her curiosity and was just emerging from the heart of the crowd.

"It's a woman who stole a child," she answered.

"Pf-o-o-o-o-h," the air escaped from Adey's lungs. "Is she inside there?"

"Yes, she is with some policemen, and two doctors who are giving the child a check-up."

"Thank God," said Adey aloud as he turned and walked away. Then he saw Wara approaching, a friend of his whom he had not seen since after their secondary school days. He had heard Wara was already a nurse after a few years in the Government College of Nursing in Batemba.

"Good morning, how are you?" greeted Adey.

"Fine and how are you too? Wonderful! Long, long time. So how is everything? My goodness!"

"Not too bad," answered Adey with a feeble smile. "So you are in Nju'nki. We just heard you had been posted, but nobody could tell exactly where."

"That's true, I am here."

"I've just heard that a family friend of ours has been admitted here. She is called Mungeu', the owner of Mungeu' Ventures."

"Mungeu'!" exclaimed Wara surprised.

Adey sighed.

"Maybe she is the one I've just heard of. I heard a popular lady in town was admitted in the early hours of the morning, but I didn't check. Just check in private Room 2 of 'A' ward."

"Okay, let me check and see," Adey spoke as he hurried off.

As Adey came closer, the first person he saw was Ndomnjie whose pictures he had seen so many times as Mungeu' always talked of him. He was pacing up and down in front of a door with his hands in his pocket and his eyes on the floor deeply in thought. Frightened and confused, Adey hurried past as if he was interested in the last room along the line. He thanked his stars he had never had the opportunity of meeting this man Mungeu' called her foster father else it would have been terrible now with this sudden encounter. Adey was sure that with Ndomnjie present, and in such a mood, he must have heard of Mungeu's condition and she had attempted an abortion, else what could suddenly bring her to hospital like this? Adey could not think of anything else that could suddenly carry a healthy girl to hospital with blood all around. He saw his life crumbling like the ruins of a once majestic building should Mungeu' mention his name as the boy responsible for the pregnancy. Should this happen, then there was no doubt he would soon be a wanted person. What a scandal, he thought with a sigh.

Adey had hurried past block "A" and all the while, he could feel eyes boring into the back of his head. He was already in front of the next block and exhibiting gestures with his head and hands as if admiring the old hospital buildings. Then he stole a glance behind, but Ndomnjie was in too much of a mental maze to care about his surroundings. Adey wondered if at all he even saw or heard him walk past. Carefully, Adey positioned himself behind a pillar from where he could watch Ndomnjie clearly without being seen. A young woman emerged from the room behind Ndomnjie. "Yefon!" Adey whispered with certainty to himself.

An hour had gone by with Adey still in the same position when he heard hasty footsteps from behind. He made a swift half turn with the picture of a policeman brandishing a truncheon on his mind. It was Yefon. Adey relaxed a bit, but he was still shuddering for he did not know what Yefon would say to him.

"Yefon!" whispered Adey from behind the pillar.

"Stay there, I'll be back," she whispered as she walked past without even looking at Adey.

Time passed and yet there was no Yefon, then the door of private Room 2 opened. Adey pulled his head back in one swift movement as he saw Ndomnjie walk out. He was talking to Yefon. Ndomnjie pulled out a wad of bank notes and gave them to Yefon before walking off, throwing both hands open in front of him.

From his appearance, Adey could imagine Ndomnjie's lips working as he talked to himself while walking off.

"How is she?" Adey questioned. "Sorry, I'm Adey from Batemba."

"I could tell."

"So how is she?"

Yefon curved her lips downwards as she shook her head. "Very serious," she said sadly.

"What happened, Yefon?"

Yefon looked up at Adey and she could see the tears welling up in his eyes. "I'll tell you, Adey, but you must promise to keep quiet about it."

"Don't doubt me."

Yefon cleared her voice before starting. She went through every detail until how very early that morning she had struggled before deciding to carry Mungeu' to hospital.

"Why did Munny have to do this?" Adey was talking to nobody in particular. Tears flooded his eyes. Mungeu' was really in danger, Yefon had told him, for she had already lost much blood and there was no blood yet to be given her. She was, as of then, just receiving glucose.

"She had many good reasons, you among them, for doing what she did," said Yefon, "but you will never understand because you can't see things from her perspective. You can't think of what her family members would do if they should hear Munny is pregnant again. True, they don't even know where she is, but you will be fooled if you think it means her father does not care about her."

"What has been done to her since she was admitted?"

"Nothing, just the drips she is now on. The nurses want her to speak. They know it is an abortion attempt, but they want her to accept it. When Munny refused talking, they left her alone saying they couldn't help her. I find this very strange. In fact I know some are simply jealous of her and her achievements and just want to humiliate her."

Adey was eaten up by fright. Mungeu's case was taking a strange turn. The names of three other girls he had known from different schools around Batemba who had died under similar conditions came to his mind. He prayed silently within him that Mungeu' should get well. "Can I see her now?" he asked.

"Not today," answered Yefon. "She can't really talk well and even when she tries to, you can see she is in a lot of pain, so maybe tomorrow. More to that, I'm sure to be alone with her tomorrow."

"What of Ndomnjie?"

"He has to go to Bongola early in the morning for some medicines and will be spending the night with his wife who collapsed when she got Mungeu's story. Until now she is still not herself."

"This is terrible," said Adey as if to himself. "I'll see you tonight to know her condition."

Adey tottered out of the hospital gate as if in a trance. He ignored the porter who wanted an explanation for his delay since the time for visitors to leave was long past.

Outside the hospital yard, he heard the sounds of cars driving past but could not see them. He was sure he was in a strange dream, but his legs kept on carrying him forward.

Back at his friend's house, Adey rested in bed waiting for the hours to tick by.

Meanwhile, as Adey walked off, Yefon turned and walked into the private room where Mungeu' was.

Mungeu' opened her eyes and spoke, as soon as Yefon was seated, with a faint voice. "I'm sorry for all the trouble."

"No Munny, it's alright, what choice had you? How do you feel?"

"Worn out," Mungeu' whispered calmly, "and there seems to be a furnace inside my womb."

"*Ashia ya!*" comforted Yefon. "You'll soon be alright."

"I can remember when I wouldn't talk, you were threatened. What else did the nurse say? I can't recall all."

"They said it was an abortion attempt, and if I didn't say exactly what happened then they weren't going to attend to you."

"Did you tell them anything?"

"Nothing as yet, but I think it's time we tell them. Do you realize you are still losing blood?"

Mungeu' did not answer but turned her head and for a while gazed through the window on the left side of her bed. Yefon followed her eyes and saw them: a multi-coloured lizard was running after another. The one being chased lacked the beautiful body of the male lizard in pursuit and it ran along with its back almost humped and that part of its tail joining the rest of its body high up in the air. They were scampering up and down along the sidewall of the next block. Then suddenly, the one being chased lost its grip and fell all the way from a few inches off the roof to the ground. Hearing a splat as the lizard hit the cement floor below, Mungeu' winced. The multi-coloured lizard stood where it was on the wall, nodded thrice as it stared down below where the other had landed; it swung around and immediately dashed off after another female as she ran past.

Yefon sighed as she lowered her eyes onto Mungeu's who was now looking up at her.

"Did you inform Ndomnjie and his wife?"

"Yes I did. Ndomnjie was here twice and has just left. He came here, looked at you and wept bitterly before leaving. Before he left he was already shivering like one with malaria. He told me he was confused and I could see that." A few minutes ticked by before Yefon continued, "Ndolo collapsed when she heard of your situation and as Ndomnjie said, she has been unconscious since then. Of course, you know she is hypertensive and also diabetic."

Mungeu' suddenly looked pale as she learnt of Ndolo's condition. It was then Yefon realised she had been hasty in breaking the news. Mungeu' was now crying and Yefon feared for her because she knew she was not strong enough.

Mungeu' was still crying when Yefon spoke. "Adey was here for hours but couldn't come in because the nurses were here."

"Adey! Oh my God," Mungeu' whispered. "When did he come? How did he know? Who told him?" The questions flowed. "Please do let me see him the next time he is here." She shut her eyes after the request and, but for the rhythm of her breathing, remained immobile.

A number of young female nurses hurried in and out of Mungeu's room with obviously no important mission to accomplish. All they were interested in was to see and then go out and make scandalous stories that would mystify their positions as nurses in the eyes of ignorant patients and visitors. Yefon, aware of their intentions, stared at them and wondered where they keep the ethics of this supposedly noble profession after they swear the Nightingale oath.

## Chapter Seventeen

It was already dark when Adey walked in through the gates separating the wards from the outpatient consultation unit. The porter, an old man with a glowing pipe in his hand, was nodding asleep. As Adey walked along the verandas, the buildings looked like big transparent monsters. Through the open windows he could see the lighted entrails of these monsters—patients in weird shapes, some with legs in the air, others with heads raised, and others struggling and raining abuses at nurses who appeared confused and obviously angry that they had to face such mad patients, ones suffering from cerebral malaria.

Adey approached "A" ward cautiously, as the fear of encountering Ndomnjie again made him chilly. All he wanted was to see Mungeu'. Days had slowly gone by since they last met, and to Adey, the days were like weeks. He walked past private Room 2, straining to catch the slightest sound from within. There was none. "What could have happened?" he wondered. Is she already better and has been discharged? There was a flicker of hope and joy as he turned to walk away, but just then the door creaked open and Adey swung right round to see Yefon emerging with a bucket in her hand.

"Good evening," greeted Adey, "where are you off to?"

"I want to get some warm water for Munny," she answered.

"How's she now?"

"She looked better this afternoon but became very disturbed when I made the error of telling her of Ndolo's condition. Since then she closed her eyes and until now has not opened them."

"Ndolo?" Adey sounded confused.

"Yes, Ndomnjie's wife."

"I see. Yefon, can you tell her I'm here?"

The door creaked shut behind Yefon. It was after about five minutes that Yefon reappeared with a troubled look on her face.

"What's wrong?" questioned Adey anxiously."

"I don't know—I don't know how I can put this."

"Why? What's going on?"

"She said she didn't want to see you. I've pleaded with her in vain."

To Adey this was a nightmare in real life. Adey was no longer seeing Yefon who was standing in front of him. The hospital was going round and round and round. He was falling, and then something gripped him in midair. Yefon placed Adey on one of the two chairs always standing in front of private rooms.

"Adey, please be a man. Don't let this happen to you. What will people say was the cause?"

"I was a man, Yefon, until I met Munny, and we've become one person. How then can Munny refuse to see me? I who have been in a strange dream ever since all this started, only hoping to be myself when all would be normal again. Now she refuses even to see me? Why would she do this to me? Is she now blaming me that much?"

"Not really," Yefon tried to appease him.

"Not really? Not really? Yet she will not see me? Are you sure she heard you? Did you hear her well ... that I wanted to see her and she said 'no'?"

The cement floor, coated with dried mud from visitors who had hurried up and down the veranda, absorbed his tears as they glided down his cheeks and sailed off his chin all the way to the ground. Adey, who was still seated where Yefon had placed him, covered his face with both hands and wept as if he could see his life ending. "Well," exclaimed Adey as he stood up wiping his eyes and nostrils with his handkerchief. "I'll try again tomorrow, but please try before then to talk to her." He spoke without looking at Yefon.

"I will," answered Yefon, still stunned by the sight of Adey, a boy she had heard was all manly, in tears. "There is a sure route to every heart," she whispered to herself, as Adey walked off dejectedly.

Yefon returned with a bucket of warm water, with which she repeated the task she had performed earlier on that morning, but this time she cleaned all over her mistress's body and then placed her back comfortably on the bed. Yefon herself then lay down on a mattress on the floor next to Mungeu's bed before speaking. She told Mungeu' all that had transpired between Adey and herself. As she spoke, Mungeu' listened with her eyes on the white ceiling. Then she turned, painfully, to look on the floor at Yefon who had long stopped talking. Yefon was fast asleep.

A few hours had gone by when Mungeu's breath started escaping from her lungs in gasps, accompanied by a hoarse sound. Yefon thought she was dreaming, then she heard Mungeu' calling her name. She got up with a start, looked around the room confused, then got her bearings, located Mungeu's bed and clearly, this time, heard Mungeu' calling for help.

"Sister! Sister!" Yefon called, running into the office separating the ward from the private section. She bumped into the motherly nurse who was already running in from the general ward, where she had been quieting another patient. She was a woman somewhere in her late forties.

"What's wrong? What's wrong?" she asked.

"My mistress," answered Yefon, "she can't breathe."

"Take it easy," said the nurse as she hurried into the room. Mungeu' was still on her back and with each breath she closed her eyes tightly as if the air was some rough metal that scraped its way into her lungs. Yefon saw Mungeu's tears drip down by her ears on to the pillow. Mungeu' was in excruciating pain. Yefon cried as she helped the nurse with the oxygen cylinder.

The nurse took Yefon by the hand and led her into her office. "I think you should get her family."

"Why," asked Yefon suddenly alarmed, "you don't mean she is dying?"

"No," said the nurse calmly, "just go for them."

"She refused talking to her guardian this morning. Even then, he is presently with his wife who is also very sick. Is there anything very wrong Sister?"

"No, not quite. It's just that I don't like the way she is breathing now, coupled with the continuous bleeding. She has lost so much blood."

"Can't you call for a doctor?"

"Nobody knows where the house of the doctor on call is."

"Not even the ambulance driver?" questioned Yefon.

"No! The ambulance driver on duty is new."

Yefon spent the night looking after her mistress who with the fresh air being pumped into her lungs managed to fall asleep.

Night was gradually giving way to day. Yefon sat with her head in her palms and her eyes bloodshot. She had not for one moment shut her eyes but had patiently watched all through the night until dawn was approaching.

Mungeu' asked for the cylinder to be disconnected before asking for something to eat.

"Yefon!" she called out.

"Munny," answered Yefon who was still close by.

"Please help me. I'd like to see Adey."

"He'll soon be here. He promised to come very early this morning."

"What of NM?"

"She was here and asked to see you, but I felt she shouldn't see you in such bad shape. It would only trouble her the more."

Yefon had not finished her sentence when there was a gentle knock on the door. She hurried to the door and pulled back the bolts before fidgeting with the key that slept in the keyhole.

"Come in," Mungeu' heard Yefon saying. "She has just asked of you," continued Yefon. "How did you get in so early?"

"I lied. I had to beg the porter that I left a flask here that I need in order to bring tea to my patient. With that he let me in." Just then, Adey heard Mungeu's breathing. "My God!" he sounded frightened. "Since when did she start breathing like this?"

"Last night. We have not slept."

Adey's eyes moved from the cylinder to Yefon and back.

"We had to use that to make breathing slightly easier for her," she explained, "she just couldn't breathe well."

Adey approached the bed with feeble steps and stood at the edge with his eyes on Mungeu's face. He could not believe his eyes. His hands flopped down to his sides. Mungeu' was no longer the girl he knew; she was all worn out. Her lips were dry and scaly. Only her hair remained the same, long, black, and shiny as always, but scattered all over the pillow. Seconds had ticked by without Mungeu' moving, then slowly she turned her head towards Adey. Her eyelids fluttered open and she stared quizzically at the figure by her side. Recognition struck home.

"Adey!" she whispered.

Adey could not answer but went down on his knees, taking Mungeu's hand into both of his. "Why did you do this to me?" he questioned in a low voice. "What did I do to deserve all this Munny?" Adey lowered his head and as he kissed her slaked lips, his tears dropped on her face. With his face still over hers, he laid the packets of chocolate, Mungeu's favourite, with a single rose flower on her chest.

"Thank you," she whispered, and for the first time since in bed, she struggled to move, hiding her pain. Yefon helped her and she snaked her arm round Adey's body. "Pardon me my husband," she whispered, " I had to do it for I had no alternative. I'm sorry for what I did yesterday. I just couldn't face you. I was afraid I would die of pain if you came in. Tell me you forgive me."

"With all my heart, and you?"

"You never did hurt me Adey," said Mungeu'.

"Just tell me you do forgive me."

"With all my being," said Mungeu', "kiss me again."

Their lips met and she shut her eyes. Her hands fell to her sides. Adey sat down beside her. She was crying again and this time she could not control herself as her chest kept on jerking in spasms.

"Munny, why the tears?" Adey pleaded.

"I'll miss you."

"Why? I'll always be by you."

"I don't think I'll get well again."

"No Munny," Adey pleaded, "you can't talk like that."

Mungeu' felt her eyes pricking. She tried not to cry, but the tears kept rolling down her cheeks. She no longer fought against them and so they flowed freely on to the pillow. As she cried, she spoke, recounting every stage of her move from the very last time she left Adey, until how she got to the hospital.

Adey heard the sobs, turned and saw Yefon leaning against the wall, staring with unseeing eyes. She too was weeping. Adey embraced Mungeu' and with his arms about her, like orphans, they wept.

"Don't blame me Adey," Mungeu' begged. "I wanted to save us both from all that people would have said, from the insults, and, above all, from the wrath of my family. They would never have understood, no matter what we could have said or done. I didn't want the memory of my mother tortured by unkind words which I'm sure my parents would have uttered. Anything can be said now and the strange customary squabbles about unmarried mothers chanted. I will not be there to receive those blows. In any case, I never suspected it would turn out to be like this, but let God's will be done. If I should die, then pray for my soul for I did all that I did with..." Mungeu' was moaning, with a voice that pierced Adey's heart.

When Mungeu' next spoke, it was to call for Yefon. "Yefon, please keep all that has passed to yourself. As you know, Adey is the father of my child who would have been. He was always against what I did and wasn't even aware when it all started. Promise me to be quiet."

"Munny, I'll be quiet, but why talk this way?" Yefon asked, looking tired.

Mungeu' smiled calmly.

Adey walked then ran to the nurses' station where he repeated Mungeu's story. Strangely, the nurses had kept their promise not to attend to her until she confessed what she had done. It was a recent and offending trend in the way female nurses related to young female patients they suspected had attempted an abortion. How this helped was anyone's guess as the girls, ignored in their plight, just died, yet nobody seemed capable of challenging these nurses. Within minutes Mungeu' was prepared and strapped to a gurney. With Adey by her side, she was rolled down the corridors to the operating theatre with partially recovered patients and their visitors staring.

Lying in the operating theatre with the doctors and nurses around her, Mungeu' looked from face to face after she felt the sharp prick on her arm. She could not identify anyone; they were masked from their noses down to their chins.

"Pass me the ...," she heard a firm and confident voice saying, when something blocked her throat. Mungeu' tried to breath, but the effort was almost in vain. She was choking, and then she coughed. She saw the heads raised and the eyes looking from face to face. Something had trickled down the side of her chin to her throat. Then she felt dizzy and could see, feel, or hear no more.

About three hours had gone by when Mungeu' was placed on a bed in the reanimation unit for the effects of the anaesthesia to subside. In the process of carrying out the D&C, the need for an operation had presented itself for there was a strange swelling, to the left of her navel, which felt like a hot water bottle. As the effects of the anaesthesia cleared, Mungeu' began moaning. The pain was unbearable. Mungeu' asked the nurse standing by her bed to do her the favour of letting her talk to Adey and Yefon. The nurse withdrew, a door creaked open, then Mungeu' could hear her talking to Yefon.

"Are you Yefon?"

"Yes."

"She would like to talk to you and Adey."

"Adey is not here. He went home and–oh there he is just returning. Hurry up." Yefon beckoned.

Adey hurried, pulled off his shoes and shoved his feet into another rubber pair of shoes shown him by the masked nurse. With Yefon by his side, they were shown into a room where Mungeu' lay on a bed receiving glucose into which some drugs had been injected. One after the other, the nurses left the room.

"Yefon!" Mungeu' whispered, "I feel all is lost. In any case, there is a letter in my box, in which I have given a sort of account of all what I would like known. I wrote that letter when I made up my mind to take this step. Give the letter to Ndomnjie. Please can I talk to Adey alone?"

Yefon left the room completely at a loss as to why Mungeu' should sound like somebody giving her will after what seemed to be a very successful operation. But for a trickle of blood that was on that part of the sheet directly under her chin, everything appeared normal. Mungeu's voice was even clearer and she appeared to be breathing more comfortably than before.

"My darling," she called looking at Adey, "I love you so much that I was ready for anything just to see you free from trouble. Forgive me for disobeying you. I did it because I was sure I was doing the only thing I could do to free us in the eyes of the public. Let's not regret, for I believe the forces controlling the events of life are larger and stronger than we are. Were I to have another chance, I'd say let's be very careful next time. I'll miss you Adey, but be a man. My unlimited love for you has led me to this, but I'll always love you and I'm happy you've loved me right through to the end, so ..." Mungeu's voice was strangled by her coughing as more blood ran down her chin.

"Sister! Sister!" called Adey as he ran to the door.

The nurse rushed in and, identifying the problem, immediately dried the blood and hurried out for the doctor.

Mungeu', now breathing with difficulty, smiled. "Don't cry, Adey," she pleaded, "Take off this ring," she said slowly stretching out her left hand, "you gave it to me, and I have cherished it more than any other gift I have ever had. Give it to your next friend," she said after Adey had pulled off the ring, "and tell her I loved you with all my heart. And because she will have this ring, treat her as you would have treated me had this trouble come to pa-a-p-a-ss." Her last words were distorted by pain. She was coughing again, and this time Adey could see she was in a lot of pain for she was twisting her body and gripping the wound just under her navel as she coughed. Adey bent forward and took her hand. Mungeu' turned, her eyes full of tears, and looked at Adey whose face flooded as teardrops rolled down to his lips. "Adey! Adey!" she whispered as if from afar. Then Mungeu' started stretching and flexing her right leg gently and at the same time gently blowing out air from her lungs as if trying to put out a flame. She was no longer talking but continued in this manner, with a faraway look in her eyes for a while before her chest suddenly sank as she exhaled one last time. Her leg stopped its to and fro movement and collapsed on to the bed. Mungeu' was still staring at Adey but with a kind of glazed look. Adey suddenly got the message. He slumped on Mungeu's chest wailing. Then suddenly he lifted himself and stared into those blank eyes. As he wailed, he placed his lips on her cheek, still warm and resilient to the touch.

The doctor who had just rushed in touched Adey from behind. "Excuse me," he said as he picked up Mungeu's wrist. After listening for a while, he massaged and applied pressure with the base of both palms to Mungeu's chest until he was sweating, but those eyes continued staring as if in mock encouragement.

Slowly Adey walked out of the room, put on his shoes and walked out of the intensive care unit. He saw Ndomnjie, closely followed by a yelling Yefon, running down the corridor towards the intensive care building. As Adey approached the edge of the veranda, which was the highest point from the lawn below, he heard, as if from a distance, Ndomnjie's voice as he screamed in disbelief. Adey continued gazing at the Western horizon unperturbed by all the noise behind him as people rushed to the intensive care unit to catch a glimpse of the young woman they heard had just died. He heard the tac! tac! sound on the roof and then down across the road he saw children running around, shouting excitedly. It was going to rain. Adey saw men, women and children running in every direction, some jumping into taxis as the powerful wind blew down the heavy raindrops from one part of the town to another like the slow transfer of sound from the left to the right speaker of a powerful sound system.

Just then, he heard somebody trying to hush Ndomnjie. "Please calm down and grip yourself with both hands. I think you should be strong and try to make arrangements for the corpse to be moved instead."

"Thank you, thank you." Ndomnjie whispered, "Yes, they will have to move the corpse. Please, can you help and see to it that the body is transferred into the mortuary?"

"That's no problem. I'll do it."

"She will spend the night there and some time tomorrow. I'll leave for Batemba with the body." Regaining more control of himself, Ndomnjie asked his friend, Asukwo, another Batemba man, resident in Nju'nki, where he suddenly came from.

"My daughter just put to bed a baby boy a few minutes ago. Since there's no husband, I had to be the one begging and bribing those midwives to do their work, even though I am their colleague."

"No problem, provided she can deliver safely. Okay, *Werekeng*, he addressed Asukwo with a title of respect, help with that. I'll rush back now to make the necessary arrangements before informing the president of our village meeting here in town."

Down across the road from the theatre building where Adey was, stood a girl beside the wall of a house. There were other people there too, all sheltering from the rain. Adey recalled the day he first met Mungeu'. "It was just like today, but then, it was early in the morning," he confirmed. It was dusk already; he had spent all day in the hospital.

Over twenty minutes had gone by while Adey stood planted to the spot when all of a sudden the lights came on, attenuating the encroaching darkness that had slowly swallowed up the hospital surroundings. Adey had been soaked by the rain, the drops carried to him by the roaring winds. He was thinking of how he could meet Mungeu's parents to tell them his mind, to tell them what he thought of them and the rest of their kind and to hell with this whole nonsense about "country-fashion catching" him if he insulted elders. Adey jumped off the veranda and walked out of the gate leading into the hospital from the maternity end. Then suddenly he was running and talking to himself at the same time. Those he went past on the road turned to look at this young man running and talking to himself. Whatever he was mumbling, Adey ended each sentence with the word "fools."

★★★

Before going to bed, Ndomnjie was sure he would leave for Batemba, with the corpse, by noon the following day. He had arranged with the carpenter in the neighbourhood for the coffin and had spent the better part of the night packing Mungeu's property. Even Yefon's two-room apartment was now empty. One of Ndomnjie's many twenty-ton trucks and two pickups usually on hire for importers to use in transporting goods from their coastal warehouses into the different towns of the hinterlands were ready to transport Mungeu's possessions back to Batemba. One bus was also there to carry a few friends to and from Batemba for the occasion.

It was midday when a convoy of about four vehicles glided to a halt in front of Mungeu's apartment. The news of her sudden death "after a brief illness" had spread very quickly and her neighbourhood was packed full of friends, customers, and Batemba elements in Nju'nki. As the convoy came to a stop, Ndomnjie and the general president of *Nda- got* , the cultural union of all Batemba elements in Nju'nki, hurried into the room that had served as Mungeu's parlour to ensure that all was set for the body to lie in state for a while, as preparations for the transportation of the corpse back home were made. All was intact. Ndolo, forced onto her feet by the news of Mungeu's death, had summoned her mother from Bokai, a small village between Nju'nki and Idenamba, the border town closest to Nigeria, along with three other women—a friend and two sisters of hers—for help. Along with Mungeu's apprentices, they had emptied the parlour and neatly packed all of Mungeu's belongings into trunks that had been stacked beside her sewing machines ready for transportation.

Ndomnjie dashed in and out of the different rooms to see for himself that all was ready. With the help of some other close male friends of his, Ndomnjie and the president carried the coffin into Mungeu's parlour and placed it on two stools that had been set for this purpose. One stool must have been directly under Mungeu's chest and the other, her calf. Ndomnjie had just cleared his voice to address the crowd that had immediately followed the corpse into the room when a scream was heard. Yefon was aware of the arrival of Mungeu's corpse and had kept away from it, convincing herself like the other apprentices that she was busy doing other things and would not see it until later on. Unconscious of the fact that the open coffin in which Mungeu' lay was already lying in state, Yefon walked out of the inner room straight into the coffin and there in front of her lay Mungeu' ready for interment.

After the scream Yefon crumbled to the ground in a heap. She was rushed into another room where a group of men struggled to revive her. Ndolo-Mabel, as attached as she was to Yefon, was right behind her when she screamed and fainted. She walked up to the left side of the coffin, leaned against it and stared at the immobile face of her mother for a while, then stretched out her hand and touched her jaw. After calling twice and receiving no answer in return, Ndolo-Mabel burst into sobs and then turned round as if to say "somebody help me," but all the faces which her little drama had contorted with pain and tears were all very strange to her. Ndolo-Mabel seemed to realize her plight. She turned back to her mother shaking and calling her, "Mama! Mama!" A woman who was also sniffing tore herself from the crowd in the room, but Ndolo, having heard Ndolo-Mabel's voice, rushed into the room and got to her first. Ndolo-Mabel clung to her neck and buried her head in Ndolo's shoulder as she bent and lifted her off the ground. Ndolo carried her out of the house trying to quell her sobs, but it was quite a task for a weeping woman to calm down a crying child.

Ndolo heard her husband's voice from the room where Mungeu' was lying in state, trying to hush the mourners. "Listen! Listen! Please." Ndomnjie waited for a while before speaking. "Everyone in here is aware of the ill luck that has visited this house, but it is music to which every family and compound dances at one time or the other. This is our friend and sister lying here today ..." Ndomnjie went on to narrate a little about Mungeu's life before and after she came to settle in Nju'nki. People wept until Ndomnjie himself dabbed his eyes with his handkerchief a couple of times. He ended up by thanking all those present for their concern, including Mungeu's customers for having patronized her business, and last of all the *Nda- got* members for their financial assistance towards settling the mortuary bills, that for the coffin, and the transportation of the corpse to Batemba. He ended up by asking all those whom Mungeu' might have been owing to rest assured that their debts, if there were any, would be settled and that such persons, and those who may be owing Mungeu in return, should see him later on.

At the end of Ndomnjie's speech, the coffin's lid was put in place and the corpse carried out into one of the Toyota pickup trucks which Ndomnjie had provided. Some male members of the *Nda- got* group, six in number, joined the corpse behind under the tarpaulin shelter. Yefon, who would not part with the corpse for even a minute, joined them. Ndomnjie was to drive the pickup, and with him in the cabin were his wife and the president of *Nda-got* who sat by the door. Meanwhile, friends of the deceased and other members of *Nda- got* crammed the bus to capacity. The bus was to be in front, followed by the first pickup truck, then the second which served as the hearse, and then the twenty-ton truck carrying Mungeu's belongings. Before the convoy rolled on, Ndomnjie saw to it that everything was in order. Mungeu's now vacant apartment was locked and Ndolo's mother and younger sisters given instructions on what to do in their absence. "We will be back in three days time, maybe sooner."

The passengers in the bus exchanged looks behind his back as they wondered at this strange young man who was weeping, gesticulating and talking alone. Nobody knew why he felt the pain of Mungeu's demise more than her other acquaintances. It took them a long time to finally calm Adey.

"You are going up too?" asked a woman.

Adey could hardly talk as the tears started rolling down his cheeks again. Embarrassed by the sight of a man in tears, the woman left him alone as the bus' engine sounded.

As the engines of the different vehicles coughed alive, Ngoh, the photographer who had taken pictures of Mungeu' as she was in the mortuary and as she lay in state in her parlour, rushed in with his bike, waving at Ndomnjie to stop. He rode up to the side of the van and handed over a khaki envelope to Ndomnjie. Ndomnjie asked him how much the pictures would cost him, but Ngoh waved off the question, telling Ndomnjie to consider the gesture as his own small way of contributing towards the financing of events that marked the final journey of a townswoman from the coast back home. Ndomnjie thanked him profusely before putting the pictures into the pigeon-hole of his vehicle. The sun had long crossed the peak of the sky and was just beginning to descend towards the West when the convoy, with the other friends and well-wishers who could not make the trip to the grassfields waving, glided out of town with many other vehicles, motorcycles and bicycles leading the way. Ndomnjie was a few hours behind his estimated departure time, but it was only a tentative plan, and there was nothing at stake. The corpse was escorted thus until they got to about a kilometre out of town. The others then made way for the four main vehicles that were undertaking the trip to roll to the front. Ndomnjie came out and waved at the crowd on behalf of the corpse before the convoy embarked on its journey. Those who had dropped off hooted their goodbyes until the convoy was out of sight before they turned and mournfully went back to town.

## Chapter Eighteen

It was past midnight when the convoy rumbled into the Batemba suburbs from the direction of Fosamou—the neighbouring town. In the darkness the late-night town shimmered like a lake of light in the valley-bed down below. The passengers gazed with admiration, some for the first time, from the top of the surrounding hills through which the tarmac meanders before leading down precariously into the valley township. Ndomnjie now led the way guided by Yefon, closely followed by the other vehicles, to Pa Anye's compound on the outskirts of Batemba towards Bachiri, the neighbouring town from the south. But for a brilliant electric bulb in the courtyard, the compound was otherwise in darkness. Ndomnjie, followed by the other pickup and the twenty-ton truck, wound his way into the courtyard with the corpse while the bus emptied its bowels on the edge.

Ndomnjie, having stepped out of his truck, was still taking in the entire compound as his eyes moved from building to building when he heard numerous bolts clicking from the different buildings in the compound. Angwi, the first wife, approached the pickup besides which Ndomnjie was leaning, followed by the second and third wives who both appeared at a loss. But when Pa Anye swung open his doors, Angwi stopped dead in her stride and all eyes turned towards him. With faulting steps, since he was busy taking in the strangers in his compound instead of where he placed his legs, and a drooping mouth betraying his surprise if not confusion, he swept his compound with his eyes, from the left where his wives were, through the middle where the group of men and women were with the convoy, to the right where the bus was parked.

Ndomnjie and the president of *Nda- got* approached Pa Anye who after having slowly descended the steps behind his back door was also walking towards them, his eyes not having touched the ground.

"Evening Pa," greeted the president, "or should I say morning since it is already after midnight."

"E-v-," started Pa Anye before clearing his throat. "Evening!" he greeted finally.

"I'm the president of *Nda- got* Nju'nki branch," said Awasom cutting short Pa Anye whose lips had already parted in a bid to ask them to identify themselves. "We are sorry to enter into your compound unannounced, but it is not at all times that a man can tell how he plans to spend his tomorrow. If we had planned this journey ourselves, we would have told you we were on our way. But instead of a marriage proposal, we have come to you in tears."

"Your daughter, we have brought your daughter back to you." It was Ndomnjie who spoke.

"My daughter?" Pa Anye asked in a suppressed voice and looked all the more perplexed.

At a loss as to how they could put the message to Pa Anye, Ndomnjie took Pa Anye by the elbow and led him to the back of the pickup truck where Mungeu's coffin, on which rested a framed picture of her, was.

"Oh my child, my child, my child!" lamented Pa Anye as he collapsed screaming, with his hands sliding down the tailboard, which he had gripped in a bid to take a closer look at the picture. "U-wu-wu-wu-wu-wu-wu-wuy!" Pa Anye screamed as he slapped the ground with his palm. "Wey! Wey! Wey!" he wailed. "What have I done wrong to deserve this?" he cried aloud.

The president and Ndomnjie held Pa Anye between them, lifted him off the ground, and led him back into his house as the neighbours started trickling in to find out the cause of all the noise at that hour of the night. The women and the children in the compound who had taken turns in identifying the contents of the van standing in the courtyard were already on the ground, rolling about in tears.

After a while, Pa Anye, the president and Ndomnjie emerged from the building looking grim but determined. They dished out instructions to the women and the children of the compound and together they went to work arranging the compound to accommodate the crowd that was already gathering. Chairs of different kinds, many more brought in from the neighbouring compounds, were lined round the courtyard, leaving the centre bare. In Pa Anye's parlour, two benches were positioned and Mungeu's coffin removed from the van and placed on them. Women started sitting, waiting with legs outstretched and buttocks on the ground, in the space between the coffin and the chairs lining the walls. The wailing and keening continued late into the early hours of the morning, rising with the arrival of every new mourner and subsiding after a while. The night wore on.

When the first rays of dawn, ushered in by the crowing of cocks, hit the courtyard, the hitherto dormant crowd's breathing became obvious as individuals occasionally extricated themselves from the mass, moved around a bit yawning, stretching and sighing, before taking back their places.

It was not until the sun raised its head from under the thinning blanket of darkness, its warm breath dispersing the chill of the night from the limbs of the mourners and the landscape as a whole that the mourners came fully to life. The tent they had been constructing to keep the courtyard sheltered in case of rainfall was immediately completed. The food that had been prepared during the night and left on the hearth to maintain its freshness was also dished out to the mourners with special attention paid to those who had brought the corpse from the coast. Frothing palm wine brought in by friends and relatives was stored in the rooms belonging to the different wives, depending on who brought the wine and for which member of the bereaved family. People scuttled around looking for water to bathe or at least wash their faces, before considering the steaming pots, dishes, and frothing jugs of palm wine.

Adey sat on the ground next to the wall of the house from which Pa Anye had emerged. Every once in a while he would stare unseeingly at the gathering crowd and then would burst into a foolish, apparently unprovoked laughter which caused everyone around to stare at him in wonder. But for Yefon, no one seemed to recognize or even care about him.

★★★

The day, to Mabel, was just like any other. She was already very busy this morning when the phone on her table rang. It was her manager.

"Miss Anye, could you come over please."

"Yes sir," she answered.

Mabel walked over to the manager's office and knocked on the door.

"Come in!"

As Mabel approached his table, the manager scrutinized her face and decided she was unaware of the situation in her parents' compound.

"Good morning Sir!"

"Morning! Please sit down."

"Thanks," said Mabel completely at a loss as to this early summons by her boss.

"So how are you today?" asked the manager as he struggled to decide whether to give the news to Mabel.

"Fine Sir," Mabel answered her face cringing in wonder.

"No! No! Don't look like that. In fact I'm just trying to find out if you've been to your parents' compound since yesterday?"

"No Sir. Why?" asked Mabel, her surprise mounting and changing into suspicion.

"I think you should go there now and find out for yourself. As I drove past this morning, there was a large crowd there but since I was expecting this call from the general manager, which I talked to you about yesterday, I couldn't stop to find out," the manager lied. He had in fact stopped and found out that the corpse of Mabel's stepsister, who had suddenly disappeared years ago, had been brought in last evening.

"Thanks, Sir. I will go now," said Mabel.

"Ask the driver to drop you and come back immediately, since I'm virtually on my way out."

"Thanks, Sir."

When from a distance Mabel saw the crowd in her father's compound, she knew at once that whatever it was, it was certainly not good news. The crowd was void of elation and she could see some women barefooted, with their headscarves tied round their waists instead. As they drew nearer, she became surer and surer that the women were keening. Death! "But who?" Mabel wondered. "Nobody in the family had been sick," she did a mental check. She worked her way through the crowd unconscious of the persons she quietly nudged aside as she approached and stepped into her father's house from where the keening was emerging. Mabel staggered through the keeners on the ground to the side of the coffin.

"Munny! Munny! Munny-y-y-y!" Mabel called out, her voice rising each time until she ended up screaming before dropping on her knees by the coffin and clawing at the floor.

"Why? Why didn't you answer my calls?" Mabel's voice came out as if she was choking, then she fell on her face. The president and another man who had just walked in to see the corpse picked her up and carried her into a neighbouring room.

When Mabel finally recovered, the grave being dug next to Mungeu's mother's behind her crumbling house had just been completed. The thunder repeatedly rumbled overhead and on each occasion was closely followed by the crackling sound of lightning as it flashed violently across the sky, painting the picture of a major light chord dwindling into tiny thread-like nerve ends. With dishevelled hair, dirty clothes and folded arms, Mabel followed the coffin to the graveside. Like one in a trance, she followed the burial to the very end, unable to utter a word, not even to answer the prayers that were chanted. Just before the grave was refilled with earth, Ndomnjie and his wife, Ndolo, professed the part they had played in Mungeu's life. He confessed that he and his family had packed all of Mungeu's possessions and that they had handed everything over to her parents. "However," Ndomnjie pointed out, "Mungeu' had always told us that should anything happen to her, then her business should be handed over to Yefon who would run it to see to it that her child had a future. It was her wish that a sister of hers, by name Mabel, whom we have never met, should assist Yefon in managing everything if she is alive and has the time. This is because, as Mungeu' told us, she was at the point of death when she last saw her. Her love for that sister of hers was too deep, for which reason she named her daughter after her." Ndomnjie then pointed out that the little girl who had been clinging to his wife since their arrival was the deceased's child whom he would equally leave behind with Yefon according to Mungeu's dying wish. "I trust, therefore, that as soon as all is calm again, you the parents will hand over everything to Yefon who, under Mabel's supervision, will try to realize the will of your late daughter whom she has loved and served for so long." Turning to Yefon, Ndomnjie said, "Do not let Mungeu' die. She will only die when this business, which to her was her life, is left to die. It is now in your hands. I have done my part. Interestingly, I first picked Mungeu' up here in Batemba, when as a taxi driver I helped transport her to Nju'nki, not knowing that we would never be separated again from that first meeting. I have returned her to where I first picked her up. May Batemba know, this was one brave woman, generous, and full of love, the qualities she herself has been in search of all her life yet never seeming able to find them in many that came her way. It was a great honour for my family to have been a part of her life. May her soul rest in peace. Even then, we promise to remain a part of her daughter's life for as long as we live." With his speech ended, husband and wife each picked up a handful of earth and dropped it on Mungeu's coffin before stepping back to join the rest by the grave.

By midday, the day after the burial, with the rites of burial done and the funeral in high gear, the convoy from the coast started the long and tedious trip back.

When Adey saw the grave being refilled, he walked out of the courtyard unnoticed. He was still talking and laughing from time to time. Then all of a sudden, he started running with his eye fixed in the distance. "She is not dead. It is a lie. She is not dead. People just don't die so suddenly, no. I'm sure she is gone ahead to my place for a visit and is there now waiting for my return."

With unseeing eyes, Adey inserted his key into the lock of his room door, unlocked the door and walked in. Then he stared at the table carrying the turntable. He thought he could still see Mungeu' standing by the turntable selecting records to play. In the darkness and silence of the room, Mungeu' floated round like a soap bubble and stared at Adey with a weak smile in her eyes. He was going to go to her but felt so weak. He sat on the edge of his bed and stared instead.

"You think you are dead, they think they have succeeded in killing you," Adey spoke with a cynical smile as he brandished his left forefinger in a knowing gesture very close to his left eye, "but I'll see to it that you come back to me. Don't worry, just give me time, give me time, give me time." Adey kept repeating his words with his voice dying into a whisper. "I'll get you back, one way or the other, I will. This cannot happen. It's unfair, but give me time." Adey could hear the silence in his room ringing in his ears. Then there was a scurrying sound in the darkness. Whatever it was had many legs at least, for it sounded like many fingers scratching a sheet of paper.

It was much later on in the night that Adey stealthily left his room. He had spent so much time thinking of how to bring Mungeu' back to life with his face assuming strange looks and his thoughts cascading his being with every new suggestion in connection with this strange plan of his. Quietly and appearing unperturbed, but with determination in his face and a supercilious air around him, he walked on defiantly, with his chest thrust forward, swinging his arms like a soldier, only they were bent at the elbows with folded fists and thumbs pointing to the sky as he marched towards the heart of the town. With his shirt in his hand, he stopped from time to time, stared steadily at one spot while murmuring to himself with a faraway look on his face in spite of the raging storm. Once more he stopped, as he stared with a lot of concentration far ahead of him, his lips working, and then he smiled and nodded, while appearing completely oblivious of his surroundings. The thought of going back to his room crossed his mind every once in a while, but there was a certain overpowering feeling of estrangement which convinced him he could not face the room, in fact the entire compound with the occupants, in his present state of mind, and so he kept on walking, walking, and talking to himself.